Minor Prophets

Minor Prophets

Blair Hurley

New York, NY

Ig Publishing
Box 2547
New York, NY 10163
www.igpub.com

Printed in the United States of America
First Printing

ISBN: 978-1-63246-149-0

To Kamil, for the adventure of a lifetime and to Mallory, for our best adventure

PART I

Baptism

2002

WHEN NORA IS EIGHT, and they've been living in the woods for a year, her father holds out a rifle to her, almost longer than she is tall, and asks if she's ready. She nods and shoulders the gun. She's been practicing for months.

Her mother didn't want her to go that morning. She said, "It's not right. Killing things, so young." But her father replied, "She needs to know how it's done."

A few hours later, her first kill is slung up on a hook in the yard, the porcupine limp and heavy, half as big as herself. She's never skinned an animal bristling with quills; you could get it so wrong. She hesitates, runs her hand down one of the spines, unsure of how to proceed.

"Like this." Her father pulls out a quill with a hard jerk. He shows her the tiny backward-facing barbs along the quill's length. "They'll slide into you and not come out," he says.

Nora jostles with her twin brother Henry to touch one of the quills, both of them sliding their small hands carefully along the barbs.

"Like a fish hook," her father says. "It only goes one way. It worms itself farther in, a millimeter an hour. Like when you think an evil thought. When the devil gets his hooks in you. Once the sin is in you, it only ever goes deeper."

A dog on the compound was struck in the face with a porcupine once, and came limping from the woods, whining. It took days for the quills to dry up and fall out. Nora wonders if their tiny spines are still inside the dog somewhere, traveling through its bloodstream, flicking in and out of the red chambers of its heart.

Her father spins the knife in his hand so that the handle faces her. "Your first kill, you make the first cut," he says.

Nora has seen him do it so many times. She's always hanging around the yard while he chops wood or consults with the other men, talking new irrigation ditches, more root cellars, gasoline storage sheds, gun lockers. She's watched him slide the knife along the belly of a deer, the care, skill and attention it takes, the importance of saving every usable piece. There's an elegance in his movements when he does it, a brutal usefulness.

She hesitates for a moment too long, feeling the responsibility to make good use of the animal life, Henry breathing loudly behind her. "Come on, don't be such a girl," her brother says.

Nora grasps the knife, holds the spiny skin back, and cuts. The guts bulge out warmly from the incision, still so close to being alive. She's opened the animal's insides to the cold fall air.

Her father takes over, enlarging the cut and removing the intestines. He cuts out the bladder, which is full and glowing yellow with the afternoon sun behind it. It looks like something saintly, the animal's soul contained.

Then Henry makes a quick motion and the bladder upends itself, splashing the warm liquid down Nora's shirt. The shock makes her lip tremble. Tears hot on her cheeks, her brother holding the white little organ, surprised at his own act.

Her father is wiping his own jacket in silence. Women's tears always bore him. His attention, the fierce loving glow of his gaze, fades, a light shifts away when her mother cries. She's seen it. "Look what he did," Nora pleads.

Only then does he sigh. "Henry." And his hand comes out and smacks the boy in the jaw. "We have to work together," he says. "We're preparing for what we'll have to face."

The door of the house opens; her mother stands on the threshold. She's been peeling unripe potatoes all morning, their grassy stains all over her apron. "I need her," she says.

Her father straightens, running the side of the knife along his crusty jeans. "Go on," he says to Nora, without bothering to look at her. Henry will stay outside cutting up the porcupine, her prize, but she is expected inside.

There is this divide she's learning between what goes on inside the house, where her mother rules, and what goes on outside it. The woods, the fields filled with high grass, the shushing lake shore, the people they live with on this windy property in the Upper Peninsula of Michigan, all belong to her father. When Nora crosses the doorway, she belongs to one or the other. The line between them is exact.

A woman from the compound is sitting at the kitchen table, knotting and unknotting her fingers. She's one of the younger ones, slim and wide-eyed, her dark hair falling wildly in her face. She doesn't move to brush it away; she keeps her head low instead, almost to her knees. "Nora, honey," she says, soft and sweet as butter. Her mother sends Nora to the stove with a jerk of her chin, where she's dropping plant pieces into a pot, not peeling potatoes after all. A bitter smell fills the kitchen, like burning tree sap. "Nora, keep stirring."

Nora moves to the pot without question.

Her mother often confers with the women of the compound, providing counsel and advice that her father can't give. She travels from trailer to trailer like Little Red Riding Hood, a basket on her arm. "You'll bleed," she says.

"Will it hurt?" the woman asks.

A measured silence follows. Her mother has never been one to offer false comfort or grace. Her silences can fill a room, can speak like a line of verse.

"Some," she says finally. "Enough."

Under her instruction, Nora adds more ingredients to the pot: willow bark, juniper, St. John's wort, a handful of musty-smelling mushrooms. Her mother explains to the woman when to take the draught and how long it will take to work. Nora is not sure why she's here, except that her mother wants her to see this.

"God forgive me," the woman says.

Her mother rests a hand on the woman's shoulder. "He's forgiven worse," she says.

Eventually, Nora is released back to the world outside. At eight years old, she has a contempt for anything female, and escapes from the kitchen with relief.

She runs gladly past her father's mud-streaked pickup toward where he is holding up the spiny porcupine pelt. Men are standing around him with guns in holsters, dogs barking in excitement at the smells in the air. There are always men here, needing things from her father, and he's always directing them, reassuring them, making plans with them. She belongs to them, the way they shift and spit in the damp earth, the creaking of belts sighing into the air around her, the tender way they cup the nape of her neck in their giant, clumsy hands, like paws.

"What are you waiting for?" her father asks.

Nora takes the pelt, draping it over her shoulders like some ancient prize of war.

"First blood," one of them calls to her, and they all laugh, her father too. "She'll be a terror now."

When she'd held the gun that morning, eager to join her first hunt, her father had put a hand on her shoulder. "Remember, when you fire a gun, you do something you can never undo," he said. "You can never go back. Are you ready for that? Can you live with the consequences?"

The porcupine trundled low and unbothered through the trees. It had no knowledge of its impending death. Sweet, really, these bumbling creatures put here for us to master. Her finger on the trigger, her belly low in the brush. Her father's warm gravelly voice in her ear. "You've got it," he said. He meant the power to look coolly at a living thing, the power to pull the trigger. She breathed out and pulled. It felt as momentous as birth.

Chicago,

September 2016

THE LETTER COMES WHEN Nora is returning from a nine-hour overnight shift, where she'd sat and held the hands of dying people in cluttered bedrooms smelling of urine and cherry-flavored opiate syrup. No return address; the stamp, Christ on a radiant cross. She's dopey with fatigue, but slits her finger along the edge automatically, and out drops a single index card with three typewritten lines:

PENTECOST, 2017
THE DAY IS AT HAND
PREPARE YOURSELF

She doesn't realize her hand is shaking until the card begins to tremble. "Nora, honey, are you all right?" asks Masha, passing through the kitchen. "You're as white as a ghost."

All the nurses from the agency live in the group home together; it's a kind of halfway house for women new to the country or otherwise struggling to get a foothold in their careers or their lives. Nora nods, slips the card back into the envelope and goes to the little bedroom she shares with Kiki. She sits on the bottom bunk and presses her hands between her legs to still the quivering; sirens rush past the window, a bird sings. Nora doesn't know where songbirds make their nests in

14

these apartment buildings jammed up next to each other, but somehow they adapt, they find a way.

Kiki, from Barbados, has a little flip calendar on her nightstand with the Catholic holidays labeled. Nora turns the pages, slow at first, then faster and faster. Pentecost will be May 20th next year. It's September: playoff season, one of her patients, a Cubs fan, reminded her today. Another year, another reason to hope. Leaves are shriveling on trees. An election is nearing its ragged end. The wind that blows down the long, broad avenues means business.

Prepare yourself. The invocation of her childhood, the prayer her father began and ended every sermon with, a warning and a command. He had a talent for unwavering eye contact and firm handshakes, a certainty in his blue eyes. She hasn't heard from him in nearly three years. This missive could be from him, or from any of his followers. They've finally found her, and they want her to know it.

⁝

At Kiki's aunt's house in Cicero, Nora sits in front of a computer, sifting through birth records, arrest records, driver's licenses. She had to find her own information this way when she first arrived in the city three years ago. With a homeless shelter's assistance she got a birth certificate from a hospital in Indiana, and from there scrabbled together a social security number and drivers' license. Her parents had started her off in life with all the usual records. It was only later that they sold their house and burned their social security cards and took her and her brother as far north in the continental United States as you could go.

She henpecks her way along the keyboard. She doesn't know what happened when she left; it's been easy to pretend there was no way to. But now they've found her. The letter is a warning, a premonition. All this time, they were close. The past and what's buried there was only an online search away.

With her documents and numbers, Nora sifts through the available data while Kiki and her aunt move about the small kitchen, the smell of cornmeal pudding and saltfish, bright and lemony, wafting through the house.

The news is thin. A former church member pops up in a local paper, protesting restrictions on his second amendment rights. "A man's got a right to defend his home," a Kyle Laughlin says in the *Muncie Herald*. She can't be sure if it's the same Kyle. Mostly her people are secretive and don't trust the press. They stay away from social media and don't use credit cards. They're hoarding gasoline and bottled water in their basements and preparing for any number of plagues. They only talk to their own. All they can hear from the outside is silence.

Oh, Kyle, and all the men like him that she knew. *Alas, O sinful nation, a people whose guilt is great!*

This year, though, there's been an increase in the number of Rust Belt special interest stories, as journalists try to pin down the typical American Midwest voter. There's a wearying number of interviews conducted in small town diners or with individuals leaning out the windows of pickup trucks. This is shorthand for Americana these days: people who have been preparing for the big blowup for a long time, making runs on gun stores, speaking ominously of collapse and corruption, political cesspools, promising that there's violence in the air. A minister in Muncie is predicting the meltdown of the Middle East; another is telling his congregation to stock up on weapons and water for the coming race war. Who's with me? You've felt it too, the promise of something ugly on the horizon, they say. Who are these people? What are they saying in rural Wisconsin, in Northern Michigan? What do they want, what do they fear? Everyone wants to know and no one knows.

She hasn't checked on any of her own family yet, afraid that the act of searching will somehow lead them to her. But is there anything left to lose? She types her father's name into the search bar.

A list of preachers attending the Midwest Bible Conference of 1996; an ancient website listing real estate holdings in Indiana, another in Michigan. But then, something new: a local Michigan newspaper's police blotter, reporting on a shooting incident at a remote location in the UP. The story was reported partially and never followed up on, but there's one line, all that's needed to stop time: Francis Delaney, her father, deceased.

In the kitchen, Kiki and her aunt are arguing over how much hot sauce to use. Kiki says, "Nora can't take your spice, Auntie. Give her American-spicy."

Their voices seem magnified; Nora's breathing, loud in her ears. There's a summary of a coroner's report, the cause of death a gunshot to the heart. Part of an armed standoff with police, but that sort of language is used for both hostage situations involving dozens of people, and domestic disturbances in which a gun is found on the property. Nothing is said, it's not clear who is responsible, who pulled the trigger. The case is closed. For more detail, she'll have to call the local sheriff's office or come in person, bring ID, prove she's a family member. And if she does that, whoever sent her the letter will realize she's looking for information.

Kiki's younger cousins drift in and out of the kitchen, playing on their phones or stealing cashews in handfuls from the dish on the counter, getting shooed away. The smells and sounds of somebody's home, foreign in their peacefulness. Nora wants to hide the grainy government PDFs she's looking at on the screen, the black outline of a human body with a star-shaped entry wound over the chest. There are no photographs of the scene, thank God.

She stumbles across a scan of her father's driver's license, his clear eyes, his direct, luminous gaze. There are some faces in this world that inspire trust. A certain look, a lucky roll of the genetic dice: eyes that look like light from another world is passing through them.

Prepare yourself.

Internet preachers and televangelists are saying on Christian forums that the signs are looking portentous. The state of Israel, the current election, the markers of climate doom in the air—take your pick. The country is splitting apart into the entrenched camps of the believers and the godless, just as the prophets predicted. This weird little corner of the internet is crackling with an excitement not seen in decades. False prophets abound. It's easy to jump from one to the next, one click, one YouTube video suggesting another. This is how you get pulled in, how you convince yourself of the story. Why not? Who can say for sure? Her father trafficked in these sorts of paranoias and doomsday preparations, leading people into wonder and then doubt and then a dawning certainty. She can feel the old exhilaration in the frenzied Facebook posts. It quickens her blood, fills her body with a dangerous heat. End Times preachers are on the march. And they know her name, they know how to find her.

"Nora, come help," Kiki calls from the kitchen.

As she is about to close the computer window, a new link catches her eye. It's a forum for the survivors of cults and "coercive ideologies." *Step out of the darkness and share your experiences,* the site urges. *Together, we'll find answers.*

Kiki is approaching. "What are you doing, anyway?"

Nora closes the window quickly. "Nothing. How can I help?"

The news of her father's death is too grim to drop into this peaceful Sunday afternoon kitchen. Nora instead starts chopping onions. Kiki's aunt is happy to put her to work, because she focuses hard at any task she is given, with none of the complaining of the other young folks arriving for family dinner. Nora beats batter, washes okra, slices through cucumbers with the knife pressed into the hard uncomplaining skin of her thumb. She knows how to bone fish and pluck and gut a chicken. There is work to do in this house. That is something Nora understands.

Gradually, the house gets louder. The older adults still speak with their strong musical Barbadian accents, but the kids are full American Midwest, fighting over video games or baseball. They're South Siders, so they're usually White Sox supporters, but this year everyone's excited about the Cubs.

Someone turns up the radio, and heads nod together to a languid beat. Kiki's handsome adult cousins chop vegetables beside Nora, getting friendly, trying to figure out who she is, get her story. She smiles and looks away and Kiki shoots them warning looks. Eventually, they back off, puzzled that Nora could be immune to their charms. She is not immune, but she is not willing, either. She remembers the dizzy, fervent feeling she used to get when she thought about saving herself for God, keeping herself pure for his voice to speak through her. Attraction was always a threat, her body's lies about what it needed.

She loves being among Kiki's family, though. Swaying a little to the fuzzy music, jostling for food at the crowded table, banging elbows as she brings a fork to her lips. Occasionally she pauses to watch the others eat. They're so ignorant of real hunger, they stop mid-bite to talk and argue, forgetting about what's on their plate. It has taken her a long time to eat with pleasure that isn't tinged with desperation. The first few times Kiki brought her here, Nora put biscuits in her coat pockets until Kiki's aunt caught her and packed up a Tupperware container for her, *tsking* gently.

When the food is eaten and the dark sweet tea comes out, Nora sits back and listens to the worries come out, too. Whose kid is flunking

Spanish, who is wrestling with green card difficulties, trying to bring over a mother-in-law, who has another hearing this week, a meeting with the immigration lawyer. Who's going to pay for that? How can I save for a house and pay for the lawyer too? Kiki's aunt says to Kiki, "You're not paying for that boyfriend of yours to come. He can save up the same way you did."

"We're doing it together, Auntie. That's what couples do." Kiki is waiting for her boyfriend Vincent back in Barbados to join her; she saves a bit of her paycheck each week and sends it to him.

"And look where that got me! I put your uncle through school!" her aunt snorts, and her sons look at each other; no one wants Kiki's uncle to slip into this room, even if it's just in conversation. He's living in Tampa with his new wife and his new children, and only enters the house through phone calls and occasional checks in the mail, arriving as randomly as good weather in Chicago.

At the head of the table, her aunt presses a hand to her forehead. "Don't waste your time on him. You'll always be holding him up. Get yourself an American man who can provide."

Kiki looks away. Last week Nora asked her, "Don't you want to visit home? Use some of that money you're saving for a ticket."

Kiki shook her head. "I can't go back until I've saved enough. I promised myself I wouldn't return until I could bring Vincent here with me." And she pressed her hand to her forehead, her aunt's same gesture of proud forbearance. "I wonder sometimes if Barbados is still there waiting, or if it's gone. You know what I mean."

Nora fled when she was nineteen. It's been over three years since she saw her home in the UP. The country she left behind no longer exists. But she wonders, just the same, what survived, and who.

⁝

When they're driving home that evening, Kiki says off-handedly, "So you don't like Tom, okay, fine. Tell me your type so I can set you up."

Nora's neck grows hot. "Tom is nice."

"But not for you. Don't lie to me, I can tell." And she always can. "You want some Midwestern corn fed man like the ones you grew up with?"

"That's okay."

Kiki touches Nora's arm, a quick, irritated gesture. "A bunch of the girls are going out tomorrow. I want you to come with us."

"I can't," Nora says. Which means, *I shouldn't.* There are so many things she knows aren't supposed to be for her—strange music and strange men included.

"Sometimes," Kiki begins, her voice wistful, "it feels like my real life is happening somewhere else. While I plod on here, in a dream. All this labor and waiting. You feel that way, too, don't you? But you can't wait forever."

Nora can't hide it any longer. "Kiki, I just found out that my father is dead."

Kiki's hands tighten on the wheel, though she doesn't look away from the road. Chicago traffic takes concentration. "I'm sorry, Nora."

They're silent for a moment; Kiki is watching Nora out of the corner of her eye, trying to figure out what she's feeling. What *is* she feeling? She doesn't know. There's a creeping numbness in her hands, her feet. A solid ball of ice in her stomach. Is this grief? Or is it anger?

"I guess it's not that much of a surprise," Kiki says, finally.

"What do you mean?"

"Isn't that the way these things always end?"

Nora turns to the window. "I don't know what you're talking about."

"Prophets have a way of dying by violence."

Since leaving, Nora has learned of the anti-government standoffs in Idaho, Branch Davidians in Texas, white supremacists in Oregon—all those groups that collapsed in on themselves in disaster and death. They all seemed foolish to her, just another bunch of men with guns, thinking they could fight the world and win. Her church, her people, are different. They have no political ambitions; they aren't racists or anarchists. They are—were—getting ready for a war not with men, but with fallen angels. Their battleground was their own souls. They held together with radical, God-charged love.

"He wasn't who you think," Nora says.

Kiki doesn't challenge her. She just sighs, hands at ten and two on the wheel, always conscientious and careful. Her father is a semi-drunk who lives in Jamaica and sends her wrinkled airmail letters, sometimes wishing her well and updating her on his life, sometimes asking for money. They keep a thread of communication open, even when it's difficult. Kiki holds no illusions about whether he is a good father. "Who was he, then?" she asks.

"He wasn't—a monster," Nora answers.

"What am I supposed to think?" Kiki snaps, impatient now.

Nora promised herself she'd never let her father make her cry again. But here the tears are, impotent, stupid.

Kiki says, "Come out with us tomorrow night. You need to get your mind off your troubles. Don't let the bastard take up any more space."

"I can't."

"Why not? It's because you're still afraid of him, and his judgment. When are you going to see what he really was?"

Kiki digs in her closet and holds up a blouse. "It's time," she says.

"Time for what?"

"To go out."

Nora stares at the offered shirt: turquoise and semi-sheer, with little embroidered hearts on the sleeves. "You think just because my father is—" she can't find the breath to say the word.

"Yes," Kiki says firmly. "There's nothing holding you back now."

Nora's tried to explain to Kiki before, if you grow up reading the Bible as literal truth, then it's like living two lives at once: the world around you, and the world of miracle and ruin, of tiny choices—asking a question, doubting, desiring something or someone—magnified to the size of sin. (*Know ye not that your bodies are the members of Christ? Shall I then take the members of Christ, and make them the members of a whore?*) She grew up with the sense that anything that's yours can be taken from you by God, or by the devil. This body that she walks around in, careful not to touch or look at too long, is not hers to keep, not hers to defile.

"Why did you come to Chicago, anyway?" Kiki asks. "You want a normal life, yeah? You've got to live your life. We're going out."

She presses the shirt to Nora's chest, and Nora takes it.

They laugh and scream on the rattling L to Kingston Mines, a legendary blues club. Once there, they can barely make themselves heard over the howl of the music. An old black man in an elegant white suit bends over his guitar, crooning to it, the guitar seeming to respond, twanging back in its own language. The room hushes, grows warm. The song meanders in and out of its own melancholy, each note smooth and golden, voluptuous with meaning. The crowd leans into the music, and gradually Nora does too.

The other nurses chat with the skinny young men at the bar, happy for conversation. Their days are so full of dying, it's nice to lean back and laugh at something stupid and hopeful a man has said. But they turn away from the men who lean too close. They don't want any guy stuff tonight. So they form a protective wall with their elbows and shoulders, blocking out any man who tries to corner one of them. To Nora, they seem helpless: untrained, unarmed. But there are two ways of looking at city women, two realities they share. They're soft and jaded at once. They've seen worse, they know what violence and death is, know how to ignore both. Their happiness tonight is a shield that buffers their way through tight crowds as they sidle to and from the bar with drinks held high over their heads like travelers fording a river. They drape their arms over Nora's shoulders. "What do you think, honey? Will we make a blues fan out of you?"

Nora smiles shyly, unsure of what to say. This morning these women were wearing surgical gloves and siphoning fluid from people's bodies. Tonight, they have put down their medical bags and became something else, girls shrieking and dancing in the hot mass of people, girls with lovely eyes smiling at men who buy them drinks. Her own transformation is lacking; she seems to only be herself wherever she goes.

Nora leans on an elbow and pretends to listen while a stubbly guy in a porkpie hat tells her how he came to Chicago. He makes it out to be an epic journey, when really he's just from Joliet, a clean-scrubbed suburb forty minutes away on I-90. This is always part of the story, though, how you came to Chicago, how you fell in love with the city. Nora relaxes into a story she's heard before, smiles when he tells her she has nice eyes. Let the promise of the night present itself.

The man has his hand on the small of her back. Somehow he's separated her from her friends, he's shepherding her to the door. What an easy target she is; she's been cut off from the herd like a knock-kneed antelope. But then Kiki cuts her elbow between them, guiding her back to the dance floor.

They stumble to the L at 3:00 AM, exhausted, and drape themselves over the empty seats, sated for a while by something nameless that they needed. In the morning they'll be back in the rooms of dying patients. But tonight they're flying over the city, rushing over a thousand homes and stacked apartments, all-night diners with lonely people hunched in booths eating stacks of waffles, clubs where the music comes thumping out the doors and then dopplers past them, low and dreamlike. Someone has cracked a window. Before she knows it, Nora is climbing the seats, leaning out into the freezing winter air. She wants the night to last and last. "Crazy girl," Kiki laughs, but doesn't stop her. This night is for her. Nora howls out the songs they've heard: "Ohhh, you told me that you loved me—"

At home in their shared bedroom, with Kiki snoring in the bunk bed above her, Nora clicks the link she sent to her phone, for the forum for cult survivors. She taps and scrolls and skims, the details strange and familiar. She's looking for clues, signs that her mother was here.

There's a gaggle of fundamentalist Mormons, describing the horrors of their child marriages, the children they left behind in order to flee. A few psychedelic New Agers, waking up slowly from a twenty-year hallucinogenic dream. The Heaven's Gate followers who weren't there that day for the mass suicide, who still aren't sure what happened or why they survived. There are Moonies and members of the Universal Love Temple, the Twelve Tribes, the Order of the Solar Temple. The Family, The Farm, The Brethren. Debates rage across the forum on what constitutes a cult: whether a fundamentalist Baptist is allowed to join, or a former member of the Aryan Nations. One is too mainstream, the other a political action group; it does not carry the same burden of miracle, the promise of radical bodily salvation. A man from a back-to-the-land commune in Southern California writes that he grew up picking grapes in homemade hemp clothing and praying to Gaia the earth goddess. He writes, [I still don't know which of the mothers was my mother, and which of the fathers was my father.]

Nora can taste the bitterness coming off the forum in waves. The anger in the all-caps descriptions of the Mormons' custody battles, the shunning and secrecy in extreme Amish spinoffs, the militant control of information and selfhood everywhere. [We couldn't get calls from home. We couldn't read a newspaper without permission. They took our passports, our driver's licenses. Our every thought and feeling was subject to control.] Who is that anonymous poster mourning her separation from her children? Who is the poster who was Catholic once, and was drawn into a harder strain of Christianity? Any of them could be her mother, but nothing definitive jumps out.

For almost all of the groups there was a single figurehead, someone charismatic and deadly who pulled the people in, drained their bank accounts, stole their children, and ruined their lives. David Koresh, Jim Jones, Warren Jeffs, Ti and Do; the leader who comforts you, seduces you, makes you fall in love, then makes you afraid to leave. He's a shape-shifter. A father figure, a messiah, a tender guiding hand, a visionary, almost always male. Inscrutable and indomitable and unknowable. All these leaders blend together into one semi-divine con man, huckster, devil.

[Our leader said we were all dirty from our time in the outside world, and every time we left we had to scrub ourselves in front of him, naked, so he could make sure we'd gotten every part.]

[Our leader said I was a bad influence on my kid, so he took her away and had another mother raise her.]

[Our leader said he'd poisoned the drinking water to test our holiness. We had to prove our faith by drinking it anyway. Then when we didn't die, we felt like gods; he told us we'd survived the poison through the power of our faith. I think about that a lot. I drank what I thought was poison for another human being on this earth. I did it willingly. I already threw my life away once.]

Nora can hear a kind of longing in their words. The worship still there, hovering around the edges of their stories. The leaders are legendary, the deeds and misdeeds mythical, miraculous in their cruelty. She scrolls on, marveling at the things people do to each other, the things people let others do to them. How would her father have measured up? What kind of loyalty would he have exacted from her if she'd stayed?

Someone posts, [Do you know the children's finger game 'this is the church, this is the steeple?' All the people in the world that mattered, I could hold inside my hands. The world, contained. And I fucking loved it.]

The guy from the commune posts, [There's something beautiful about giving your entire life, everything you have, in submission to a principle.]

There's a flurry of angry replies, scolding him for glorifying the experience. [That's dangerous talk.] Nora feels a little sorry for him, the way everyone is ganging up. She sends a private message, just one trembling line: [Sounds like you still miss it. I know I do.]

She gets up from bed and walks to the bathroom at the end of the hall and sits on the toilet with her hands pressed between her thighs. Listening to the echo of her breath on the tile, feeling the safety and privacy of this dim little shared bathroom, the riot of toothpastes on the edge of the vintage pink sink. She could disappear here. She could stay forever. Just lean against the wall and close her eyes.

Or she could start asking questions about her own life and what was done to it.

When she returns, he's written back. [Constantly. Do you remember what it first felt like? To belong to something beautiful?]

Genesis and Exodus

BEFORE THE UPPER PENINSULA, they lived in a small, rusting town in Indiana on the east side of Lake Michigan, full of vacant lots and closing factories and little old ladies standing out by their mailboxes in the hot cicada-roaring summers. She remembers weedy front lawns, sandwiches with white bread that balled up on the roof your mouth, the mysterious ambient cry of the ice cream truck that was always one street over, but which way? She remembers crowds of other kids, screaming as cold water jetted out of sprinklers, dashing into each others' arms in endless, violent games of Red Rover. The feverish joy she felt when the other side chanted, "Red Rover, Red Rover, send Nora over!" She was good at plunging headfirst into the other side's locked hands, breaking their grip. She didn't mind scuffing her knees, or the pain from the fall. The older kids offered a grudging respect for the way she hurled herself at the wall of sweaty arms, holding nothing back. She was good at playing dead during street games of war, when they shot each other with stick guns and fell, tragically, clutching their hearts and moaning.

Her brother Henry, thin and slump-shouldered, stood on the sidelines during these games, complaining that they weren't fair, kids were always breaking the rules. They were twins, small for their age, but it was all right to be small and a girl, trouble if you were a boy. Henry couldn't keep up in the races or the wrestling matches. Nora tried rushing in once when the boys began to roll and kick him in a tangle on the street, screaming at them to leave him alone; it only made things worse, they really beat him up that time, pressed his face into the dirt, shoved handfuls of gravel down his pants, crowing that he let his sister fight his fights. That night she crept to his room after bed and said, "Sorry, sorry," and held his hand. He cried a little. They could still cry in front of each other, then. And they didn't tell their parents; they knew this was governed by the brutal hierarchies and struggles of children. They were on their own.

After that day, when the other kids made fun of Heny's ability to throw or hit or his scrawny legs, Nora let it go, with a sliding look to him in the silent communication of twins, telling him she was there even if she could do nothing. He retreated inside, the thin red spine of the children's Bible propped up in front of his nose on the table. When the games drifted apart, she joined him, and together they unrolled a piece of long white butcher paper on the floor of their bedroom and worked on their mural of animals marching into Noah's Ark. They moved seriously across the paper, taking great care with their drawing, the coloring of the male and female of each species, the grouping of like with like. They didn't need to tell each other who should draw the giraffes or argue over the colors of tropical birds.

Sometimes when their father came home from his ministry work, he rolled up his sleeves and joined them, expertly sketching horses that seemed to leap off the page, or primates with artfully shaded faces. The three of them fell into this work together, hunched and silent, intent on drawing every animal that was saved on that ancient biblical day, the room thrumming with the deep peace of shared prayer.

Nora remembers her father's church, with its white tiered steeple and black roof, alone in a grassy unkempt field by the highway. She can close her eyes and see it boiled-white in summer, salt-stained and gray in winter, dark and lashed with rain on the nights when her father stayed late, the junior minister with a special way of tending to troubled people.

One night, Nora waited up for him at the kitchen table. When he came in the door he sat down and drank raggedly from a can of beer. His work depleted him, all the people who wanted to know things about God.

She asked, "What do they want to talk to you for?"

"All sorts of reasons," he said. "People have troubles in this world."

"What do you tell them?"

"I pray with them. A prayer said together has more meaning. 'For where two or three have gathered in My name, there am I with them.'"

Nora tongued the gap in her mouth where a tooth had recently fallen out, thinking how her father had said that a life without God is like that hole, but it's a giant hole in the universe.

"Do their troubles go away?"

"God always answers. Just not in the ways we expect. If your heart is pure and free from sin, you'll understand." He put a hand on her shoulder, his voice low with warning. "Remember: the word of God is an act. It speaks and it makes the universe. If He starts talking to you, you have to obey."

The senior minister pointed his long limp finger at the crowd. They were full in it now, the "Yes sirs" and "amens" rising. "Will He speak in you?" he demanded. "Will you make yourself a vessel?"

Nora clenched and unclenched her small sweating hands. Watching the people swaying in their seats. Just let go. Run at it, like with Red Rover. Give it everything.

She let herself flop and slide off the pew to the ground. A tidal wave was rising inside her chest. Her arms and legs tensed and clutched at the

floor as though she were a spider, crawling and grasping. Strange non-words were coming out of her mouth. *Alahabra mamdaja hallelujah .
. .* a long string of vowels. She rolled and tensed and seized. "That girl, she's speaking the Lord's tongue," someone cried. Nora's eyes were closed, her mouth moving. She hadn't known if you wanted it badly enough, it would come to you, taking your body by surprise.

Then a hand was on her shoulder, holding her thrashing body still. "There, there." She opened her eyes: a boy from the congregation was kneeling on the hard wooden floor beside her, hanging onto her arm. "There, there," he repeated. "Ride it out."

He was a junior deacon, and it was his job to quiet and soothe the people speaking in tongues, helping them through the spasms and shrieks. They called it the thrashing of the serpent's coils: it was the devil inside their bodies, fighting the presence of the Holy Spirit. You just had to hang on, let it take you where it wanted to go. The body was made of sinful matter; it fought angelic tongues, resisted the word of God coming out.

"I'm Levi," the boy told her solemnly. "You're all right. The Lord was passing through."

It was rare for the Spirit to speak in children. Nora lay there a moment more, letting the storm subside, as unpreventable as weather. Listening to the murmurs and shouts and amens around her.

Her mother grabbed her up off the floor. "Quit that right now," she said.

They drove home in silence, Nora and Henry elbowing each other for space in the back seat. "She's showing off," her mother said finally. She was always wary of the way people in their church moaned and sobbed as though their problems with God were for everyone's ears.

"She felt the Spirit," her father replied. "It wouldn't hurt you to try it yourself."

"I know you want me to pray the way those people do," her mother said, "but I just can't that way. The way I talk to God is just for me. I don't show it, for everyone to see. And I don't howl to the moon when I'm doing it. I'm not an animal."

Her father replied, "You always were afraid to feel something, weren't you. Look at what our girl is able to do with her faith. People were lining up to pray over her." Nora caught the excitement in his voice. "'*I will pour out My Spirit on all flesh; Your sons and your daughters shall prophesy, Your old men shall dream dreams, Your young men shall see visions.*' It's a sign."

"A sign of what?"

"What's to come."

"The Kingdom, you mean?" Her mother's voice was doubtful. Mocking, even. She always pretended she didn't fully believe the things her father said, that the promises the Bible made were far off and hypothetical. But Nora had seen her praying in the bedroom, on her knees and rocking, her arms wrapped around herself in a full-body embrace. She'd seen her watching when her father began to preach, his head down and eyes lowered, then rising, his throat swelling as if he might burst into song. What was that look? Wondering and fearful, something like awe.

"Don't you feel like you're living in an extraordinary time?" her father asked.

Nora's father started rousing her for the late night meetings he held for those too uncertain or ashamed to pray during daylight hours. She would get up sleepy and compliant, fumbling for her shoes before getting into the truck and riding with him to the church with its lit green door.

Nora prayed with people who sobbed uncontrollably or whispered about things she didn't understand and begged her to forgive them. She didn't know how she was helping them, but they left calmer, sated for a while.

One day, her father said to her in the truck, "Prayer is like a promise. You're telling the Lord you're here, that you belong to Him. And the voices you speak in are His answer. He's telling you, 'I'm here too. I have called you, and your heart belongs to Me.'" He reached over and squeezed her hand, a rare touch that sent her heart thudding with excitement. "It's proof," he said. "Proof of his love. You can give that to others. You can pass it on."

One night, they were coming home late from a prayer session when they saw a car idling at their street corner, lights off, motor chugging, the radio going with some old song her mother used to play when she was washing dishes, singing along. *"Why not take all of me . . ."*

They could see two heads in the backseat. Foreboding crept into their own car, a growing feeling of thunder in the air, crowding Nora's lungs.

"Stay here," her father said, and got out. Nora didn't want him to go but she knew better than to speak. She watched his long skinny legs move off into the darkness, the dim red brake lights glowing at her like eyes. She saw him lean down into the car window and then recoil and step back. When he got back in the car, she asked, "What is it?"

"There's a devil at work," he said. "Here. In our town."

When they got home, he called the police, and spent the rest of the night hunched at the kitchen table in prayer.

More people started coming to the church at night than during the day. Disheveled, confused, sleepy, prayerful, woeful, resigned, they slid into the pews in the candlelit dimness to watch Nora, falling silent when she began to moan and shriek. Levi was her partner during the day, holding onto her when the storm started to rise in her throat, making sure she didn't bite her tongue, but at night she was alone. Once when she emerged from her trance, her mouth was full of warm bitter blood, streaks of it running down her chin. She grinned, tasting the metal between her teeth.

Strangers yelling in the aisles of the supermarket. Children disappearing from school, moving away, shuffled into foster care. The calamity was striking Indiana and Ohio and Michigan, not unlike the prophecies in her father's favorite books of the Bible. It was creeping up on everyone; no one could see the scope and depth of the blight. The plagues came, amorphous and baffling: job losses, opioids, deaths of despair. In the daytime, their senior minister spoke blandly of hope and healing. But he seemed confused and dismayed, while her father was focused, filled with energy and anger. In his nightly sermons, he was stormy. You're Americans, he'd say. You've been given a bill of sale for goods you never received. You were promised things. There was a covenant in this country, and it's been broken. He quoted Lamentations: *How doth the city sit solitary, that was full of people! How is she become as a widow! She that was great among the nations, and princess among the provinces, how is she become tributary!*

It meant nobody was around to play Red Rover on Nora's street anymore. People slumped against the back wall of the convenience store and clustered in rain-sodden tents under bridges. Her mother wouldn't let her go alone to the store to get Red Vines or milk. The lawnmower disappeared from their shed. The world was changing. It was filled with an ill will she hadn't sensed before, creeping in the shadow behind God's light.

One night when her parents were out to dinner, Nora woke to bumping and rustling sounds outside her door. When she poked her head down the hall she could see the babysitter asleep on the couch, her head tilted back, her mouth open, the TV washing grayly over her face. Nora tiptoed to her parents' bedroom door. Inside, a strange man was standing by the dresser, holding a black garbage bag. He wasn't wearing all black or a ski mask like the burglars on TV, just jeans and a stained T-shirt, his skinny torso sunken into his hips like a crooked question mark. He had a day's growth of beard and his eyes gleamed in the half-light. He looked afraid and lonely and she wanted to help him, the way her father said they were supposed to help the least among us. So when he put his finger to his lips, she nodded, and he climbed out the window and slipped away, running across the evening lawns striped with moonlight.

In the morning, her father drove to the pawn shops to see if her mother's jewelry had been turned in, returning grim and empty-handed.

Nora drifted, playmateless, through the house, hanging in Henry's doorway while he read, his chin tucked down into his chest, his children's Bible open before him.

"Listen," she whispered one night. "I saw the robber."

He put his finger in the book and looked up. "What?"

She paused: the house empty, their mother in the back shaking sheets out on the line. She heard the solid *thwap* of her flapping them in the air.

"He looked so sad," she said. "Desperate, like one of Dad's people. He looked like he needed our help." Then she paused. "Are you going to tell?"

She knew Henry's thinking face, they were twins after all, and sometimes they could tell what was running through the other's mind.

"No," he decided. There was nothing in it for him. "Besides, he's going to meet justice in the end."

"What do you mean?"

"Dad asked me to look for signs in the Bible that judgment is coming. He says I have a gift for exegesis." He allowed himself a small, modest smile.

"Exe-wha—"

"He says we're living in extraordinary times and the Bible predicted all this."

"All what?"

He showed her the Bible passages he had found:

Ah, sinful nation,

a people laden with iniquity,
a seed of evildoers,
children that are corruptors!
They have forsaken the LORD,
they have provoked the Holy One of Israel unto anger,
they are gone away backward.

And:

Therefore wait ye upon me, saith the LORD, until the day that I rise up to the prey: for my determination is to gather the nations, that I may assemble the kingdoms, to pour upon them mine indignation, even all my fierce anger: for all the earth shall be devoured with the fire of my jealousy.

"Dad says we're living in the sinful nation," Henry explained. "The unrighteous are going to be punished, and the righteous will be repaid."

Nora stared at the words, stroking her finger down the tissue-thin page. She knew the Bible was full of stories she loved: Noah and the flood, the warring angels and the creatures in the garden, going up to Adam one at a time to be named. But now she remembered what her father had said: the word of God was an act. It could make or unmake. What if the flood they'd been drawing so diligently in their mural was real? What if it was coming again?

"We'll all have a part to play, before the end," Henry said, pushing his glasses up his nose.

One late night, they sat in the cab of the truck in the church parking lot, which was filled with cars as if it were a Sunday morning. Her father stared straight ahead, before speaking. "I need you to try something this time," he said. "We could help these people better if we could tell them what they're going to face. I need you to prophesy."

"Prophesy?"

"When you listen to the Lord and speak. I want you to do that. But make a prophecy. Tell us what the Lord is saying in simple words. It might feel like a performance at first. But if you believe in it, it'll become real. I think the Lord wants to fill you up with the Spirit and give us a warning about what's to come. These people need to see that."

"But what do I say?"

He touched her hand. That thrilling contact. "The Spirit will tell you. Make yourself empty and let the Spirit fill you up."

The church was half-lit and filled with the souls who had been coming to pray with her and her father. These were not the scrubbed up and nicely dressed men and women who filled the pews on Sunday mornings. They wore afterthought beards and had pockmarks on their thin, hollowed faces. Limp hair in scraggly ponytails, their bodies shapeless under salt-stained coats. Their faces blank and expectant with need. If her father's hand weren't firmly on her head, she might have turned and run down the aisle, back to the safety of the car.

Her father began his sermon. The words themselves didn't matter all that much, as long as the cadence was right, the certain key phrases that made the congregants nod their heads. He started speaking about the ways the church had let them down, how the world had fallen away from the promise they'd been given. He said "righteousness." He said "redemption." He said, "The tree is poisoned at the root." He said, "I know you're angry. I'm angry, too. In the old days, we could point a finger at the source of the poison. But now it's everywhere. It's inside us. It's in our children. It's in our schools, our government. We're living in a ruined world. This was the world the Bible warned us would come."

The congregation grinned or grimaced in sympathy. Her father told them, "Your lives are full of pain and you don't know why. You did everything right and yet you suffer. You wanted something for yourself and someone lied to you and told you you'd get it. The world is darker and dirtier than the world you were led to expect. It's times like these that we turn back to God and realize He's been there all along, waiting for us to accept His plan. He has a plan for you, and He's waiting for you to accept it and join us. You know it, don't you? You can feel it. We're here tonight because we feel the threat and the promise. We're the only ones who are really listening."

His eyes slid to her, clear as a shout. Nora stood up and walked to him, her breath loud in her ears. This was not a game of pretend, it was not Red Rover; it was real and he needed her. Just decide to do it. Decide.

Her hand shot up over her head. The other clawed at her throat, so tight it was hard to breathe. Something was bubbling out of her—a voice, not her voice. Let this mood take you, this hovering unsettled frenzy in the air. Let your knees weaken, your body collapse on the shallow run of wooden stairs up to the dais. (Later, in the mirror, she'd find yellowing bruises climbing ladder-like up her spine.) "Ah, sinful nation!" she cried. "Offspring of evildoers! The earth will be devoured by the fire of my zeal!"

Prophecy, pouring out of her. Then the tongues. The people around her ferocious with joy, stamping their feet.

Proof.

"Didn't I tell you?" her father said afterward in the car. Nora was exhausted and sliding into sleep, the street lamps gliding past her head in the high-up window. His hand stroking her hair, moving in circles, like a spell he was casting over her for protection. "I knew you could. You're special. My God-given girl."

Her mother was standing in the kitchen in her paisley robe. "Go to bed," she said, but Nora just crept down the hall and crouched outside her bedroom door.

Her father said, "Listen, Kat. Remember when we met? How it felt. Like predestination. We knew we were meant to be together. We knew when we had Nora and Henry. We just didn't know what we knew. We've been picked: our family, our kids."

Henry's whistly breath was on Nora's neck. "What is Dad talking about? Where were you?"

"At church," she whispered. She couldn't tell him everything, it was too much, and she didn't understand it all anyway. "He's talking about us," was all she could say.

"It's her," her father said. "All those other times I tried to get a flock going, I didn't have her yet. Remember your Isaiah: '*And they shall hang upon him all the glory of his father's house, the offspring and the issue, all vessels of small quantity.*'"

"That's me," she whispered to Henry. "I'm the vessel."

She felt her heart beating in the dark, and could hear Henry's heart beating, too, and for the first time she knew they were different. Not just their clammy naked bodies or his glasses or her light mouse-brown hair and his dark. It was something she could do. Something she could be. It was thrilling and frightening at once.

"Nobody is going to help these people if I don't take up the task," her father said. "They're starving. We have to show them the radical possibility of their own salvation. But there's no getting clean here. You know that."

There was a long silence. "Frank, what are you saying? What do we have to do?" her mother asked, and her voice was different now, probing and unsure.

"And I could do it. With her I could do it," he said. He wasn't even listening.

"What about me?" Henry asked, too loud.

"Sssh!" But it was too late. Her mother swept into the hall, sending them back to their rooms with a pointed finger.

In her bed, Nora listened to the throb of her own pulse against the pillow, unable to sleep, her body beating like a clock. She had heard the urgency in her father's voice, but she didn't know what he meant, or what he was going to ask them all to do.

⁑

A friend of a friend had a property he wanted to sell. A remote spot battered by the weather off Lake Superior in the winter, the area not safe for camping because the ground was pockmarked with holes from old mines.

Men gathered at the kitchen table arguing about it, maps curling at the edges. It was perfect, her father declared. Protected and lost, full of spiritual potential, ready for the coming storm. Nora wandered in and out of the conversations as she passed from the kitchen to the bedroom and back again, dragging her doll by the arm. Whatever happened to that doll?

It was 2001. In September, after the towers fell, her father's following tripled, and plans moved from hazy hypotheticals to realities. Nora was young enough for the events of that Tuesday to be peripheral, its portents only fuzzily understood: getting sent home early from school, her mother sitting at the kitchen table, watching footage looping on the television, kneading bread dough past the point of use; she and Henry bouncing a tennis ball against the side of the house, the only sound on the street the hard *chock* of the ball hitting the clapboard siding, like one key on a piano tapped over and over, until their mother came to the door and yelled at them to stop.

Wordlessly, she and Henry looked at each other, and in the way they had sometimes of knowing what the other would do, they left the tennis ball and walked into the grassy vacant lot behind their house, where overgrown catgrass stretched tall into the ruins of a house behind theirs that had burned down years ago. The shell of the structure was dangerous and unstable and their mother told them to stay away, but it was the kind of place that drew children, with its crazily leaning walls and dark holes in the roof open to the sky. They poked around in the cool shade of the house's lee, finding signs of human habitation they had never noticed before: cigarette butts and beer cans and mysterious piles of burnt metal spoons. Strangers, enemies, had found their way here. They were everywhere.

Their father summoned them from the backyard. Nora and Henry left the burned house guiltily, expecting punishment. They found their father squatting in the untended grass, looking like he belonged there, a creature of the outdoors in his element. When he saw his children, he called to them in a voice of such tender sorrow that they forgot to be afraid of his anger, and came to his knee, one on each side, and he pulled up shoots of crab grass and whistled through the small openings in order to make them smile. He told them they were safe, that he would always protect them.

"But how do you know?" Henry insisted.

"Because you are loved by God, and love is a kind of protection."

Nora wanted to believe him.

"What's to stop them from coming here and hurting us?" Henry asked. Nora didn't know if he meant the faraway attackers who believed in a different god, with fervent beliefs she could scarcely understand, or the strangers breathing all around them, filling their town with unholy light.

"They're not ever going to find us," their father said. "Because we're going away. All of us, our church has decided." He pulled them closer. "We were right. It's begun."

They both leaned into him, content for a while, enclosed in the heavy warmth of his arms. Listening to the buzzing of cicadas, their frantic end times song.

That evening, Nora's father called her into his bedroom. "This is the sign we've been waiting for," he said, and there was not one trace of a smile on his face, no more warmth in his voice. "You know that, don't you. This is what God told you to warn us about."

She shivered in the cool, unlit room. The solemnity of the moment was too big for her; she wished she hadn't prophesied anything. Words were just words, and she was just a kid.

"I'm going to need you," he said.

She swallowed, straightened, and nodded.

⁂

Nora still remembers the rainy spring day the following year when the trucks lined their quiet street, men and women standing outside grinning and uneasy and exhilarated, like kids who have just lit a firecracker and are waiting for it to go off. Crates and bags making every truck groan on its hinges. Levi dragging sacks too heavy for him to carry, the rain plastering his hair to his bumpy skull. Her mother dashing in and out of the house forgetting things. She and Henry jammed in somebody's cab, waving to their neighbors in their yards. "We almost forgot," Henry said, and held up a rolled scroll of butcher paper. It was the Noah's Ark mural. Nora clutched it, wrinkling the paper, grateful for Henry's flash of brotherly tenderness.

Goodbye, house. Nora recalls the way it looked, all hunched up and small in the rain like a dog somebody was leaving behind.

When they passed the church, she began to cry.

"Ssh now." Her mother held Nora and Henry tightly, one in each arm. Even as she held them she was looking out the window, somewhere else entirely. She explained how there were two kinds of churches, the church militant and the church triumphant. The church militant was the church Christians carried with them on the earth, and the church triumphant was the perfect church manifested in heaven. "We carry the church militant with us," she said. "It's inside us, and we carry it with us wherever we go."

A Catholic notion, Nora learned later. Something her mother would never fully let go of, occasionally getting into shouting matches with her father over it, when she insisted on her rosary and her little bent deck of prayer cards. "You're always saying you have to feel the Lord's presence in your life," she once said to him. "This is how I feel it."

Nora still thinks of the church militant as the rainwashed little building with the white steeple and the green door, though she has never been back. She is carrying it around inside her, even though she is fourteen now, and the woods have been home for years, and their church meetings are in a barn on a grassy hillside ringed by old-growth trees, with mourning doves cooing in the eaves, the smell of hay and barley warming in the crooked shafts of light that filter through gaps in the roof. Now they ask her to call upon the voice and prophesy whenever they are feeling afraid or angry or just want that savage joy again. It is all inside her, all the believers, all the people who love her, inside. *This is the church—and this is the steeple—open the doors—and see all the people—*

On Why We Left

Everyone was excited.

The lonely people and the families. The kids chasing each other under trucks and through their parents' legs. There was a feeling like Christmas in the air. We didn't know what to do with ourselves, we were so happy. We were leaving for our true home, taking control of our lives, freeing ourselves from the devil's grasp on the world.

Because that's what it felt like, living here. There was something wrong with the world. We could taste it in the water. We could hear it in the humming of our refrigerators at night, see it in the black mold creeping down our shower tiles, the strangers idling in cars on quiet street corners.

We believed you when you said the devil was to blame.

We were already starting to think and feel as one. Before we left, we gathered on someone's damp front lawn and folded ourselves together to pray, arm and arm and arm. The hairs rose on the backs of all our necks when you told us he was on that street with us, whispering in our ears.

We cried when you told us the judgment and the restoration of heaven was near, and that we would live to see it. We were God's people, fearfully and wonderfully made, and we knew we were meant for more.

You didn't tell us how hard it would be. You didn't tell us that the devil was everywhere, and there was no getting rid of him. Or maybe we took him with us, into those woods.

Chicago, October

"TELL ME ABOUT YOUR WIFE," Nora asks.

Her favorite patient doesn't open his eyes. He's in his chair by the window, his hair trailing in long damp wisps after his bath, listening to a recap on the radio of the last game. He saw it on TV, but he likes to relive it the next day. They're nearing the end of the series and it's looking real for the Cubs.

"She had the best voice. She had this throaty laugh like Lauren Bacall. I'd be downstairs and hear her upstairs chuckling at something the cat did. I could hear it a mile away."

Nora doesn't know who Lauren Bacall is, but she nods along as Mike describes the sounds his wife made that only he knew. Coughs and *tsks* and rainy day humming songs. "You don't know what you'll miss," he says. "I'm afraid my last thought will be something stupid. I'll still be thinking about baseball when I should be thinking about her. Remembering her voice. I don't have any recordings of it, you know. I try to bring it to mind, try to make it live again. But I can't. When we made love, she screamed, really screamed. Like a wildcat."

Mike opens his eyes, and he and Nora look at each other, not sure how they've arrived at this unexpected intimacy. "No one else alive knows that," he says.

"I won't tell anybody," Nora promises. Her patients, like members of her church, have lost many of their inhibitions; when the world is going to end, embarrassment loses its power. She's listened to old ladies testify about all the men they've sinned with; men describing the way it felt to prick the skin between their toes with needles and fill their veins with liquid light.

"That's the problem. There are all these things I remember about her," Mike says. "And when I go, it all goes with me."

They sit quietly with the knowledge of this, the clock ticking on the mantle. Nora does not like offering bright chirpy truisms. Her father once told her, "You ease someone's pain by saying, 'Yes, it hurts.' To affirm someone's world, that's a powerful thing. That's how you make them love you." Finally, she says, "We don't just carry our own lives. We bear witness to others. You tell me about her and the chain goes on." She stops. She doesn't want to use her father's tricks. She hates how she still knows the old moves by heart. "My father died," she says, abruptly. Whatever fragile friendship she has with Mike can't be real unless he knows.

He sucks in his cheeks. "I'm sorry, angel. I remember when my father died. I was twenty. Not so far off from you, right?"

She nods, standing and busying herself around the room clearing old bandage wrappers.

"He worked at the Morton Salt Company," Mike continues. "Thirty-five years, can you believe it? Same job, factory foreman, for thirty-five years. Chicago born and bred. Salt of the earth." He laughs. "His hands were always cracked open, these cracks—" he traces phantom lines on his own hands, then seems to catch sight of the creased, swollen claws. "Then, a stroke. He wasn't an old man. Young men died of things like that, back then."

"Do you still miss him?" Nora clutches a handful of bandages.

"Sure I do. That never goes away. You think about something he might have said or what advice he might have to offer. You wish you could talk to him, sometimes. Now I've outlived him. I don't think he'd have any more advice to give me. But still, you wish you had his blessing. You hope you've lived in a way—that he would be proud. But you never stop wondering." Mike is still staring at his hands, turning them this way, that way.

Nora laughs a little, a half-choke. "So you never really get over it," she says.

"What you do is, you go through the ritual," Mike tells her. "We had the wake, and the funeral, and people laughed and got drunk and told jokes about him. That's the way the Irish say goodbye to a fellow. You walk home drunk and tired after the wake, and you go to the funeral and sit hungover in church, and the priest says the right words, and then you throw a handful of earth onto the casket. You have to bury him, you see. It helps you say goodbye."

"Is that what you want?" she asks. "A good Catholic send-off?" She tries to ask her patients about their wishes, in case they haven't told anyone, or have failed to write an advance directive. It's surprising how many people pass without telling anyone what they actually want for themselves. They always think there's more time to make the unpleasant plans, and then there isn't any time left.

"Not me. I don't want anyone to kick up any fuss," he says. "None of the God stuff, none of the superstition. No prayers and no opening a window to let the spirit out. I suppose I'd rather not go alone. You could be there. Or Emily, my daughter."

"You have a daughter?" Nora's astonished; he has made no mention of her all this time. The pictures on the mantle show him and his wife with a young girl, though. "Where is she now?"

"She's not far. But we haven't spoken in years. Lucky her." He smiles a little, always trying to shore up the tenor of their conversations. "I was no angel while she was growing up. I had a beast on my back. I drank. She got out as soon as she was old enough and she's only visited a few times since."

"Have you told her you're sick? I bet she'd come."

"Maybe she would." He's still staring at his hands, rubbing them as if they've grown cold. "But I don't want her to feel obligated. She put up with a lot."

"If you leave her without saying goodbye, she'll always wonder what happened."

He cocks his head like a curious dog. "Are you wondering about your father?"

"I guess so. There are some unanswered questions." She's being vague. She knows she needs to either trust him, or not. "My father's death was suspicious. Nobody seems to know what really happened."

"Well, listen. My neighbor here is a cop. An old friend of mine. You could ask him a few questions, he wouldn't mind checking on something for you. If it's those sort of questions that need answering." Mike lies back, his eyes already closing. "Lord, I get so tired these days. You think about it."

Nora helps him into bed, and then walks through the sitting room on her way out. She strokes a picture frame and her fingers come back dusty; no one has tended to it in some time. When Mike dies, his things will be put in boxes, the precious along with the worthless. No one will know what was loved.

You have to bury him.

When she hears a snore emanate from the bedroom, she sneaks back upstairs and pushes open the closed door of a room she's never seen. It's a mess of boxes, a depository of ancient workout equipment. But underneath the junk is the semblance of a kid's room, meticulously preserved: a narrow twin bed with a faded floral bedspread; a shelf of yellowing paperbacks, books about horses; an electric typewriter, a model horse, a dream catcher, the cheap plastic kind you get from carnivals, hanging on the wall. He's kept it all: his daughter's childhood is here, tenderly preserved.

Does a father's love ever extinguish itself?

Nora crawls under a NordicTrack's arm and lies down on the bed. She closes her eyes and breathes in the dust.

⁙

On their first meeting, Kiki—who had been assigned to train Nora—took one look at her patchy men's flannels, and long hair braid, and said, "Some sort of backwoods girl. What are you doing here?"

They went together to the Target on State Street and picked plain, functional blouses and stockings and slip-on shoes. "You are the guest in someone else's home," Kiki said. She wouldn't let her enter the building until Nora had memorized everything in her medical bag. "I don't like training new nurses," she said, frank and annoyed, her thin dark brows arched high. "People are dying, and they don't deserve some trainee coming in and shitting all over their final moments. They deserve someone who is taking this job seriously."

"You must have been new, once," said Nora, timidly.

"Yes, okay, I was not always the angel of heavenly mercy. So we have work to do."

Nora followed Kiki into a cramped third-floor walk-up in Little Italy. A middle-aged man greeted them at the door and showed them into the dim, windowless bedroom. "Mama, you have two nurses today," he said. A tiny woman sat stiff and upright in bed, awash in blankets and glaring at the wall.

Kiki moved into the room without hesitation. "How are you today, Mrs. Alviani?"

"Good, until you came," the woman spat, without changing expression. She was concentrating fiercely on a spot on the wall and her gaze would not waver.

"She hates me," Kiki whispered to Nora. "Some of them will hate you." She moved to the bedside and built up the pillows around the old woman, so that she wouldn't have to work so hard to stay up. Nora stood by awkwardly while Kiki moved smoothly, assuredly, through a vital sign reading, a re-up of pain medications. She eased the nightgown up and over the woman's head. Nora was shocked at how thin and wasted the old woman's body was; she looked like a victim of starvation, with her ribs jutting, her breasts flat sacks, her powdery, ashen skin hanging limply off her bones. She stood, mute, until Kiki nudged her. "Don't stare. Hand me that towel."

Kiki gave the woman a quick towel bath and re-dressed her, while Mrs. Alviani glowered and swore in Italian. "I'm sorry, it's not a good day today," her son said. But Kiki was unfazed. "Mrs. Alviani, I hope your pain is manageable. You can take two of these pills if it gets worse, and remember to take these for constipation. We'll be back tomorrow."

On the sidewalk, Kiki tallied the medications in her bag. "Normally I do this in the kitchen on my way out," she said. "But in this case—she wanted us gone." She paused, looked Nora straight in the face. "Don't ever stare like that again. It's rude. Rude doesn't even cover it."

Her Barbadian accent, warm and melodic, made her words sound gentler, but Nora's face flushed hot all the same. "I'm sorry."

"You might feel the urge to look too long. Or even to laugh, sometimes," Kiki said. "But don't ever, unless they want to laugh at themselves."

"Why was she so angry?"

Kiki shrugged. "Wouldn't you be? She's dying."

"That's not your fault. You didn't do this to her."

"Who is she going to blame? God?" Kiki frowned. "Don't start getting all high and mighty, thinking they should be grateful for you. You can't think that way. You've got to think about the job that needs doing. And the job isn't always to give this pill, don't give that one. Sometimes they want ice cream even though the doctors have told them they can't have ice cream. So you give them ice cream." Kiki leaned on the wrought-iron railing outside the house, adjusting the things in her bag. "And after you leave, you can say what you want about them. The old white ladies are always the worst."

They both laughed, the dying woman in the apartment still on their minds, the laughter seeping out anyway. After a short silence Kiki said, "When it comes down to it, I think hospice is the purest form of medicine. All those other tinkerers and mechanics—the surgeons, say— are trying to cure something that can't be cured. They're just putting things off. We're what happens when we come up against death. We look it in the face, we don't pretend. No more 'cautiously optimistic' and 'we have every reason to hope.' Doctors are afraid of death, I think. When they get to the end, they don't know what to do or how to help. Then we come in, when somebody decides to give up. We have to show them there are still ways to make choices, to make the days matter."

They ate hot dogs at Devil Dogz, a hole in the wall place in the South Loop. The hot dogs arrived in metal holders, toppling over with the weight of their heaped cheese and relish. Nora didn't even know how to hold the hot dog, or what part to eat first. She still found outsider food foreign and vaguely obscene, the meat so far removed from the animal it came from. Kiki watched, amused: "I thought every American knew how to eat a hot dog. Just where do you come from, really?"

Nora told her a little about her childhood in the UP—just the smallest part, the pieces outsiders would understand. Pentecost, the compound, the believers. Kiki listened, her eyebrows climbing. "You all lost your heads," she said finally. "Like something my Mama says. *Bazodee*. It means crazy. But crazy in love." She took a messy bite of her hot dog, and sighed. "What can you do, about family?"

Nora shadowed Kiki for three months, and it took her all that time to figure out how to be good at her job. On the surface there wasn't much to it: cleanliness and pain management, schedules of stool softeners, twisting off the caps of orange bottles, hoisting frail weightless people in and out of beds. But it took more than that to really do things right, which she witnessed in Kiki's adaptability, her calm, knowledgeable presence. In homes upended by panic and grief, Kiki demonstrated how to fluff a pillow and take a pulse; how to give an enema and treat a bed sore; how to draw fluid from a lung; and how to mark the time until the medication kicked in and the pain was gone. If this doesn't work, let's try this, she would tell them. How about a meal, a heating pad, a walk around the block? How about a phone call to your children, or some quiet time free of their presence? How about some fresh air and sunlight. How about we sit quietly and I'll hold your hand, if that is what you need. Let the time pass, be present in the enjoyment or endurance of each moment.

They all needed something that Kiki hinted at, but couldn't fully explain. Something not quite medicine, not quite blessing. There's a holiness that sometimes creeps into a room when a person is dying—when a husband holds his wife's hand and won't let go even when her clothes have to be changed. Or a parent with her child, a daughter who has almost lost consciousness, but who still kisses her mother's forehead when she leans in close. The way a son rubs lotion assiduously into his mother's cracked hands. Love in diligence, in the way people speak or don't need to speak. It leaves Nora breathless, this charged and lonely beauty that can enter the rooms of the dying. She's sure that some form of God is present even when she's sure on other days that there is no God. And Kiki with her warm hands and her kind, listening face, is an instrument of God as surely as she is her own solitary self.

On the shelf of slumped training manuals in the nurses' house, Nora pages through earnest introductions struggling to define this sacredness. *Hospice. Archaic: a lodging for travelers or pilgrims, especially one run by a religious order,* one book tells her. *These are the most important patients you will ever attend to as a nurse. They are on a journey to somewhere unknown.*

"There has to be a witness to the dying," Kiki says. "That is the job."

⁏

It's Halloween. The doorbell has been in a steady chime all evening, the sound of laughter outside, screams from kids running around in witch and zombie costumes. Most of the other women enjoy handing out candy, but Nora hides, unnerved by the devils and ghouls and goblins about, the late-night teenagers looming in doorways with leering skull masks and pillowcases full of eggs.

She holds her phone under the covers, texting with her friend on the cult survivors forum. She told herself she was doing reconnaissance, looking for her mother on there. But now, chatting with CommuneKid87 is why she keeps coming back.

[What did you used to do for Halloween?] he asks.

[It was an evil night. We lit candles and sang for hours. We had to keep the devil at bay.] She tells him her father died. But she doesn't tell him it was by gunshot, or that she has no idea who might have done it.

[He would have wanted a funeral, surely,] he writes. [On our commune, when someone died we had a Tibetan sky burial.]

[What's that?]

[You give the person back to the universe. You open up the guts and leave the body in the open, where the vultures can get it. It's our last gift back to the earth.]

[Sweet Jesus.]

[We're only renting, :)] he writes. [We got in trouble with the authorities a few times, you can imagine. We had to defend it in court, show that it was a real religious ceremony, that we hadn't made up. We showed them clips from the movie *Kundun*.]

Nora tries to picture what kind of funeral her father would have wanted. A Pentecostal one, surely, full of holy rolling, shouted prayers and fervent grief. For Pentecostal Christians, Pentecost is the most important day on the calendar. It's the Greek name for the ancient Jewish holiday of Shavuot, a festival celebrating the wheat harvest. But on Shavuot in the Gospels, the Holy Spirit entered the apostles and made them speak in tongues, affirming Christ's resurrection for all who doubted. It's the moment that proves our relationship with God is personal and real, not just a metaphor. It also affirms God's physical, literal presence in the world, and His sovereignty over our bodies in this life as surely as in the next one. Her father believed in that physical intimacy. He explained it to her once, pressing his fist slowly into her hand, then interlacing their fingers into a double knot. This is how close we are to God, he said. Very few people understand that, and have felt the Spirit move in their lives. But you and me, kid. You and me.

And if the story of the tongues is literally true, then so are all the others: the burning bushes and pillars of salt, the devil's whispered promises in the night, the leviathan heaving itself onto land, the whore giving birth to the end of the world. Pentecostals have a reputation as the scary ones. They're all in, living the truth from the beginning to the end of the story: the first revelation (*Let there be light*) and the last (*Surely I come quickly*). If the stories are true, then eschaton, the final event in the divine plan, is part of the story, as certainly as creation. Even mainstream Pentecostals believe in the rapture and the day of judgment on some buried, intimate level, the way you can know you are going to die someday and also not know. Nora would go to bed every night with her shoes on, so she'd be ready. For war, or fire, or Rapture, she wasn't sure.

[Did he have time to make amends?] he asks. [To ask for forgiveness, for what he did?]

She wonders if the person who shot him gave him his chance. Did he beg for his life, or did it come, out of nowhere, like a thunderbolt?

[I wasn't there,] she writes. [I'll never really know.]

[There must be others who were. Don't you want to know what happened?]

[I ...]

She stops typing. She can't explain that it would be too risky to ask. That they could take her back again, could demand she pay her price. There was something she was supposed to deliver, and these people have reason to expect reparation. She didn't know at the time that when you defied the church's rulings, or refused to be exorcised, there were consequences. Reduced rations, no hot water in your trailer, the hard, dirty work like shoveling garbage and burying dead animals. The deacons watching you on the hillside with their guns on their hips. The others walking by, so careful not to look.

She writes, [I should tell you. I was one of the people making promises. I told people they'd be saved if they joined us. It was me. I was the recruiter.]

His answer comes a long, dark minute later. [Why are you telling me now?]

[There has to be a witness,] she responds. [Someone has to know the truth.]

Kids are walking by the house, singing their creepy Halloween songs. *The worms crawl in, the worms crawl out . . .*

The doorbell rings, but no one's downstairs to get it; everyone's out on rounds. By the time Nora opens it, holding a bowl of chocolate kisses, no one is there; the kids must have moved on to the next house. Someone has kicked their pumpkin. Its mouth is smashed in, the eyes torn and sagging. She stands in the doorway for a moment, searching for figures in the shadows.

They have her address. They could be watching her play with pagan holidays, trying her best to live a normal life. She's a seed planted in foreign soil and they know it. "Come out," she calls, and feels stupid, her voice so thin and frightened, her breath clouding in the night air.

Then a light comes on across the street, in the old duplex apartment building that she thought was vacant. Just one light in a window, on and off. Blink-blink-blink. Like a signal.

She's being watched. Telling her they know she's there.

She waits, hardly daring to breathe. She remembers the old flashlight system the deacons had on night watches, how she'd be walking through the woods and see lights blinking in a particular rhythm and know she was protected.

No one comes out of the darkness; the street is quiet. They're waiting for her move.

It's almost a comfort, to know they are here.

She blows out the candle in the wounded pumpkin, turns out the outside light and locks the door.

The Bottomless Pit

September 2008

(133 days until the world ends)

LEVI STANDS BESIDE NORA, tall and lanky in the waving yellow grass of the meadow. His .22 is slung easily over his shoulder; he squints as he scans for rabbits. He's fifteen, expected to do the work of the other men, but now, with the end of the world approaching, the adults are so busy that she and Levi are sometimes forgotten, left to wander the deer trails on their own.

They've lived here for seven years, long enough that the world outside is a faint and puzzling memory. Did she really line up with other kids for ice cream handed to them out of a truck? Did she really once go to school? The closest thing they have now is survival school, where a member of the community gathers up the kids and teenagers in the barn to practice woodworking, or fire-building, or tying tourniquets with swift jerks of scraps of fabric. Nora has a battered notebook smelling of fish oil that lists the random things they've been taught:

Can make a water filter with cotton, sand, gravel, and activated charcoal.

Can boil spruce needles in water to make enough vitamin C to prevent scurvy.

Insects: widely available and high in protein. Grubs and larvae same. Live in rotten tree stumps. Follow bears, woods' most resourceful omnivores.

Boil acorns for two hours to remove bitter taste.

All parts of dandelion -> edible.

Nora stays low in the grass, listening for the tiny scratching of mice and the chewing of rabbits, Levi a gawky sentinel, watching for enemies. If you know what to listen for, the woods are never truly silent—birds calling, squirrels chattering, the rush of the river, even the chewing of grasshoppers working their way down stems of grass. Above it all is the guttural roar of ATVs rumbling across the compound, men on four-wheelers dragging loads or patrolling, the noise rattling Nora's ribs.

This fall has a charged feeling of melancholy and anticipation. Her father and Henry have determined that the time of Revelation will come in the new year, 2009. Everything—last grasshoppers, last cat grass, last season of whirligigs spinning their way down from the maple trees—seems to glow.

This morning, before her father left, he called out to her and Henry sitting at the kitchen table. "John 4:3."

Nora could picture the narrow column of spidery text on the page, the old words like friends, marching across her mind's eye. She was at John 3:16—*This is how we know what love is*—and John 3:19, a little further down—*This is how we know that we belong to the truth*—but Henry beat her to it, as always: "But every spirit that does not acknowledge Jesus is not from God. This is the spirit of the Antichrist, which you have heard is coming and even now is already in the world."

Her father nodded, and Henry pushed his glasses up his face and smiled that small, self-satisfied smile that makes her hate him sometimes.

"You get some things from work, and some things from grace," her father said, touching her head. "You're all grace, girl."

From their spot in the meadow, Nora can see their world as if laid out on a map: to the west, the fields where women are working, pushing little hand plows through the thin, rocky soil, trying to coax enough to eat out of the ground. Women weeding, kneeling in the rows, bending and reaching and pulling all day, their hands and faces creased and black with dirt. To the south, a cluster of prefab structures: their house, and Levi's trailer, his father in the yard, chopping wood. They're close enough to hear the dull chocks of his axe, his small figure in silent motion. To the north, her father is unscrolling blueprints and talking about the new silo, the new root cellars. Will there be enough time to get them built? He looks different from the other beefy, bearded men who surround him. He has a fragile look, shoulders sunken and slender as a girl's, a pale goose-pimpled torso she sees him slapping with cold water in the mornings. Large black glasses and an architect's pencil tucked behind his ear. Long-fingered, delicate hands, good at sketching, at making diagrams in the air with his hands, at pointing and planning. The men gather around him, leaning over the plans spread on a wooden table, intent.

"Did you hear?" Levi asks.

"Hear what?"

"There's been a defection," he says, eyebrows raised, deadly serious. But then he clams up because her mother is climbing the hill, her long skirt catching in her legs. "Nora, come help," she shouts.

"I'll see you later," Nora says to Levi.

Nora and her mother walk the long wooded paths with a basket of supplies, tending to the women who need their assistance. Bringing linseed oil and duck fat, rosemary and sometimes antibiotics, whatever her mother has collected in her private stash. While Henry studies classical Greek in his room, Nora often stands with her mother at the stove, learning to sift and distill herbs and oils, grinding spruce bark, willow, and wild mint. She has learned not to overwork the bread and to separate egg yolks with half a cracked shell; the whites make a good adhesive. She can pasteurize milk and skim off the rising curd to make sour, hard little cakes of cheese. She knows how to seal her boots with duck fat in winter and make a yeast mother that can be torn and multiplied, again and again. We'll need people who know these things, her mother says. This is how to dress a wound, press your hand on someone's head to detect a fever; darn a sock and fix a leaky boot, feed a cold, steam a cough, cauterize a wound, soothe a hurt or a worry just with your arrival in a house. The body heals itself, if you let it. The soul is in God's hands.

When the women of the compound need something from her mother, they slip a prayer card into her hand, a secret signal her father and the deacons have never noticed. Nora often accompanies her, sitting and drinking birchbark tea while a woman talks about her problems—kidney issues, aches and pains, bleeding, or lack of it.

Today, they begin with Hannah. Nearly blind from decades working in a dimly lit textile factory checking for sewing mistakes, Hannah saves warm pocketed caramels from a secret supply. A lifetime of swishing Coke before bed has taken most of her teeth. When she laughs her mouth is a startling open pit. Her mother digs in her basket, comes up with tiny hotel-sized bottles of brandy to dab on her gums. Hannah keeps them awhile, talking about the pills she and her son were taking before she came here, both of them busted up with back pain from years of work, or in his case, football.

Next, they visit Joan and Dinah, who live in the next trailer over. Joan has a long black braid thick as her arm, and is half Métis, half Ojibwe. Dinah has a buzz cut and wears men's flannel hunting coats. She is usually slicing into one of her kills when they arrive, the guts still warm. She offers them a raw sliver, which her mother refuses with a small shake of her head. "You can't eat raw meat from a farm," Dinah says. "They screw it up with steroids and chemicals. But what you hunt here in the woods is clean."

Joan and Dinah have their own story of predestination. How they were living together and a man broke into their house one night. He had a gun, and ordered them out of bed. They learned later he'd been watching them for several days. They were up to something sinful that they have never shared. The man told them they looked happy, and that he wanted a little bit of their happiness for himself. I won't kill you, he kept saying. We're all gonna walk out of this, if you do what I tell you. We're going to survive.

Afterward, Dinah bought a gun, and started going to a shooting range. All the bright shining things they believed in couldn't protect them from the world's cruelties. No amount of psychological insight was going to explain why people did the things they did. The devil was not a metaphor.

"Don't ever spend time with a strange man after the sun sets," Dinah tells Nora. "After sunset, men turn into bears."

"Even Dad? But what about—"

"When you grow up, you learn how to handle bears," her mother interrupts, short and sharp. She gives Dinah peppermint oil and sweet honey and sage for mysterious aches and pains.

"And for the depression?" Dinah asks, her voice low and humble.

"Pray," her mother says. And hands her a bottle made of dark amber glass, with a skinny notched neck.

Her mother gives fenugreek to George, who keeps the cows; the herb is known to help lactating women with their supply. Nora likes running into the barn and scratching a few warm rumps while George pours the mixture into buckets. He always speaks gently to the cows, calling them his beauties. It's hard to keep cows going on the compound. Not enough grass or range, not enough bulls to keep the stock varied, no warm sturdy buildings. They lose several calves every year.

George explains how you need the calves to get the milk. "People forget that. Gotta keep these ladies producing. I read the birthrates are dropping. Fewer things getting born in the world. What's one of the surest ways God punishes the wicked? He curses the women with barrenness."

George lost his wife and daughter in a car accident. He stopped eating, stopped milking his cows, just lay on his couch listening to televangelists. The soothing cadence of their voices assured him that there was a plan, and that this was part of it, if he'd only look long enough to see the pattern. He started reading the Bible again, trying to do the math of when end times were going to come. But it was difficult when you didn't read Hebrew or Ancient Greek. He found a website late one night, something Nora's father had put up, which announced in giant letters, HOW'S IT GOING TO END? ARE YOU READY?

While Nora is patting the cows, her mother tells George about a farm near Marquette that is giving away its hay supply for cheap because some of it got infested with weevils. "Might not be good enough for feed stores but it'll do for us," she says.

George nods, rubbing the back of his neck. "I worry about my beauties. When it's all over. When we—go, if that's what's going to happen. What'll happen to them?"

"No one knows for sure what'll happen," her mother says. "It could just be the beginning of a long period of trial. I think of it more like that. Like another, harder phase, as if this one isn't hard enough."

"I don't want to abandon them," George says. "If we're all getting raptured, I'll shoot them. I'd rather they be somewhere warm. A warm dark place with no hurts. I'll settle for that. What do you think, angel?" he asks, turning to Nora. "What should we do?"

Her mother sniffs with irritation. "Don't ask her that."

On the walk back to their place, her mother passes a hand over Nora's tangled hair. "It mats up just like a dog's," she says. From time to time, she will rip a hairbrush through her daughter's hair. Despite the roughness, Nora leans into the brush, hungry for the hand steadying her head, feeling a sharp happiness at any scrap of tenderness.

"I brushed it," Nora says, knowing she hasn't done so in days.

"You got this hair from your grandmother. Hers was the same way."

This is the first mention Nora has ever heard of her mother's family, and she wants to make it count. "What was she like?"

"She was an Irish Catholic woman from back east. A real tough lady. When I married your father she threw me out. She said he was a slick snake-wrangling preacher and he'd drag us both down to the devil." Her mother's fingers move through Nora's hair, trying to ease out the knots. "Our family had a history of that, estrangement. There was a whole strain of cousins I never knew because somebody down the line married a Protestant."

Nora says, "Maybe if she'd met me, she would have seen what we were doing. Maybe she would have understood." A grandmother sounds nice, even a cruel, hard one.

"She was trying to protect me," her mother answers. "That's what we do. This life we lead, it only works if the women look out for each other. No one else is going to. The Bible has plenty to say about men, but it forgets the women."

When her mother releases her, Nora runs back up the hill, where Levi is waiting as if he hasn't moved in all this time, the gun at his hip.

"Let's go east," she says.

They walk the sandy, pine-needled path by the lake, slipping past deacons, past the women who straighten with hands on their backs when they see children, asking where they're off to, who's watching them, shouldn't you be working?

Along the iron-red shore, the little laps of lakewater have eaten caves and inlets into the cliffs over time. When they're peering down at the openings, a man pops his head out of one of the caves. They jump back, nearly slipping over the edge.

"What do you say, kids?" he asks. It's only Kyle, a church member who makes his home in a cave. He left his wife to be here; he couldn't convince her to come along, that they'd be safe when the world ended. He could live in one of the trailers on the property, but he wanted to practice self-reliance, he said, and build his own shelter, which he has been trying to do on the shoreline; right now, it's just a ruined, sagging mess of tree branches and tattered patches of moss. He only shows up for church meetings; otherwise, he can be seen wandering the shoreline gathering driftwood, muttering about Numbers and Acts.

Kyle shuffles out of his cave, scratching at his wild beard. "Shouldn't somebody be watching you?"

"I'm watching her," Levi says, stepping forward. Kyle looks him up and down, the long wiry knobbiness, the rattail braid snaking over one shoulder, the determined jut to his jaw, and seems doubtful.

"Don't you stay out after dark around here," he says. "You know what's out there. In the woods."

"What?" Nora takes a step forward.

"There are unnatural things. Bad spirits you have to watch out for. And the big one, the main man."

"The dev—" she starts, but Kyle puts a finger to his lips.

"Don't speak his name," he says. "It gives him power." He looks over their shoulders, grim. "When he's close, you know it."

Nora and Levi turn the way Kyle is staring, into the green haze of trees beyond the lapping water. It looks the way it always has. But Nora knows what Kyle means. There's a feeling you get when it's late and you're heading back through the trees and you feel a light, cool breath on the back of your neck. The dark drops around you, swift as summer rain. And if you stand for a while in the quiet of the woods, you hear the soft yips of the wolves that run wild through the UP, one of the last places in the lower forty-eight that still have them. It's an unearthly cry, a song of inhuman melody.

"Sometimes you hear the wolves crying," Kyle says, "the ones we've killed. Sometimes you hear deer that we've shot and men who died in the mines calling from under the earth. Sometimes you hear someone paddling a canoe in the water. That's the ghosts of the Ottawa Indians. This was their home, you know, and the white men took it away. Everywhere on earth that man has sinned, there are spirits."

"Come on, Nora." Levi tugs at her arm. He doesn't trust Kyle, with his twitchy unrest, his anti-social habits.

"Be careful," Kyle calls after them. "These woods are full of bad things."

They head into the dense tree cover, curiosity pushing them forward onto unfamiliar paths. It's getting late, the sun low and rose-colored on the horizon, just a glimpse through the old-growth forest. "Let's go back," says Levi. "Your mom and dad will worry."

"Just a little farther," Nora implores. She wants to drop off the edge of the world she knows for a moment. To journey beyond the water-logged map pinned to the wall in the church, outlining the farming lands and the places where military drills are conducted.

A crow calls in the trees, an obscure warning.

Suddenly, Levi throws an arm up before her and cries, "Watch out!"

Nora is one step away from a dark slit in the forest floor, a crevasse extending down into blackness. It isn't round like a well, and seems to be part of the loamy earth with fallen leaves around it, natural and not, unknowably deep. They creep to the edge and drop a stone; listen to it fall, soundlessly, for an age before the tiny distant tick of its landing. "What is it?" she breathes.

"I don't know," Levi whispers.

They don't say it, but they're both thinking: this is where the devil lives. The time is close and this pit has opened for his entrance into the world. Nora leans further, wanting to see the bottom, until her balance shifts, the ground slides; she's about to fall, but Levi's arm tightens around her waist, holding her up.

"Say a prayer, Nora," he says urgently.

She fumbles for something that will keep the devil down in the dark where he belongs. "We drive you from us," she begins. Her thin little girl's voice shakes:

whoever you may be,
unclean spirits,
all satanic powers,
all infernal invaders,
all wicked legions,
assemblies and sects.

A low, lonely sound rises up from the darkness. A moaning. They turn and run, panting and wordless, not looking back.

Later that night, when she tells her father about the hole in the forest, he says, "It's a ventilation shaft. There were iron and copper mines all through this area, in the old days. Most of them are closed up and buried. But every now and then, you find one." He shakes his head. "There are stories the locals could tell you. People died down there, in cave-ins, or if they hit a gas reservoir."

It's reassuring to hear an earthly explanation. But it doesn't take the teeth of the memory away. "What's down there?" Nora asks. "Are there bad spirits? Can we pray to drive them out?"

Henry's lip crooks. "You mean the devil." His eyes drift the way they do when he's summoning a verse. "Revelation 11:7. *And when they shall have finished their testimony, the beast that ascendeth out of the bottomless pit shall make war against them, and shall overcome them, and kill them.*"

"Enough, Henry." Nora's mother rubs her shoulder. "There's nothing down there. Just iron and dust and darkness."

"But the devil is real," Nora insists. "I've felt him. I've heard him speak."

Her mother looks at her father, who is standing by the window, his back to them all, and Nora knows that he is keeping them safe from enemies earthly and supernatural.

"He's real, all right," he says. "You've seen his work."

That night, Nora wakes to a scratching at the small window in her bedroom. Sounds like a possum or a raccoon. When she creeps to the window, Levi is standing there in the darkness. She knows him by his long-necked silhouette, the rattail trailing over one shoulder. It's cold enough to see her breath outside but he's there in his usual ragged canvas coat and a t-shirt.

"What are you doing here?" she hisses. They aren't supposed to be out alone at night.

"What was that place? What did your father say?"

"It's just a ventilation shaft, from an old mine," she says. "They're all over the UP."

They both heard the moaning from beneath the earth, though: there was something alive down there, calling for them. Nora remembers the cool firm grip of his arm around her, the shock of his touch hauling her back to safety. "Thanks for pulling me back," she whispers.

"Do you think—" His face is white and piqued in the cold air. He looks scared. She wants to reach out through the narrow gap in the window and hold him the way he held her.

"Do you think in heaven, we'll be married?" he asks.

She doesn't know if he means "To each other." But she wishes it, deeply.

"I think—I mean, we're all supposed to be," she says. "When the world is free of sin, and every creature paired with its mate." Henry said something about that, once. Either that, or they'll be creatures of light and air, and bodies will no longer trouble them. She's afraid, sometimes, when she pictures herself peeling free of her body. How will her soul know the parts that are insubstance and the parts she no longer needs—breath, heart, fingertips? She fumbles for the crack in the window, trying to slip her hand through.

Then a dog barks, a flashlight jitters across the ground, and Levi is gone, running in the dark. She doesn't realize until he's left that she forgot to ask what he meant about the defector.

⁂

Last spring, they welcomed a new member, a young woman named Rachel. She was tall and slim, her knees close together when she walked, her hips sliding in a way the other women's didn't. Nora had seen her leaning on the outside of her trailer one day, and she stopped to meet the new arrival. Rachel told her stories about Chicago, the city where she came from. The elevated train that was always roaring next to her apartment, rhythmic and soothing, like a constant clattering heartbeat. She lived across from a rooming house for men only. She would walk by it every night coming home from work, passing through groups of men hovering and talking, their eyes on her, weighing, undressing, doing things to her in their minds. Sometimes they asked her to join them in their little rented rooms, and sometimes they offered money, and she told Nora, leaning close so no one else could hear, I was broke, and sometimes I did. It was always so sad, though. Lonely. You wouldn't know, those rooms with the chipped old radiators and the scummy windows. Sheets that never got clean. So many men looking for comfort.

A week after Rachel's arrival, Nora's father called a church meeting. The spring air was cool and mysterious. A few men smoking in the yard, an air of anticipation as Nora passed through their company. She hurried inside to the front bench, where her mother and Henry were seated. She could feel the congregation watching the back of her neck, waiting for her to move, shift, speak.

"Friends," her father began, his voice quiet at first, the sighing air of the barn thick with dust and hay. He was wearing his ordinary canvas work clothes and his hunting jacket, but had removed his cap to reveal his oily brown hair. Don't trust the prophet who puts himself above other men, he always told Nora. "We're here today because there is someone who has come to us unclean. And one person's sin affects us all. Come forward," her father said, and gestured. Rachel walked slowly down the aisle like a bride. When she was almost to Nora's father, she wobbled and fell to all fours, her hair, long and dark, hanging lankly over her face. She swayed in the dog-like pose, sobbing softly.

The congregation murmured with nervous excitement.

Nora's father did not bend to Rachel or offer his hand. He looked out, instead, to the crowd watching her. "This woman is guilty of fornication, and of selling her self," he said. "She has come to us to take away her sin."

All Nora could look at was Rachel, her head low, her slim body swaybacked, her hips high and elegant.

Her father's face shone in the bright bare bulbs dangling from cords in the rafters. "We have been given the great gift of immortal life," he began. "We are made of spirit. But we have also been given bodies." He looked sorrowful, as though he had been reflecting on this quandary for a long time. "We are not without flesh," he continued, "and flesh is what makes us long for its touch. We are a union of matter and spirit, and we worship our own bodies because they are beautiful and they were made by God. These bodies drive us to seek pleasure— greedily, carelessly. Lust makes us steal pleasure for ourselves, or worse, to sell ourselves in cold transaction."

From the front row, Henry's voice rose thin and cracking: "*Thou shalt not bring the hire of a whore or the price of a dog into the house of the Lord thy God for any vow, for even both these are abomination unto the Lord thy God.*"

A discontented rumble passed through the room.

Her father raised his hands. "This woman has paid the price for her sin. She has come here for our protection."

The words settled in the dusty air; the congregation leaned forward with close attention. "We're building a sanctuary here," he said. "We have promised to love the spirit, not the flesh. We have invited the Holy Spirit inside us. We are building an ark. If one of us is weak—if we let the devil in—then we're all vulnerable."

Her father closed his eyes. They were with him now, hanging on his words, feeling what it meant to have opened themselves to danger by letting this woman enter their church. Nora pressed her temples.

"He's here." Her father almost whispered it. "He's in this woman."

The congregants began to pray, whispering and murmuring,

heads bent over laps or straining toward the ceiling, reaching up to heaven. Nora pressed her clasped hands to her forehead. Her father was going to ask her to speak. It was coming, he needed her now.

"He's here with us, right now," her father roared, and the congregation moaned. They were looking at Nora, hoping for some kind of a sign. The sounds began to rise in her throat, rasping and ferocious. "Drive him out, drive him out," her father chanted, and the crowd prayed harder, reaching a rhythm, *In Jesus' name, In Jesus' name.* The force of it, when they came together, seemed to create a wave of heat that pushed Rachel down to the floor. Nora pressed her cheek to the wooden bench beneath her, digging her nails into the boards. "Out, Satan," her father shouted, and a force pulled Nora from her seat and sent her stumbling to the front of the room, the feeling she got when running through the woods, breath gone, her body acting without her control or consent.

Then, a long, throaty laugh purred out of her, mocking and wise. "Hahahaha."

"He's in her, he's in her," the crowd chanted. Nora laughed in response. "Let me out," her voice said, "let me out." This voice was not afraid of her father. This voice saw the whole bunch of them praying as some kind of charade. This voice was unimpressed by crosses and incantations. This voice knew things, wanted things.

Everyone was now pressing close around her, praying over her, pressing down her head with their heavy hands. The devil was speaking through her, spitting with malice—and then, suddenly, the Spirit voice was back, babbling and praying, wrenching the Fiend loose.

"He's gone," her father panted. "We drove him out."

A ragged cheer rose in the group. A few weary "hallelujahs." Everyone exhausted, smiling; they'd been through something together, triumphed over an old enemy. Nora lay limply in her father's arms. People clustered around her, reaching out their hands, touching her everywhere they could reach, holding her to the earth. "Pray for me, Nora," they asked. She was cleaned out, empty; nothing left.

No one noticed Rachel, climbing shakily to her feet, walking out of the barn.

After the frenzy died down, Nora walked by herself to Rachel's trailer. She found her in her usual spot, leaning against the side, smoking a cigarette. Something lonely and brave in the way she was out there, shivering in the chill, gazing off into the lantern trails amid the trees. "Sure you want to be seen with me?" she asked.

Nora nodded. "You're clean now."

"Clean." Rachel stretched out the word, long and slow, like expelling smoke. "Still, people talk." She smiled, a small crook of her mouth.

Nora rubbed one boot with the other. She wanted to ask Rachel how it felt to have the devil in her and then be scrubbed clean. Did she feel it like Nora felt it? Wonderful, breathless, raw. Like falling through the ice on a frozen lake. Splashing alcohol on a wound. A memory of pain, and the ecstasy of its erasure. The way it grabbed you and then let you go. Now it was something they shared; the ill wind had passed through them both. Did that make them the same?

"When my father said you've already paid the price for your sin," Nora asked. "What did he mean?"

Rachel exhaled, a long sigh. "I just wanted somebody to be kind to me. I was lonely. I just wanted a little comfort," she said. "But the devil, you know—he's in some men. Your father said I'd be safe here. That I'd be welcome. But people are people, aren't they?"

"You are safe here!" Nora answered. This place with its long strings of barbed wire, its nightly patrols, its armed and ready men, protected from whatever the world could throw at it. They were cocooned in spiritual armor.

Rachel laughed. "You don't even know what safe means. Just like you don't know what clean means."

Nora's body throbbed with shame. She was only a girl, and knew so little. This was a grown woman in front of her, a woman who had seen things, who had lived in cities and shrugged up alongside sin.

"I'll tell you something," Rachel said, looking at the end of her cigarette as if its tiny spark held a secret. Her voice—raspy and sultry—was not like any woman's Nora knew. It was rich with danger and knowledge. "After what happened to me, I put another lock on my door. I stopped going out, I didn't speak to strangers anymore. I wouldn't get on a train if I was the only one in the car. I moved up here, where I thought nobody would find me. I got to feeling I'd pay almost any price to feel safe. Make whatever bargain. I was so tired of feeling afraid. I started going to church. Your father told me my problem was spiritual, that I was afraid because my soul was hanging in the balance."

"It is," Nora said, fervently. "It is."

Rachel didn't look at her. "Do you really think God can mend all wounds?"

Nora only knew what she'd been told, the promises her father had made. "He's the only one who can," she said, and it sounded strangely flat.

"When your father said the devil was gone tonight, did you believe him?" Rachel asked. "Are you sure there isn't a little shred of him left in you?"

Nora is walking on the ridge with Levi. It is fall, the day after they found the pit. They pause to watch the women moving, bent double, across the field. Nora shades her eyes with her hand, looking for the solo shape who is always a little apart, doing things her own way and at her own time. "Where's Rachel?"

Levi turns. "That's what I was going to tell you yesterday."

"What?"

"She left," he says.

"What?"

"She's gone. Just packed up and took off, last week. She deserted us." He spits into the pine needles. Levi has no patience for defectors.

Nora shakes her head in shock. She knows that Rachel has never really fit in among the women, always keeping a slight separateness from the gatherings in kitchens and storerooms. She didn't mend or sew or bake, and looked past the other women with a bored indifference when they asked if she'd help make crabapple preserves or fix the holes in a large pile of deacons' socks. Still, for someone to abandon the faith, after all the work they'd done to free her from sin—and with the time so close now, just months away. And after Nora had the devil ripped out of her. This loss feels personal.

"If you're saved," she asks Levi, "Can you be unsaved?" For all the intensity of her performances, Nora suspects that his faith is purer than hers; that he knows things for certain that she doubts.

"If you weren't meant for heaven," Levi answers. He crouches swiftly in the grass, bringing his rifle to his shoulder in a tight military gesture he's learned from months of drills. Nora searches for the shiny black dot of the rabbit's eye—everything else blends into the grass, but Levi's focus is keen, his hand is steady as he settles the rifle in its God-determined place, as though an invisible thread connects him and the gun to his prey, a line in the air to its death. Straight and certain, pre-destined.

She plugs her ears, waiting for the shot.

Later, she finds her father outside the house with some blueprints stretched on sawhorses, sketching, and demands to know why no one told her about Rachel.

He looks over his glasses at her, mild in the way he can sometimes be with state troopers or social service workers, containing his storm elsewhere. "You don't have to know everything that goes on here," he said. "You don't have that right."

"But I could have tried to save her. I could have talked to her. Maybe won her back."

He shakes his head. "You can't save everybody, Nora. Some people aren't bound for the chariot. Her time of judgment is coming soon." He shades his eyes and searches for the sun in the sky, as if to mark its passage. It's getting late.

In bed that night, Nora closes her eyes, holds her breath and counts to ten, just like she is a child again, not a girl who's felt the devil speak in her own mouth. When she breathes again, the world is still there. The sighing sound of the house settling around her. Her father, her mother, her brother, their breath filling the air around her, all holding the world up.

On the Forms He Takes

Sometimes, we say, the devil takes the form of a wolverine. The most vicious animal in the woods, with the most powerful bite: we don't dare hunt him, because if you miss, or only wound him with your shot . . .

We can hear the squalling at night as he marauds through the woods, stealing prey from wolves and raping lady wolverines, making more angry, cursed offspring.

Sometimes the devil walks out of the hills as a sharply dressed man with a black suit and a snakeskin briefcase. He likes to cheat people out of their inheritance, steal the clothes off their backs without ever really stealing. He convinced the Algonquin to sell their lands to the white men. He sold the iron out from under the mountain until the mines collapsed. He's got the paperwork for you all ready in his briefcase, all you have to do is sign right here.

When you read a book that isn't the Bible, he's leaning over your shoulder, helping you sound out the words.

When you're thinking things at night that you have no business thinking, about the pleasure you get from the sound of someone else's breath, the strong line of his jaw, the way he tucks his overlong hair behind his ears, the feel of skin on skin—he's the one watching in the corner, grinning in the darkness. You can just make out the shine of his teeth.

He's riding in the passenger seat of your truck when you're driving at night just to drive, the trees stark and white in the headlights. He's whispering your loneliness to you. He's on your back, making that itch that creeps all over. Your body is all want. You can try to pray him away, but alone, you don't have the power. He hears the quaver in your voice.

He knows your heart better than you do. The devil is both creature and kin.

Acolytes

October 2008

(110 days until the world ends)

"NORA. TIME TO GET up, girl."

Her father speaks quietly as always, but his voice still penetrates her deepest sleep. She's already sitting up, pulling on her jeans before she's fully conscious. The dawn is only a gray-blue promise in the window. It's October and they're running out of time, and every hour is precious.

She takes a piece of bread off the kitchen shelf and butters it while he sits at the table in his fishing vest, cleaning a rifle, sliding the bolt home, checking the action, his movements unhurried, precise. The tackle box is on the table beside him. So they'll be fishing for followers today. The imperative to find more faithful, when the end is so close, thumps in both of them like the pendulum of a clock.

Her mother appears in the kitchen in her nightgown. "Where is it this time?" she asks, her voice low and weary, not really asking a question, not hoping for much of an answer.

"A few hours' drive," he says, without looking up from the gun, making sure the safety is on before he shoulders it. "A fishing spot. My guys tell me there's a big gathering there on the first day of the season, a chance to reach a lot of people."

"Why do you need her?"

Nora chews slowly, keeping her eyes on the bread.

"They need to see the power of the Lord's grace."

"Grace," her mother says, and in her mouth it sounds like something forbidden, unclean. "She's a kid. She doesn't even know what that means."

"I know what it means," Nora protests, but they aren't paying attention to her.

"She doesn't have to. He moves in her, speaks through her."

"But how do you *know.*"

The word is loud and strange in the dark kitchen. Her father stands up and walks slowly toward her mother, growing taller with each step, the rifle rocking on his shoulder.

"If you believed in me, you wouldn't ask that," he says.

Her mother seems to shrink a little, contracting like a plant starved of water. She turns away from him and bangs a pot into the sink, and doesn't turn back when they lace up their boots and tramp out the door.

In the truck, driving through curtains of blazing orange trees, Nora asks her father how he met her mother. Surely there was something that drew them together, some touch of destiny that led to the making of her and Henry.

"I was preaching in a night ministry in Massachusetts," he begins. "Your Ma is from a town on the ocean there. I was preaching to people coming out of prison during the day, and at night I'd go around to the bars and parking lots and under bridges, wherever people congregated that needed help. I met her in a bar one night."

"Was she beautiful?" Fairy tales have told her this is always part of the story.

"She was."

"What made you—"

"We were both looking for a radical change in our lives. We started going on camping trips all over the state, the wilder the better, looking for places where God was hiding. She'd read a book that said God was easier to find in nature.

"One time we were hiking on a mountain ridge and we could see all the way down the slope to a lake below. We saw some hunters stalking a mother bear with her cubs. They were bad at it. They got off a few shots before she charged and was on them. We saw it all from fifteen hundred feet up and couldn't do a thing. I believed in God but I hadn't seen before how His wrath was real, how He could destroy things if you didn't respect his creation. It meant something. And He wanted me to see. I knew then I had to spread his Word before it was too late."

His hands clench the steering wheel. "Your mother saw the same thing, but she will never understand what I felt. She thinks faith is something you keep for yourself, not a gift you're meant to give."

Nora doesn't say anything, staring straight at the road ahead.

The RV camp is crowded with first day fishermen, families with kids struggling with their baits and flies, and loners in trucker hats and battered old hunting gear preparing their bait with silent efficiency.

Nora and her father pretend that they're just there to fish. They set their tackle box on a bench and start tying flies. It's a steady, quiet process that takes skill and dexterity. Nora works deftly while men drift by and talk to her father, men with north woods accents and a casual Midwestern friendliness. He chats to anyone who stops at their bench about the decline of good whitefish in the area. The men are mostly from downstate, though a few are from Wisconsin or farther away— Idaho, Ohio. They come to the UP every year because it still has the real wilderness that is being lost in other places. Her father says, "It'll be the safest place in the country, when the big one comes."

The big one?

"We're getting ready," he says. "You can read the signs. Just look at the way the country is going. Look at the election. It's on the way, all right." He delivers his lines calmly, with casual conviction, while he works on his flies. He looks like one of them, with his tattered fishing vest, his scruffy beard, the calluses on his thumbs. A few men shake their heads, move on. But some linger.

"The thing is, if a man reads his Bible, the signs are all there," he continues. "It's an historical document. It's all about the fall of empires and nations. And we're living in a time when more people have fallen away from God, from faith, from community. When the president says people like us cling to our guns and religion because we're bitter, when someone like that is in charge—" he shakes his head. "The abandonment of values always precedes a collapse. We've got to be prepared for it. We've got to reach out and take ownership of our survival."

Then Nora raises her head and says, "The Spirit clearly says that in later times some will abandon the faith and follow deceiving spirits and things taught by demons." She knows there's something disquieting about a kid spouting these dark verses, so she keeps her eyes down, her hands busy with the flies. Like she's not quite of this world.

"My daughter," her father says. "She's always had a gift. You can believe me or not, but she prophesies. And we've been told to get ready."

Nora feels the old crackle of excitement under her skin as they begin their work together, each knowing their part, the give and take, the building of omens and messages, the dire promise they have to share. They are watching and listening, waiting for their people to reveal themselves. Their people—the ones who subscribe to mimeographed newsletters about new world orders and listen to talk radio when they're driving through the woods late at night. The ones making feverish calculations on the backs of envelopes about prophecies and timelines. The ones who drive past JESUS SAVES billboards and notice them and nod. The ones who wonder.

"If I could shut my mouth and stop talking about this, I would," her father says to the men still gathered around him. "But it's too important."

Nora wanders in and out of the circle with cards that describe their church. "It's time to make your life mean something," she says as she hands out the cards. "Time to take your future back. There's still time to be forgiven."

It's getting dark; they've been out here for hours. The clouds draw low across the sky, making it heavy with threat. A few more fisherman pull their boats up onto the lakeshore and grope for cigarettes in their pockets. They're watching her, waiting for some sort of sign.

Nora closes her eyes, trying to find the right words. She keeps her favorite ominous Bible verses stored in a pocket of her memory:

"And in that day they shall roar against them like the roaring of the sea: and if one look unto the land, behold darkness and sorrow, and the light is darkened in the heavens."

There's a beautiful order to these lines, each word correlating to life out there, in the waves of spring rain that wash across the fields, in the forest fires, in the believers and sinners. If only she can help others see that divine order.

Later, when they're handing out flyers with maps to their compound and invitations to join them for a Sunday service, Nora notices a group of teenagers gathered by the shore. They're standing by a grill pit, holding beer cans, talking and laughing. One girl keeps looking over, catching Nora's eye and then turning away. She's wearing jean shorts so high you can see the whole length of her smooth legs. Her hair is long and silky and drifts over her face in the lakeshore breeze. She doesn't even bother to toss it out of her face.

Nora heads determinedly over to the group. "Have you heard about what's going to happen to you?" she asks them. "It's known. It's written in the book."

"So we've heard," someone says, and they all laugh.

"I could pray for you," Nora says.

"Like the way you did back there?" the girl says gently.

"I have the gift of the voice," Nora says. "God speaks through me."

"I'm sure," the girl says, and though her voice is still gentle, it is filled with sly contempt. "Look, you don't have to try to convert us, okay? Tell your father not to send his windup doll."

Nora opens and closes her mouth, but realizes she must look even more like an automaton, smiling and opening and closing. She turns and walks away; the laughter resumes. She hears the word *freak*. The girl's voice rises above the others. "Don't, it's sad," she says. "Poor thing, it's fucking depressing."

Her father is still speaking to a group of fishermen who are putting pamphlets away in their tackle boxes. "Come see us sometime," he says. "When she speaks, it's something you can't believe. You'll see God speaking here on earth."

It's completely dark when they get back to the truck, all the pamphlets and cards gone, a few phone numbers collected.

Her father drives one-handed, working a wad of small bills into his coat pocket with his free hand. Never ask for money is his rule, but if people want to give, it's a way of helping them feel more invested, and he won't say no. It's rude to refuse a gift. And once you've given a dollar, you expect something in return. They'll come to see the show.

Nora slumps in the passenger seat. "Am I a freak?"

"Who said that?"

"Those kids back there."

"You're going to meet a lot of confused people in your life," he says.

"Don't listen to them. They're afraid of your goodness. They're terrified that one day the clouds are going to open and God is going to look into their souls and see what they really are."

"What are they?"

"Empty."

Her father turns on the radio and starts to hum along to the music, soft ballads and Celtic songs with sad fiddles. Nora can feel the happiness in his absent humming. "We did it, kid," he says. She drifts off to the sound of his voice.

When she wakes, it's pitch black outside. They could be at the edge of a cliff. They could be in a mine shaft. Then the headlights wash over the house, the walls stark and splashed with years of winter salt. Her father half-carries her inside, her legs heavy with sleep.

Her mother is sitting at the table without any lights on.

"Katherine," her father says, formally. "We got held up." He gives Nora a little shove down the hall, and she knows better than to object. She listens to the rest from the safety of her bedroom.

"You can't use her this way," her mother says. "She's not your pawn in some game."

"You think any of this is a game?" her father answers.

⁂

The next morning, Nora wakes up to an empty house. The sun is high in the sky; her father and Henry have gone to work. They're building a new storehouse; she can hear the buzzing of chainsaws in the distance.

But where is her mother?

Nora makes breakfast for herself, burning the oatmeal and forgetting to add milk. She wanders out into the yard, but her mother is not tending the garden or chopping wood. The truck is here; she hasn't gone into town. Her basket is on the table; she is not out visiting a woman who needs her help.

Nora walks for a while through the woods, her breath getting louder and louder in her ears, a thrumming in her throat. Once, when she and Henry were little, they were picking blueberries with their mother in a dense, thorny meadow. The two of them arguing over the berries, and the buzzing of cicadas, masked the approach of a mother bear until she was almost on top of them, hungry and furious, her cubs nearby. "Run," their mother yelled, and they tore across the meadow as fast as they could, but the bear was close behind, the shout of its huffing breath in their ears. They turned at the edge of the meadow to see their mother standing in front of the bear. She barked "No!" and swung the metal pail in her hand, smashing it into the bear's nose. Startled, the animal reared back, and they all ran on into the woods.

When they were clear of the bear, Nora asked, "How did you know that would stop it?"

Her mother shrugged, mysterious as always, still breathing hard, her frame going up and down, her eyes alight. "When you have children, you know what you have to do."

Nora finally finds her mother by the lake. She's standing on the beach with her arms folded under her coat, looking out over the water. One of the fishing boats is hauled up beside her, wet and covered with lakeweed.

"Were you out on the lake?" Nora asks cautiously.

Her mother turns to her. "I was thinking about it," she says. "I was thinking about going."

"But you don't have your pole." The only reason to go out there is to fish. There's no such thing as leisure boating here.

Her mother doesn't answer. It is one of those times that she's far away, living some other life that Nora doesn't know. "Before I was born, was there a time you went camping with Dad, and you saw a bear attack some hunters?" she asks.

Her mother shivers. "Yes. Yes, there was." She doesn't say anything more. Nora stands close, and her mother's arms come out of her coat and pull Nora inside it. "What if we went somewhere warm?" she asks. "Henry too. What if we went to Florida, or Mexico? We could leave today. We'd lie on the beach and feel warm for once. And nobody would ask you to talk to God. You could just be."

Nora laughs. The absurdity of leaving when the time is so near. "We can't. They need us."

"What if we went anyway? Who could stop us?" Her arms are tight around Nora's body, holding on.

"It's not safe."

"Nowhere's safe," her mother says. She unfolds her arms slowly from Nora's body. "Go get the bread started," she barks. "Go on." With a small shove she sends Nora back toward the house, while she stands there a while longer alone, looking out at the water.

⁝

With the time rapidly approaching and new members joining every week, her father wants more prophecies. "People need to know they've come here for a reason," he says. "If they're going to join us, uproot their lives, they need promises."

"Can't I just—"

"Nora." His voice stern. "This is what God has asked of you."

The last time he asked her for prophecies, she prayed fervently, clasping her hands and digging her nails into her palms until little bloody crescents welled up. What was the voice of God, and how did it come upon her sometimes and not others? She closed her eyes. "Make me a vessel, make me a vessel," she chanted under her breath. An increasing desperation. She couldn't fail.

But when she opened her eyes, she was still empty.

She got up, brushed off her knees, and wandered over to Henry's room. His back was to her at his little desk; he had three different Bible translations open, carefully tracing a finger along one line before moving to the next version and tracing the same line, then furiously jotting down notes.

"What are you reading?" she asked. A stupid question. It was only ever one book.

"Acts." He didn't look up.

"What's in Acts?"

He pushed his glasses up onto his forehead and squeezed the bridge of his nose like a much older man. "Details and signs, things to watch out for."

"Like?"

"Things that might presage the End Times," he said. "Here, look." He guided her finger down a narrow column of text.

All the sinners of my people shall die by the sword, which say, The evil shall not overtake nor prevent us. In that day will I raise up the tabernacle of David that is fallen, and close up the breaches thereof; and I will raise up his ruins, and I will build it as in the days of old

"That's a reference back to Isaiah 45," Henry said. He flipped quickly, knowingly through the dogeared book. "See?"

I will go before you and level the mountains; I will break down the gates of bronze and cut through the bars of iron. I will give you the

*treasures of darkness and the riches hidden in secret places, so that
you may know that I am the LORD.*

Nora leaned closer; Henry's smell came to her, brotherly and
familiar, a little metallic. He was keen to show her what he'd been up to,
how important it was, as crucial as laying drainage pipes or converting
more souls. "It's like cracking a code," he said. "Or a treasure map. You
follow one trail, which leads to another, until X marks the spot."

"And then what? What does it tell you?"

"Earthquakes," answered Henry. "Mountaintop removal. Coal and
steel mining. David's fallen tent, the settlements in Israel. All of these
are signs."

Nora was quiet for a moment, watching him scratch out his notes,
drawing lines from one verse to the corresponding one. Like her, he
was listening to the voice of God. Who was to say he couldn't be that
connection, the Lord working in the world to ensure that the message
made its way through her?

Nora started coming to Henry's room whenever she needed a new
prophecy, copying down the verses he pointed out. In church, she
quoted verse after verse about disaster and judgment and the iron cities
falling to hellfire while the righteous endured. Whenever she went to
Henry needing a new verse, he wordlessly supplied one. But something
was changing in his face with each request. The thoughtful, longing
look she knew became more sour each time.

Was that when things started to change between them?

The three of them, she, Henry, and her father, out hunting. Her father
showing them how to rise swiftly from a crouch and shoot grouse out
of the air, tracking their arcs across the sky and aiming for where they

will be, not where they are. The shot birds dangling from her father's fist as they walked home, one child on either side, content to share him for the day.

Suddenly, the smell of something burning, oily and too sweet. The forest was damp from the previous night's rain, no chance of a wildfire. Whatever was burning was man-made.

An ATV roared up to them, Bill, one of the younger deacons, driving. "Stupid fucking Matty, he blew the whole batch up," he said. "That load was due in town tomorrow. The trailer's totaled."

"What blew up?" Nora wanted to know.

Her father ignored her. "You'll have to make a new batch."

"We'll need to start over."

"What were you making?" Nora demanded.

Bill looked at her and grinned. "Money," he said. "Somebody's got to around here." He turned the ATV around. "Come on, boss, it's close."

Her father started to get into the vehicle, then paused and turned. "Henry, come on. We could use another hand. Nora, go on back to the house. Pluck these birds for us." He pressed the bony reptilian feet into her hands. Along with Henry, he climbed onto the ATV behind Bill.

Nora waited until they'd cleared the hill and disappeared among the trees. Then she followed the ATV's destructive trail through the brush. From the top of a shallow ravine, she saw a tar-streaked trailer, smoke billowing out the door. Her father, Henry, Bill and Matty, another one of the younger deacons, stood together. Remaining hidden, Nora slid down the hillside to hear what they were saying.

"Look at this," Bill said. "Matty fucked up the whole Goddamned batch."

"Don't use that language in front of my boy," her father said quietly. "Matty, if you messed this up, you've taken away precious time and resources from our community. Are you remorseful? Are you ready to ask for forgiveness?"

Matty hung his head like a kicked dog. "Yes, sir."

"We'll see about that," her father said. "Bill, get this cleaned up and start a new batch. Henry, come with me."

Nora watched her father lead Matty off into the trees, Henry behind them. She didn't follow. There were things that men did that she was not allowed to see. Nora remembered the time she came into the house and found her mother mixing things on the stove. Dolly, one of the women her mother sometimes helped, was at the kitchen table holding a rag poultice to her face. "He had an extra ration of oats for me, and a magazine from town," she said bitterly. "Like a bouquet of roses. Or something."

"They like to bring little gifts," her mother said. "To say sorry for what they've done. Next time, ask for something useful, like meat. Deacons get first pick, you could have had some tenderloin." She handed Dolly a mug. "Drink this. To be safe."

Dolly slowly lowered the poultice: half of her face was swollen, black and blue and shiny. "Hello there, Nora girl," Dolly said. She had a soft country voice that always sounded a little ashamed.

"Who did that to you?" Nora asked.

Dolly opened her mouth, then looked at Nora's mother and closed it again. "Just an accident."

"What kind of accident?"

"Just—hit myself. Piece of wood flew up when I was chopping. Living in the woods, things happen, you know."

"But—"

"That's enough questions," Nora's mother said, and shooed her out of the room.

It was then that she figured out what some of the deacons did, what they got away with, what her father forgave, and what the women, for some reason, chose to tolerate. It was hard, living as they did, for her to put the pieces together, and understand that the people who were supposed to protect you could also be the ones you had to prepare for and protect against. Funny how when she was walking home through the woods at night she'd hear the growl of their ATVs and think that meant she was safe.

That night, she came to Henry's door and asked, "What happened when you and Dad went off with Matty?"

He didn't look up from his books. "You wouldn't understand."

"Aw, come on. Tell me."

"No." Something unfamiliar in his voice. She slouched into his room, trying to move through the strange air between them.

"Do you have a verse for me? Just something—"

"Something for me to pray on," he said abruptly, in a high mincing voice, imitating her.

She took a step back. "Well?"

"I'll only give you one if you show me how you do it."

"Do what?"

"You know. I tried doing what you do. But if I try to speak, nothing comes out. How do you do it?"

Nora could see how badly he wanted it. They both had the same powerful, consuming need to please their father. She felt it every time he looked over at her in church and she knew she had to stand up and walk to the edge of that cliff and fling herself off. She'd do anything for that hand on her head.

"Okay," she said. Nora closed her eyes and got down on her knees and began to pray very fast, rocking back and forth a little, waiting for the Spirit to take her. Soon the words that were not words were pouring out of her.

When she could breathe again, she climbed shakily to her feet. Henry was staring intently.

"I can't do that," he said.

She wiped her damp forehead. "How do you know until you try?"

"I've tried. I get down on the floor and pray just like that. But nothing happens."

"You have to open your heart to the Lord, let Him in." That was the official explanation for how it worked. But he was her brother, he deserved to know the secret she'd been holding close for a long time. "The truth is, I imagine what Dad wants," she said. "I know he wants me to become someone else."

"Someone else?"

"Someone God loves more than anyone. And I go through it, like, what would this person do? And then it becomes real."

"So it's like acting."

Nora was quiet. It was the closest she had come to saying that what she did might be a performance. A game of pretend.

Henry looked away, clenching and unclenching his fists, a hard, unfamiliar look on his face. She realized, with shock, that he was about to cry. "I'm scared," he said.

"Scared of what?"

"I'm scared of what he wants from me." There was no stopping the tears streaming down his face. "I'm scared of what I might do."

He was begging for her help. Not able to say it, but asking in the old way they had as children when they needed each other, when they woke from bad dreams to find the other one already there by the bed with a few comforting, whispered words.

But she had nothing comforting to say to him this time. "He wouldn't ask us to do anything bad. If he asked, there's a reason for it," she told him.

Henry shuddered and wiped his eyes. A change came over his face. He mastered himself. "Yeah, I guess so."

She had failed him in some way she didn't understand. After that, she stopped coming to him for verses, and he grew quieter in her presence. Now it was up to her to flip through her own nubby black Bible searching for inspiration. The twelve minor prophets always had more doom and gloom to offer. She was surprised by some of the things she found in them—women burned and angels who became monsters. Rape and the butchering of the children of enemies. It was a dark and bloody story, and it had been all along, it was just that no one had shown her those parts before. Henry would be able to tell her what it all meant, and why their God would exact such violent vengeance. But she is afraid to ask. In church, she catches Henry's eye and sees him staring at her with a look. What is it? A longing. A loathing. She can't be sure. The silent language of twins that they used to share seems more remote and foreign every day.

⁂

It's November, deeper into the fall. The weather has grown colder. Each morning, Nora has to knock ice out of the chickens' water troughs. She does her chores bundled in an assortment of thrift store winter clothes, whatever they can get at the army surplus store in town.

One morning after her chores, Nora wanders down to the creek, where she sees a few of the other church kids clustered together on the bank. There aren't many other children her age here, besides Henry and Levi, and the others keep to their own secretive cliques. There are the boys who hunt, wearing their coonskin caps and trailing after the deacons, arguing about the relative merits of AR-15s and Bushmasters. And the girls, who are even more alien, sitting on hay bales during their slender times off from work, talking about the things they miss from their old lives, before they came here: lip gloss, Harry Potter, sports bras, the perfume samples you got from the mall and pressed to your neck. It is difficult for Nora to make conversation with any of them; to them, she's not a girl, but a performance piece, a symbol, as friendable as the chipped plaster Virgin Mary statue her mother keeps on the window sill of the barn, which her father allows, his one concession to her Catholicism.

They're poking the head of a deer laid out on the gravelly creek bed, the rack of antlers still intact, the hide loose as an old cloth draped over the mostly-gone carcass. A strip of spine, a jumble of blood and bone: that's all that left. The deer's eyes are still dark and full and glossy.

She overhears a girl asking, "Do you think wolves got him?" Nora is about to chime in to say it was probably coyotes or even skunks who finished the job, when one of the other girls says, "Or the devil got him. We should call the Holy Girl." The laughter that follows, soft and snickering, makes Nora back away into the trees before anyone catches sight of her.

She decides to go look for Bruce, the old bull moose that shows up every fall to munch the willows close to the shore. She can usually find him, battle-scarred and bad-tempered, jaws working on the willows. If his eyes shift to hers, she backs away. He's killed dogs with a kick and will charge if anyone gets too close. She knows it's him because while most moose shed their antlers every year and grow new ones, his remain year-round, a weird, stunted pair of bony spikes unlike any she's ever seen. The hunters call them "Devil's antlers," and one of them told her it happens if a moose is injured in a certain way—if he got kicked by an ornery lady moose in the wrong place, or a wolf bit his balls off. The hunter laughed when he told her this, and then changed the subject, looking uncomfortable.

Nora finds Levi chopping wood behind his trailer and enlists him to follow the creek out to the lakeshore, where the steep rocky cliffs and inlets let the water seep and roar in and out of its many mouths.

When they reach the shore, Nora leans far over the edge of the water to see the foaming eddies. Somehow, the water pulls at her, the ground rushing up. Her weight shifts, and then she is tumbling down the rock face, a tangle of arms and legs and gasping breath.

She lands hard on her right wrist in a foot of water. She tries to get up, the water lapping at her legs, seeping into her pants, weighing down her boots. Levi calls her name, then slides down the cliff face after her.

Her right forearm is strangely numb, but the pain is there somewhere around the edges, closing in. She tries to turn her wrist, but something prevents the movement. She turns the arm using her other hand, and a long gash comes slowly into view, getting deeper as more of her arm is exposed. At the heart of the bloody wound, something glinting like a tooth at the center: bone.

At the sight of the bone she throws up in the water. Levi finally reaches, clutching at her arm and making her cry out. "I'll carry you," he says fiercely. "I'll carry you back—"

They only make it a few dozen yards back before Nora sits down hard in the shallow water, feeling dizzy. Stupid girl, her father would say about her fall.

Then, suddenly, a voice: "Hey. Come this way." It's throaty and low, unmistakably familiar. They both look up; a back-lit face is staring at them from the cliff edge. It takes Nora a long moment to realize it's Rachel.

"There's a way up the cliff," she calls to them.

Nora stands up shakily, cradling her wounded arm as though it's a baby. Levi steadies her and they move up the rock face, putting their feet where Rachel tells them to. When they're close to the top, Rachel grabs

Nora by the shoulders and pulls her up the rest of the way, moving her hands quickly over her body, exploring and examining with businesslike strokes. She is wearing her familiar flannel hunting jacket over some flimsy thrift store dress, the usual smells of smoke and wild mint on her clothes. "That arm doesn't look good," she says. It's bleeding in heavy red throbs, soaking Nora's shirt. She feels like a deer up on a hook in the yard, pumping blood out. Rachel tears a strip of cloth from her dress and makes a tourniquet at Nora's elbow. "You should have done this right away," she says sharply to Levi. "Don't you know anything?"

Levi's face is as white as Nora feels. All those lessons in wound care and tying tourniquets on each others' arms and in the moment of need, he panicked. "What are you doing here?" he demands. "You left. You're not—"

"One of you anymore? I know."

The three of them stumble down the path together. "Be strong, you have to walk a little farther," Rachel says. "Left, left, left," she sings. They pass beyond the border of the compound, ducking under a lone strip of barbed wire. Past it is a grassy meadow; square in the middle of the meadow is a tiny gray house with a black slate roof. A cloud of smoke billows from a fire pit out front.

"Let's go back," Levi whispers in Nora's ear. Rachel is a deserter, not to be trusted. But Nora can't walk much farther. Rachel ushers them into the fenced-in yard. "I moved here when I left," she says. She offers no further explanation. Nora's eyes are on the pile of bones in the fire pit, trying to work out what they once belonged to. Rachel kicks something in the pile of ash, revealing the skull of a deer.

"We're not supposed to talk to you," Levi says, but something catches in his voice, making it reedy and high.

Rachel narrows her eyes. "That arm needs looking after." She's more feral-looking up close, with ash in a long streak across her forehead where she must have swiped her once-smooth hair out of her eyes. The house's paint is chipped and gray, loose tiles are sliding from the roof, and a few windowpanes are cracked.

Nora sways. She has to sit down and rest; the rough bandage is soaked, turning black. She follows Rachel inside. The front room is filled with books and drawing papers, many of them open and scattered on the table. Half-finished sketches lift, rustle and settle like pigeons taking flight from barn rafters. The drawings all seem to be of animals: deer with their ribs exposed and the guts torn out; rabbits with gaping holes where eyes should be; owls feasting on the skinny entrails of mice.

Rachel pushes aside a stack of drawings on a chair. "Once I left I started reading up on how to survive in the woods for real, and you're doing everything wrong," she says. "The way you're storing your food. The way you dug your irrigation and your sewage. You didn't pour your concrete foundations right. One big freeze and it's all going to crack." Her scornful voice is back, both haughty and disappointed. "It's obvious. I saw it as soon as I woke up and took a good look around."

"We've been living here for years," Levi says, hotly. "Our men know—"

"They don't know a thing," Rachel says, looking straight at him. "I've been talking to the locals, the way your men never have. Every eight or ten years there's a real winter, and that's when you learn who's really from here." She snaps a piece of wood over her knee, measuring the splint against Nora's forearm. She has a brutal competence now that she lacked before. To Nora she says, "This will heal fine." It's the first reassurance she's offered, and Nora feels ready to faint, relief and light-headedness swimming together. She sinks into the chair Rachel cleared for her. When Rachel unwraps the bandage, her arm is a mess of red and muscle, but it is no longer gushing.

Nora looks at Levi; his jaw is still clenched, glaring at Rachel. "When the world ends," he says to her, "You're going to be begging to come back. You don't see the whole plan, but we're going to be the only ones who are ready."

Nora has never heard him so angry. Rachel has gotten under his skin. "You think you can defend yourselves if a war starts?" she asks. "With a few AR-15s and some target practice? Do you know what's happened to other people like you?" Her voice softens, pitying. "Everybody's getting ready. Look in the basements of half the people on this peninsula and you'll find guns and canned food and bottled water stacked to the ceiling. People around here mean to survive. It took me a while to figure it out, but your preacher isn't special. Everybody thinks they'll be the ones to make it."

"Yeah, but we have God on our side," Levi says. There's contempt in his voice.

Rachel doesn't answer. Instead, she settles into a chair facing Nora, dusting her wound with antiseptic powder, placing the splint and tying it firmly with two quick, agonizing jerks. "You'll scar," she says. "Women of the woods need scars. It shows you're tough. You know, like the ones hunting bears and sewing up their own wounds with catgut and binder twine. You've got to learn how to sew your own wounds if you want to live here." She keeps up a steady hum of talk as she works. "There," she says when she's done. "Keep that arm crooked at your side while you're walking home. You'll make it okay."

"Thank you," Nora stutters out. "I'll pray for you."

Rachel waves a hand carelessly. The same hand Nora remembers holding a cigarette, city-smooth. The same hand that was pressed to the dirt and straw of the barn floor as she crawled for forgiveness. "You think you're the only ones who've heard a message from God?" she says sadly.

When Nora gets home, there's a long argument between her mother and father about what to do.

Her mother pleads, "We have to take her to the hospital."

Her father says, "Do you know what they do in hospitals? Do you know what those doctors do to you?"

"What. Tell me what they do." Her mother's voice is sharp. "Besides set broken bones."

"They inject you full of poison. They give narcotics to children, to get them addicted. You saw it in Indiana. You saw the junkies falling over our doorstep. They didn't get hooked from drug dealers hanging around playgrounds. Doctors did it. The doctors pulled out their prescription pads and did it. That is what doctors do."

"This isn't for your damn principles," her mother says. "This isn't one of your miracle jobs. She needs a hospital."

"What do you think we're preparing for here?" her father says. A long, unanswered silence follows, a silence that says the things no one will say. "She'll heal," he declares. "We'll take care of her."

"There are things you can't do. You're not God, Francis."

"Don't you dare take His name," her father says, low and quiet.

On the couch, Nora waits, heart pounding woozily. She wants her father to win, wants to believe he has the power to heal her.

"I can hear the doctors now," he begins slowly. "Why wasn't she in school? Why wasn't she supervised? What was she doing out in the woods, alone?" He touches Nora's head roughly, pressing her damp hair into her eyes. "You know what they think of us. They'll blame you. They blame the mothers. If you walk in there, if you let them, they can take your kids away, Kat. They could take her away."

"Is that a threat?"

"I'm not the one who's the threat. I'm trying to keep us safe."

Nora closes her eyes, feeling waves of pain traverse her body. When she opens them again, it's late, and Henry is standing by her feet, his mouth twisted in a strange smirk. "They'll probably have to cut off your arm," he says. "It'll turn black first. You've heard, in Ma's first aid lectures. Gangrene." He stretches out the word, his lips spreading wider and wider into a rare grin.

Then she's in the truck, her old spot in the passenger seat, her father huge beside her, driving fast. His lips move in a muttered prayer: *Jesus Christ, have mercy on me, a sinner*. It's the Pilgrim's Prayer, old and simple and soothing. Nora begins to recite it with him. But he hushes her.

Voices and faces rush past her in a bright room. She's in her father's arms, he refuses to let go even when a white-coated balding man insists. "We have the infection under control, but we need to reset the bone."

"I won't let you put her under," her father says. "And no morphine. It's poison."

There's a long tube connected to her good arm. Clear mystery fluid moving in. Nora distantly remembers the doctors' office from Indiana, the untrustworthy smiles of strangers who held her mouth open and asked her to say *aah*, who probed her belly with cold thumbs, who spread her legs and felt around. She paws at the tube in her arm, moaning. No animal would endure this, and she is an animal of the woods, shivering in the lights.

When they are finally alone, she watches her father snake the needle out of her skin, pulling the tape free. "I'm getting you out of here," he whispers, and though she's tired, her heart quickens: it's just the two of them again, making their escape. He's holding her in his arms, carrying her down a long hallway. Voices shouting, arguments; her father swipes the people away like bees. They're going to make it. They're safe, heading home.

He feeds her antibiotics from their private stash, but no pain meds. "When the pain comes, you have to be strong," he says quietly in her ear. She learns the tenor of pain: ferocious burning, and dull hammer blows; pulses of electric light. He stays by her bed, reciting prayers to pass the long night hours when she can't sleep. He tells her he's hidden a canoe in one of the caves by the lakeshore and filled it with supplies, just in case they have to escape. Just as he's preparing the church, the community, for hard times, he's preparing his family as well. He's thought of everything they need to survive. And she's going to survive this.

After the days of fever and vomiting finally pass, Nora goes with her father to see Rachel. When they pull into the yard, Rachel is already standing there in her discolored dress and her gum boots, arms folded over her chest.

Her father gets out of the truck and speaks in his church voice, the one designed to make friends, and thanks her for the help. "You got my little girl out of trouble. I appreciate it."

Rachel does not smile or offer her hand. "I guess she learned her lesson about being careful around those cliffs," she says. "I hope you didn't make her learn another one."

"You think I'm the sort to beat my kids," her father says, not a question.

"I know what you do," Rachel replies simply.

Her father pulls off his wool cap and turns it slowly in his hands, a humble gesture, something she's seen him do when he wants to be just like the people he's preaching to. "Rachel," he says, gentle with concern. "There's still time to come back. You can still be safe with us. We'd welcome you."

"Oh, you can save the song and dance," she says. No one speaks to her father this way. Nora's heart thumps with fear and thrill combined.

Her father puts his hat back on. And he does something she doesn't expect: he laughs. "You're a tough one. You think you've got us all figured out."

"You forget, I was one of you."

"You never fully believed. But let me tell you—you'll regret leaving us. For the rest of your life."

"I realized groups like yours always fall apart. All you offer is lies." Rachel reaches out, resting a hand on the wooden gate between them. Her voice is urgent. "You can't keep it together, you know. The center cannot—"

"We'll see about that," her father says. "We'll see if you come knocking on our door. You remember why you first came to me. You're a broken woman. You've felt pain. You don't need to feel it alone."

Rachel gives a short, sharp laugh. "Keep the wound clean," she calls to Nora. Then she disappears into her house.

Her father doesn't say anything until they are back in the truck, driving the dirt road home. "Don't ever let me catch you with that woman again," he says. "You hear?"

"I hear," Nora answers.

But she still wants to know what Rachel is doing out here, a freak of nature, a woman alone. She knows—in the way that something involuntary can come over you, take over, make its claim on your will—that she will return.

On When He Comes and Who He Comes To

It's so easy to listen to the devil's lies when it's late at night and we can't get to sleep, when we're sitting at kitchen tables under bulbs that cast too many shadows, wondering if we could have lived another life. Maybe if we were better. Maybe if we admitted how small and weak we really are. We are so tired of being afraid. You told us and told us how worthless we were, how riddled with sin. The wind beats at the door, and no one is coming to comfort us or save us, and he tells us we should be angry. Everything the devil says has a shred of truth.

There's no easy way of knowing who will be saved, and who will listen to the devil's story and belong to him when all is said and done. The fallen don't shine with evil light. There is this invisible division among all mankind between the saved and the unsaved, with far more unsaved. His people are out walking among crowds every day, riding buses and coming out of banks and quietly resting their hands on their children's heads.

His people are like sleeper cells in a silent war. They're an unknown majority, carrying with them a secret fire. We've all felt the urge to listen to that voice that is so much like our own. That's when he comes to us, when our lives have shrunk around us until they're so small there's scarcely room to breathe. Then, a dog will howl in the night for no reason. A crow will alight on a branch over our heads. He's on his way. He never comes uncalled.

Chicago, October

"HOW'S EVERYTHING?" SHE ASKS Mike. "Is the new medication helping?"

"Sure, hon." He sounds sleepy. Nora can't believe she's visiting a patient just to ask him a favor. "Were you coming today?" he wonders. "I wasn't expecting you."

"No, I—" she swallows. "I just, I just wanted to ask if you could help me with something. You said your neighbor was a cop. I'm trying to find some things out and I was hoping—"

"Say no more."

The retired cop is like a mirror version of Mike. Same bushy eyebrows and plaid shirt, same amused smile and thick Chicago accent. He has a round expansive belly, though, that Mike has lost. In the coffee shop where they've agreed to meet, he looks around, assessing the situation the way cops do, noting potential threats and disturbers of the peace. Or maybe she's the one he's evaluating, trying to determine why she's so nervous, what she's got to hide. He's trained to detect liars and secret-keepers, isn't he?

"Let me be clear, I don't help people get out of jail or dodge charges," he says. "I help my friends get information, and Mike is a friend. What do you need to know?"

Nora pulls out a sheaf of papers with all the relevant information she has: her father's name and date of birth, and a printout of the article reporting his death. "I need to know what happened," she says. "But it can't come from me. If I call the sheriff and go around asking questions, they'll know."

"Who's they?"

"The people I grew up with."

"You mean, your family?"

"Yes," she says, and it is true: by almost any definition, the people she's hiding from are her family.

He reads through the top sheet unhurriedly, his eyes pausing on one line and then the next. "They're some sort of militia you were part of?"

She winces at the word *militia*, but there's no point arguing over semantics. "Yes."

"And they're after you now?"

She shrugs.

"Are you in danger?"

"I'm—not sure." She raises her hands and lets them fall again, helpless. "I think they're watching me. They've tried to contact me. I don't want them to know that I'm looking for information on them."

She knows how this sounds; paranoid and half-cocked and close to crazy. He's nodding, though. "How do you think they found you?"

"I don't know. Don't people just—have ways?"

"There's usually a trigger," he says. "Some way you slipped up. Every now and then we'd have a run in with the Jehovah's Witnesses or the Seventh-Day Adventists. You'd be surprised how many of them are living secret lives right in the middle of the city. Some teenager shows up at a shelter begging not to be sent back. Claiming all kinds of abuse. Sometimes with a baby."

Her throat hollows. "What would happen to them?"

"We'd try to offer some support. If they were still minors, we could put them in some sort of home. Sometimes get them a job. But the families usually found them, eventually. There were always little clues left behind, like breadcrumbs. Sometimes, they even went back on their own. There was no stopping them." He clears his throat and folds the papers neatly into his pocket, shelving the emotional content of the task. "I can look up the particulars of the case and tell you what the local sheriff's department concluded. It'll take me a few weeks, working with these small town departments."

"There could be federal records, too," Nora adds. "They were involved, at the end."

His eyebrows climb, then lower again. "Okay, I'll check that angle. I'll let you know what I find out."

"Thank you. One more thing. You wouldn't be able to help with a missing person, would you?"

"That depends. If there were criminal reports filed, a suspicious disappearance, I could tell you what's been found out."

"But if she just left. Of her own accord," Nora says softly. "Could you find her?"

He shrugs; then the shrug becomes a shake of the head. "Some people just want to disappear."

"Oh. Yes." Her vision blurs. She fumbles for her wallet. "Thank you anyway. What should I pay you?"

He waves her off. "Don't worry about it," he says. "Mike's an old friend. You take care of yourself, hear?" He rises and puts a hand on her shoulder, the contact firm and reassuring and patronizing at once. How many frightened women has he touched this way?

After he leaves, Nora sits there, wondering what breadcrumbs she might have left behind.

A year after arriving in Chicago, she wrote a letter to Levi:

Tell them I'm sorry for not being what they needed me to be. Tell him I'm sorry too. I am okay. There is not much I can do to set things right but I think I have to be one of the outside people now and you have to let me. You can make it on your own, you always were good enough without me.

She knew he wouldn't understand, so she wrote Isaiah 47:5 at the bottom: *Sit thou silent, and get thee into darkness, O daughter of the Chaldeans; for thou shalt no more be called the mistress of kingdoms.*

She didn't need to sign it. She borrowed Kiki's car and drove to a post office over the Indiana state line and dropped it in the box, with no return address.

On the way back, she stopped in Gary for gas. She watched people come and go from the gas station and the diner across the street, no one lingering, everybody hurrying somewhere.

Afterward, she drove for a long time down suburban streets, looking for the church with the green door, or the old house with the rickety deck. She had this crazy idea that if she found it, she'd see her mother step out, arms open. But she didn't remember the address, and every street looked the same, with its rows of brick bungalows, a grassy vacant lot next to every third or fourth house.

She should have gone home. But she kept driving through intersections, passing Baptist churches and liquor stores. Old men standing on street corners and kids gathered in the greenish light emanating from the 7-Eleven. The town looked bombed out in places, half-abandoned.

She pulled over in front of a ramshackle house with a wide screen porch and rolled down her window, breathing into a fine mist of rain.

A weedy lawn, a mailbox in the shape of a pig. All of it grabbed at her, slippery and strange.

An old woman made her way out the door and down the path, stepping carefully over loose stones. "Can I help you?" She had her arms folded under her floral house coat, not friendly or unfriendly yet.

"I used to live around here," Nora said. "But I can't remember where."

"Seems like everybody I know has up and left," the woman said. "What's your name, hon?"

"Delaney. Nora Delaney."

"Oh, yes." She nodded. "The minister's daughter." It was always women like these who held the lore of a neighborhood, who knew the births and deaths and departures. "Oh Lord, yes. I remember when you all left in your convoy. So many trucks and trailers, the street was blocked for days. Where did you all go?"

The question seemed bigger than itself. "North," she said. "The UP of Michigan." She really wanted to say, *I don't know.*

The woman nodded. "Look at you, grown up. You still up there, all those church people?"

"Some of them. I left."

"Where are you now?"

"Chicago. I'm a nurse."

"Well, isn't that something. I bet your parents are real proud." She lifted one arm and pointed slowly. "Your old house is just two streets down from here," she said. "On McKinney. You can't miss it."

"My mother," she said. "Katherine Delaney. Has she—come back here? Have you seen her?"

The woman shook her head slowly. "No, can't say that I have, honey."

She thanked the woman and drove off. She almost headed for the turnpike, but at the last minute, swerved at the stop sign, heading for McKinney.

There it was: their house. Something lost looking about it. Dandelions growing riotously in the wet lawn. A cross in the front yard and an American flag hanging limply on the porch. There were yellow curtains in the windows she didn't remember, and behind them, someone moving, a shadow, a person living there. Maybe it *was* her mother, and she'd been waiting here all this time. Nora leaned out the passenger side window. The someone passed the gap in the curtains and peered out: a stranger.

Nora drove on.

Now, she wonders if this is how they've found her. Maybe they traced the envelope back to Indiana. All they'd have to do is talk to the same neighborhood woman. *Chicago—I'm a nurse.* Stupid, to tell her that. That was probably all it took to find her. Not sinister magic, after all; just patience, determination, and time.

⁝

Later that week, Nora is at the house of one her patients when the old woman's nephew shows up. The man is in his forties, with the powder blue shirt and solid, well-fed girth of a Chicago businessman. He has the kind of unassuming swagger that she remembers from the deacons. He says he is looking for an old baseball that he caught at a Cub's game, which his uncle took from him.

Once the old woman nods in agreement from her bed, Nora offers to help, following the man to the garage to dig through boxes. She feels herself shrinking as he leans over her to go through a carton of old picture frames, plastic trophies, and baseball cards. She digs beside him, intent on the detritus of childhood sports memorabilia. She finds the ball at the bottom of the box, none the worse for wear, and reaches for it.

His hand circles her waist, then slides down to stroke her thigh. When his hand moves inward, Nora expects a lightning bolt of judgment to strike her down.

"Hey," he says. "Relax. You'll like this."

It's the certainty that gets her. He's so sure that she's been waiting for someone like him to grab her around the middle, throw her down and fuck her.

She turns around. She could slap him but that would be a girl move, almost what he's expecting. She's not going to let him walk away from this and forget.

So she hits him instead, the way her father taught her, a strong closed-fist punch to the jaw, the power of her shoulder behind it. Defend yourself, he would say. The world's going to come at you. You can lie back and take it, or you can fight to survive. They held sparring matches in the yard, her father slapping the top of her head, daring her to stop him, until she got mad and punched him in the chest. It did nothing; she couldn't hurt him. He just laughed at her and quoted Shakespeare, one of the few non-Biblical texts he allowed in the house. *Oh, when she's angry, she's keen and shrewd! And though she be but little, she is fierce.*

She feels the man's jaw shift appallingly under her fist, and for an instant there is nothing so satisfying that she has felt since leaving the UP. Bone on bone. There's a clean feeling that comes after violence.

The ball drops to the floor.

"What the fuck?"

He's sputtering, holding his jaw. Staggering back stunned. She didn't break anything, just revealed a small part of who she really is.

She stoops down and picks up the ball, still sparkling white after all these years. "Here." She drops it at his feet and walks past him, back to the house, where she collects her coat and bag, placing every needle and syringe in its appointed place.

At the kitchen table, Kiki shakes her head slowly. "Nora, you shouldn't have done that. You really shouldn't have."

"Why?"

"He could file a complaint. You could lose your job."

"But he—"

Kiki raises her hand before she can finish. "That doesn't matter. He can do what he wants. Haven't you figured that out by now?"

"You're saying you would have—"

"You have to pretend it's all a mistake. You laugh, you apologize, you say whoops. Silly me. You walk away with him still feeling good about himself. You've never smiled at a man because he was smiling at you? Are you that stupid?"

Nora doesn't answer. No one has taught her the things she really needs to know about surviving in this world.

Later, she waits alone at the bus stop to head to her next client, watching the wind sweep old newspapers down the street. She knows they would be right to fire her. This job is not for children. You go into people's homes during the worst times of their lives and give yourself to them, everything you have, whatever they need. To do it well, you have to disappear. You have to be willing to do shameful things, and bring none of your own stories, your own anger, with you.

Apostates

2008

(Fifty days until the world ends)

RACHEL DOESN'T SAY ANYTHING when Nora shows up at her gate; she just lets her inside the house and puts a pot of tea on the stove. Then she sits down at an easel by the window, where she is working on a charcoal drawing of a hawk with a mouse in its jaws. The hawk is all ashes and movement, like it's on fire. Nora wanders the living room, relieved Rachel is not interrogating her. She's not sure why she's here, or what she imagined when she ducked under the barbed wire and set off across the yellow meadow. But she feels a tug of ownership over Rachel. This is the woman she saved; there's still time to win her back. Any minor disobedience is worth that victory.

She runs a finger down the spines of Rachel's collection of books, stopping at *Frankenstein*.

"Have you read that one?" Rachel asks, garbled, a pencil in her mouth.

Nora has heard her father talk about it. "It's an allegory of man's hubris," she says. "Man tries to steal the power of creation from God."

"Well, that's one way of reading it," Rachel says. "I always thought it's about how man tries to steal the power of creation from women. Men have always been jealous over women's ability to make life. So they try to control creation." She makes a clean swipe across her drawing.

There are so many books here that are not allowed at home. Fantasy stories about witches and dragons. Books filled with maps of the world, pictures of melting icebergs and apelike humanoid skulls. Books of poetry, Frost and Dickinson and Milton, and thick warped Russian novels, the tiny type running into the crack of the binding. There are books about tragic women throwing themselves off cliffs because their love for a man was too great. Women living selfishly, not in the service of others. Women wanting things. Whole categories of women Nora doesn't have names for. Whole books without a mention of the divine, the stern promise of creation and law, duty and devotion.

"When I was living in Chicago," Rachel tells her, "I met all kinds of people you'd call sinful. But they were only sinful if that's the story you choose for them. There are other stories. Everyone's just trying to get by, in their own way."

"Were you getting by?" Nora asks. The kind of small, pertinent question she's heard her father ask hunters in church parking lots, the kind of question that opens up conversations.

"Not really," Rachel says. "I don't do loneliness well." She looks away from her drawing, toward the window. "There was this man I met. He had these soft brown curls and a searing look. This beautiful man, I'd do anything for him. He was Christian and he told me he was going to save my soul. He told me he'd take care of me. I got pregnant. And then one day when I was alone in this shitty apartment we were renting, I gave birth too early. I held the baby. It was a boy, tiny and blue and barely formed, all his parts exact. The guy left me, said it was my fault the baby died. That there must have been something wrong with me. I believed him, you know."

She looks over at Nora, her gaze sharp. "I know what you're thinking. There are names people like you have for people like me."

Nora stares down at the book in her lap, trying to make her eyes read the type even though it looks like a foreign language.

Rachel rests her chin in her hand. "What do you do when you go on trips with your father?"

"He talks to people," Nora answers. "He always knows what to say to get their attention. And when they're listening, I prophesy."

"And how do you know what to say?"

There's no answer an unbeliever would understand. "God tells me."

"But how does it begin. *Really.*"

"I just start telling a story. Something I've learned about from the Bible. And it grows from there."

"How do you know what's coming is from God? Maybe you're just good at telling stories."

"If I'm good at it," Nora says, "It's because God made me that way."

Rachel inclines her head, and smiles in a sad way. "There's no changing you, is there," she says. "You'll always have a ready answer for me."

"It's because—"

"Stop." Rachel raises her hand. "If you want to win somebody back into the fold, try someone else." Then her face changes. "There is someone else, actually. A guy who left the church. He's been trying to talk to you."

"Who?"

"His wife works at the Beef-a-Roo. Maybe you should talk to him."

"You mean he wants to come back?"

"I didn't say that."

Nora walks home through the crusty snow, messing up her footprints as much as she can as she slips under the barbed wire, back into safe territory. If she asks her father about the other deserter, he'll forbid her from seeking him out. He'll quote Deuteronomy:

If thy brother, the son of thy mother, or thy son, or thy daughter,
or the wife of thy bosom, or thy friend, which is as thine own soul,
entice thee secretly, saying, Let us go and serve other gods, which
thou hast not known, thou, nor thy fathers . . . Thou shalt not
consent unto him, nor hearken unto him; neither shall thine eye
pity him, neither shalt thou spare, neither shalt thou conceal him:
But thou shalt surely kill him; thine hand shall be first upon him
to put him to death.

She's been told that time spent with apostates and unbelievers is dangerous. They have a way of softening you up, lowering your defenses. You go out among them with pity and caution, as though among the diseased. There's a place in Russia, her father told her, where a nuclear reactor melted down. Now to enter that zone for an hour is like smoking fifty cigarettes. You can't feel or taste or smell the danger, but it's poisoning you all the same.

But didn't the prophets walk among the sinners, she wonders? Didn't they offer themselves despite the risk? Isn't she supposed to be some sort of weapon of faith?

She's seen the locals all her life, from a distance, the hunters and fishermen and kids climbing on and off school buses. The girls in particular fascinate her. She's seen them smoking at gas stations, leaning on cars in the parking lot of the DQ, laughing in packs. They wear pink hoodies and low-rise jeans that drag in the wet slush of the roads, their hips plumping out over the edges, their bodies soft, generous, lazy. Hair in ponytails or side-razored cuts. Lip rings. When they see her, they stop talking and laughing and watch her with blank, penetrating stares.

She should be out there with them. Laughing at their jokes and telling the stories she's good at telling. If they could just got to know her, they'd realize that she's not just the Holy Girl.

A few days later, Nora asks Lonnie and Len, a couple her father often sends on supply runs, if she can ride with them into town. "We're busy today, we can't watch you every minute," Len says. "We have to ask your father if it's all right."

"I'll just sit in the truck," she promises. "I just want to see what's happening in town."

"Seeing more of the world just makes you want it more," Lonnie warns. "'No matter how much we see, we are never satisfied.'"

But her father is in one of the far fields and can't be consulted; the day is losing its light. Before they can hesitate any further, Nora scrambles into the cab of their truck. Lonnie and Len look at each other and sigh. She's the special girl, after all; it's hard to refuse her.

Nora holds onto the arm rest with her good hand while the truck jounces wildly all over the bumpy dirt track that leads to the main road. It's late fall, the sky heavy and iron-gray with the promise of more snow. The tops of road signs swing by: gas stations, restaurants, taverns. Fishing tackle, cash loans, bike rental. A church with its ominous block lettering: ETERNITY IS AN AWFULLY LONG TIME TO BE WRONG.

Once in town, they pass the gas station and the court house, the three bars, and the small unmarked door of the Methadone clinic, one of their best spots for handing out flyers.

Lonnie pulls into the lumber yard, and the three of them walk into the dark interior of the warehouse. It will be a long wait for what they need, so Nora heads over to the diner.

Inside, there are a handful of people scattered among the booths: an old man reading a newspaper and a mother with kids too young for school, picking absently at their fries. Nora takes a booth and a waitress lopes over to her. She's neither young nor old, with colorless hair in a loose bun. "What can I get you, hon? A burger?"

Nora shakes her head. "I'm looking for Roy," she says, trying to speak extra loud over her heart's noisy pounding. "I heard you knew him."

The woman lowers her pad. "Oh. I've seen you. You're from that group on the lake, aren't you? What's your name?"

"I'm Nora," she whispers.

"It's you. The recruiter." The woman sinks back on one hip, looking her over. "I thought you'd be—bigger, I guess. More impressive. Shooting fireballs out your eyes." She laughs. "Well, what do you know. Roy wants to talk to you, too. Let me just get someone to cover me, okay? Just wait."

She disappears into the back. Nora taps her foot on the sticky floor, preparing her moves. What Bible verses should she use, placing them like phantom chess pieces in her mind, this one here, that one there. Should she cry? The waitress seems excited to see her. You just have to wait for someone who's receptive to your ideas, her father told her. You can't win over everybody; you wouldn't want to, most people are not *your* people. But when you find one, you listen close, for the small shout underneath their words about what they need, what they're missing. They want your faith, they're hungry for it. You have to let it shine through you.

The waitress returns a few minutes later. "I got somebody to cover my shift," she says. "I'm Sally, by the way. Come on back to my place, and we'll talk to Roy." She says this as though it's the most normal thing in the world to meet a strange kid in a diner and take her home.

"Can I tell you about the plan God has for us?" The words tumble out of Nora, shaky and strange. It's harder than her father made it look. She doesn't sound certain.

Sally nods, puts a hand on her shoulder like they're already friends. "Sure you can, hon. Just come back with me and you can tell me all about it."

When they're in the parking lot, Sally releases her hair from its bun and shakes it loose with a sigh. She's thin in the face, speckled with acne scars; a missing tooth is a dark flash in her smile. She wears a black line of lipstick but no other makeup, and a shapeless down coat that has seen many seasons. Her hand is out, the door of her rusty SUV open. Nora's heart pounds a little harder. Maybe it's what her father calls the Thrill of the Hunt. When you're close to changing a mind, to winning over a soul, it's hard to turn back. You know what the word *rapture* means, don't you? You'll feel it someday, her father has told her. When you're close to getting somebody to believe, it's a rush. You won't be able to stop.

Nora gets into the car.

At first they are both quiet, surrounded by the smells of sun-warmed vinyl and cigarette smoke. They're heading to one of the trailer camps that hug the shore. It's a tourist spot, good for summer fishing, but it has its share of locals that live there, who are fiercely loyal about the strip of sandy beach, even when the four-foot winter snows have buried it.

"I'm a born and raised Yooper," Sally says, driving one-handed, tapping her cigarette out the window. "We get some unusual kinds here. People who like to disappear. People with pasts. Why'd your Dad come here?"

"He wanted somewhere where we'd be safe," Nora says. "The lake holds twenty percent of the world's fresh water."

"Is that so."

"It's remote."

"That it is."

"Nobody will find us here."

"Who are you hiding from?"

Nora has to think, quickly, carefully. The government, the unbelievers. But something broader. Strangers camped out in vacant lots back in Indiana, cars idling at dark street corners, people breaking into houses wanting blood and money. The steady wail of ambulance sirens. People slumped under bridges or in parked cars. The malice of the world.

"People you can't trust," she says finally.

Sally's lips press together. "The worst kind of people."

The SUV pulls up among a cluster of trailers, crunching on gravel and old snow. Despite the gray weather, people are outside in folding chairs and parkas. A girl sits on the edge of a trampoline, while a younger boy bounces half-heartedly behind her. They're both wearing scuffed neon snow suits.

The boy stops jumping when Sally gets out of the car. "You said you'd take us sledding. There's snow on Sugar Loaf. You said," he calls.

"I will, hon. Let's get some food first."

Nora gets out slowly, eying the kids. The girl is about her age, sitting with one booted foot up on the rim of the trampoline. Her eyes pass over Nora easily.

"Who is she?" the boy asks.

Sally pokes through the mailbox hanging by the trailer door. "This is Nora. She's from that group on the lake."

"Oh," the girl says, narrowing her eyes, not hostile, just curious. "Roy's people."

"Don't hassle her, okay?"

The girl blinks innocently. "Am I known for hassling?"

Nora has never heard a girl speak to her mother this way, parroting back her words to make them sound ridiculous. It's scary, but also a little breathtaking. Sally doesn't look up or scold her. "I'm making sandwiches," she says, and goes inside.

"You're one of the people in the woods, then," the girl says. "Do you have your own gun? Have you shot stuff?"

"Lots of deer," Nora answers. "And a porcupine, once."

"Gross," says the girl. But her tone is warm.

"Our Dad was supposed to take us," the boy says. "But he's in jail. Mom got probation. We lived with our grandma for a while."

"Maybe Roy will take you," the girl offers, sounding conciliatory.

"Does Roy live here?" Nora asks.

"Kind of. He's got his own trailer but he's always over here. He's weird. Sad all the time and praying and moaning about stuff. I'm Vicky," she adds. "You want to double-jump with me?"

It takes a few tries to master the tricky maneuver, Vicky jumping first, then Nora, before the two of them jump in tandem. But then Nora gets it, and Vicky goes rocketing into the air. "Now you," Vicky says, and they're jumping close together again, face to face, Vicky grinning at her. Nora has never been this close to another girl. They concentrate on synching their rhythm. Vicky then slams her legs down and up Nora goes, flying above the trailers, the trees, the lake.

Sally's head emerges from the trailer door. "Food. Now."

They pile into the cramped kitchen booth of the trailer while Sally makes peanut butter and jelly sandwiches. Nora watches every step closely: the soft bread emerging from the plastic bag, the jar of purple jelly, the slow, lavish spread of peanut butter. Sally hitches one hip high as she leans on the counter, still wearing her old coat. When she turns with the plates, Nora sees she's taken off her waitress blouse. Her thin t-shirt shows her full breasts, nipples pointy in the cold. She is all things foreign and forbidden at once, overwhelming and strange, too many sins and indecencies to catalog.

"Is Roy coming?" Nora asks. The sandwich hovers, its smell impossible to ignore.

"He'll be here any minute. Just eat up."

Nora's jaw works on the gummy peanut butter. The other kids press into her, noisy in their chewing. The only other sound is the intermittent whine of a house fly caught in the kitchen curtain. They listen to it try again and again to get out, batting against the window.

A car crunches outside on the gravel. Sally steps outside, and talks to someone in a low voice. Then a man ducks into the kitchen. He's wearing blue coveralls with his name stitched on the pocket—ROY, in red. His hair is oily black and pressed close to his skull. He stands in silence for a long moment with his large hands hanging by his sides. "Nora," he says, and it sounds like he's been waiting to say her name for a long time.

His face is familiar to her. The pigeon-toed way he lumbers across the small space, a casual clumsiness. She remembers a man moving across the compound that way, an axe over his shoulder. The whooping cry he gave during the drive-the-devil-out ritual. A *hallelujah* that was fervent and free. But at some point he stopped appearing at meetings, and no one spoke about him again.

"You used to be one of us," she says.

"I used to. I finally made it out," he says, and the phrasing makes no sense to her.

She lets her eyes go wide. "Don't you miss us? Do you miss God?"

He blinks slowly. "Yes. Every day." He sighs, runs a hand through his hair. "Don't you know? No, of course you don't. I'm doing this all wrong."

He reaches across the table and holds her hands, and though she wants to pull away, she doesn't. She listens for the keyhole into his story, something that will betray what he needs.

"I never thought I'd get the chance to talk to you," he says. "Or maybe I hoped I would. Maybe that's why I stayed up here, in this god-forsaken middle of the hell out of nowhere." He laughs. "Maybe that's why I'm here with Sally." He looks over his shoulder, indicating with a jerk of his chin the family pictures over the sink, Sally and her kids on a dock by the lake, their faces shiny, everyone squinting in the sun. Roy isn't in any of the photos. "When I left, I had nothing." He shakes his head. "We were all so ready to give everything we had. For you."

"Me?"

"There are people who look and sound like everybody else, but inside they're carrying something, a secret fire. They know that life isn't just—this." He waves his arm around in the air. "And you and your father, you were good at finding your people—the sort of people who are vulnerable to a good story. I used to hate you, you know. When I finally left. Sally had to remind me that you were just a kid." He's gazing intently at her. "You're the one who wins people over, not him. You know it. That's why you've come back for me."

All the Bible verses, all the prophecies she had planned, have gone out of her head. "You could come back with me," Nora says. "We'd take you back."

Roy shakes his head, smiles, rueful. "You don't know the first thing, do you?"

He pushes up the sleeve of his coverall. The weather-beaten skin of his arm is a map of conquered territory: mosquito bites and campfire burns and long white rivers of old track marks. Among the marks are a series of red horizontal tiger stripes, up and down his arm. "Those I didn't do," he says. "But I let them do it. They would heat a fork over a flame, and press it, like this." He pushes three fingers into his skin. "I asked if it was a punishment for something I had done. Whatever it was, I promised I'd never do it again. They said, This is how we know you'll keep your promise."

Outside a door slams, a car backfires, a dog begins a cycle of tired barks. The little trailer is cold but Nora doesn't feel it, she can't feel it if she's going to stay focused and win over this man. She has to get control of the conversation somehow, bring him back to prophecy and prayer. "The world is going to end," she says. "And you're going to be left out. The doors will close and you'll be outside."

"Please stop." Roy touches her arm, looking pained. "You don't have to do that. You don't have to recite these things just because they ask you to. I know they're stockpiling, getting ready for something terrible, but it'll be their end. And you're just a kid, okay? Like Vicky, like Danny." He points to the pictures over the sink again, the girl and the boy in their bathing suits squinting into the sun. "It's not right, what they're doing to you. They're playing with you. You're their little wind-up girl. Once I realized that, I knew I had to get out."

There's a red rim around his eyes. Does he lie awake and feel the fear of the descending angels? The images her father has put there, fire and judgment, the days of chaos? They're the kind of things you don't forget. Someone has to love you with majestic force and power, to rain down such punishment. How can you turn your back on such love?

Nora struggles out of his grasp. "You're wrong." She fumbles for the right verse that will refute what he has said, but there's nothing in her head. "They're not using me. I'm a weapon of God."

Suddenly, the door flies open, and Lonnie's red bandanna pokes in. "Nora? Thank the Lord. We're going." She takes ahold of her good arm, pulling Nora to safety, back to the waiting truck. Roy tumbles out the door after them. Sally is standing in the yard, hands on her head. "I just wanted to talk to her," Roy says. "She asked for me. She wanted to see me."

Lonnie turns and spits on the ground between them, making Roy jump back. "The dog is turned to its own vomit again, eh, Roy?"

"Nice to see you too, Lonnie." Roy doesn't sound angry, just tired. "She's just a kid. You've got no right."

Lonnie hustles Nora into the truck and slams the door. "There's a special place in hell for apostates. A special place, you got that? You know where they're going."

Nora sits squashed between Len and a sack of chicken feed. Roy is standing before them with his hands up, a helpless gesture. "I'm not going to let you keep using her," he calls, his voice singsong, a moan. "I know what you do up there. I'm going to tell people."

They drive in silence along Big Bay Road for a long time before Lonnie says, "Don't ever talk to that man again, Nora. He wants to poison you. He'd take you away from us if he could."

"How did you find me?"

Lonnie's hand glides on the wheel. "We have friends in town. And the next town, and the next. Your father makes friends wherever he goes, and they keep an eye on things. You're always under our watch." It's meant as a comfort, but there's warning in it, too.

"Why did Roy leave?" Nora asks.

"Why does anyone? He listened to the wrong voices. The devil talks to all of us. Some of us choose to listen. That whole family is black-hearted as sin."

Nora says, tentatively, "The kids were nice. And the woman." The peanut butter is still stuck in her throat.

Lonnie's hand comes out and touches her knee. "There are two kinds of women in this world, Nora. And both of them can *seem* nice. You can be a righteous, obedient servant of the Lord, or you can be a whore, like that woman back there. Which one you want to be?"

She's quiet for a moment. "Are you going to tell my father?"

Lonnie shrugs. "Don't have to. He'll know."

On His Origins

To understand him better, we have to understand where he came from. This is what you've impressed upon us in your sermons. Know thy enemy!

We know that there was a world full of light and angels, and there was no such thing as Hell; and then, there it was one day, a dark spot in the universe, a potential crime. He was the most beloved of all the angels, and then he was cast out, unfavored, forgotten. And he became.

The devil is the first being denied the love of God. Does that explain things?

There's a dark fairy tale you told us about a cursed book. If you ever read the book from beginning to end, a demon will come to life, and when you get to the last word, he'll devour your soul. In the story, a girl finds the book and starts to read, and feels the demon becoming heavy on her back, leaning over her shoulder and panting. She's terrified, but compelled to read on; it seems there's no way out. But the girl is clever; she starts to read backward, returning all the way to the beginning, and the demon vanishes.

You told us we were the lucky ones, we were safe here. As long as we didn't open the wrong book, read the wrong story, we were safe. There was one story that was safe and it was yours to tell, and it was all of ours.

Why do we feel him so heavy on our backs now, then, if we're supposed to be safe?

Maybe he's already inside us, waiting to come out. Maybe he's in you.

What other explanation is there for why you do the things you do?
Can we un-read our way back to the beginning?

Chicago, November

IT'S GAME SEVEN. ALL SEASON, the city has been holding its breath. Letters flashing GO CUBS GO across the side of the Sears tower. Bodegas flying the W, the one-letter flag that is hung at Wrigley Field when the Cubs win a game. Strangers leaning into each other at cafe counters, in elevators, arguing with taxi drivers about their chances. There's something contagious in the city's mood. Something sweet about this perennial hope, that this could really be the year. It has a whiff of prophecy.

Mike called her this evening, complaining of worsening pain, but Nora suspects he just wanted someone to watch the game with.

"Do you want me to up your pain dosage?" she asks. "We can keep you comfortable—"

He waves his hand. "I want to be awake for this."

She's surprised that the funny, gregarious Mike doesn't have any friends. They came at first, he says in answer to her question. "Yeah, they showed. Can't ask for more than that. But I've been sick a long time. No one wants to hang on, month after month. To the bitter end." He smiles, a brief grimace.

Rain delay, says the TV. Nora looks involuntarily out the window, but of course the game is in Cleveland. On the screen, the rain is pouring off the brims of the players' hats, misting up the cameras. A massive white tarp is being drawn over the field like the closing curtain of a play. The crowd stomps its feet. A terrible restlessness in the air, so many people waiting for destiny to arrive.

"Where does your daughter live?" Nora asks.

"In Naperville."

"But that's just half an hour away."

"I told you, we don't really speak anymore."

Nora stands behind his wheelchair, watching the outfield with its electric green on the TV, the players shifting uneasily in the dugout, waiting for the rain to stop.

"You think she's watching right now?" she asks.

His jaw tightens. "Every Chicagoan is watching right now."

Nora slips away into the shadows of the house. There's a desk upstairs in a cramped office that she's seen before, shaggy with piles of untouched papers. It takes her several minutes as she opens one drawer and then another.

"The rain has stopped," Mike calls to her from downstairs. "On to extra innings!"

Finally, an address book, and among the jumble of names, one without a last name: Emily. A phone number and a Naperville address. Nora uses her cruddy cell phone to dial the number, listening to the mechanical ring with her breath rough in her ears.

"Hello?" A woman's voice. In the background she can hear the game echoing back to her, the same sound as what's coming from downstairs.

"Is this Emily Innis?"

"It's Emily Johnson now." The voice a little annoyed, dark and throaty, like Mike's.

"Emily, I'm your father's nurse. I've been taking care of him for a while and I wanted you to know—"

"A run! A run!" Mike yells.

"Look, can this wait—" Emily begins, but Nora plows on hurriedly, "He's very sick and he doesn't have long. I just wanted you to know, if you want to visit him, you should come soon."

"I knew he was sick," says Emily. Her voice is hesitant.

"See him, while you still can," Nora says.

"You're missing it!" Mike yells.

Nora hangs up and hurries downstairs.

When Kris Bryant throws Michael Martinez out, winning the game for the Cubs, Mike is silent. He and Nora watch the players run toward each other at the pitcher's mound, ecstatic, the group growing as more players rush the field, coaches, bat boys, everyone swarming, jumping up and down together.

Mike reaches for the TV remote and turns the sound off. "Open the window," he says.

Nora has to work hard to open the front window, which has long been painted shut. Then with a crack it's free, and they feel the cool night air sliding past their skin. A collective roar spreads down the street. The sound of thousands, millions, of voices, yelling into the night. Nora wheels Mike to the window so he can add his own raw whoop, joining the chorus emanating from apartments and houses, low rises and street corners, car horns and fireworks exploding into the air. It is like a storm of human joy.

Mike looks at her, flushed. "Nora, angel. I need your help."

She knows already what he's asking for. "No way, Mike."

"I've just got to see the parade. And there's nobody left that I know—nobody who would take me. I've been waiting for this my whole life."

◦

When the train stops at State and Van Buren and she wheels Mike out, the happy drunk songs are already filling the air: *Hey, Chicago, whadya say? The Cubs are gonna win today.* They can hear the roar of the parade from five blocks away. They join the dense crowd streaming down the closed streets, Nora bumping the wheelchair up and down the curbs, struggling to make room. "You all right?" she asks Mike at every corner, and every time his blue baseball cap nods.

She has to stay alert and be ready for anything. Among so much humanity, any lapse in her attention is a danger. Crowds are a risk in their unpredictable surges, their power to crush, stampede, suffocate. But this crowd is a wall of suburban fathers carrying kids on their shoulders, women pushing strollers, old people linking arms and singing joyously as if they've won a war. She never knew so much happiness could be released by a baseball game.

"There are so many people," she calls to Mike, stunned into the obvious.

He twists to look back at her, grinning. "Didn't I tell you?"

They push deeper into the thickening crowd. A line of open-air buses is creeping down Michigan Avenue, on which the players, shaggy, bearded, hung over, a little awed, wave and smile. David Ross raises the World Series trophy in a slow, dazed arc through the air. Anthony Rizzo gives the thumbs up and the crowds roar. Mike has to tell her who these men are, ordinary-looking, sheepish, draped with Mardi Gras beads. People are climbing the barricades, trying to get closer, to touch the players, the bus, anything.

Nora and Mike move slowly into Grant Park, where the team owner is giving a speech thick with reverb and emotion, the players dismounting the bus to make rippled, garbled remarks through loudspeakers. Grown men are weeping openly, as the team's manager, Joe Maddon, speaks of the long wait, the collective hope, the extraordinary power of people coming together to witness a shared dream.

"I wish I could see them," Mike shouts. In his chair, all he can see is a wall of blue-shirted backs.

Nora scrambles onto a lamp post. The posts have been greased to prevent climbers, but she has a lifetime of shimmying up birches. She hugs the post, looking out over waves of blue baseball caps, all of Chicago together here, united and seamless, a many-rooted life form, gathered in common prayer. She'll read later that the parade was one of the largest gatherings of humanity in history, and the only non-religious event to crack the top ten. Five million souls. It would be her father's dream.

"What does it look like?" Mike calls to her.

"It's like a sea," Nora yells back. That doesn't do it justice: it's a family.

From her position on the pole she sees a large man lean close to Mike, speaking in his ear. He nods. Suddenly, the man and two of his friends have their arms around him. Nora knows what they're about to do. She waves frantically. "No! He's sick!" she yells, sliding down the pole, a gluey mess of lube down her front. But it's too late: they're lifting him out of the chair and onto their shoulders like a conquering hero. They carry him him forward through the crowd, leaving her behind with the empty chair. "Wait!" she screams, fighting with the chair, struggling to push through bodies that won't give. She wrestles and shoves and gets absolutely nowhere. He's gone.

"Ma'am."

There's a hand on her arm. The only person in this blue-clad sea not in blue. An older man with a flyaway beard, a plaid shirt and ripped jacket. He looks homeless.

"Do you still read your Bible?" he asks.

The roaring around them recedes. She's in a pocket of silence with this familiar stranger, a man she's seen before, a face praying in a barn in another life.

"I do," she says, and it sounds like a vow.

"Revelation 12:14," he says, gripping her wrist.

It sends her mind darting back to the spidery columns of text, the placement of this and that verse. *Revelation* was her father's favorite book, full of strange prophecies, many-eyed angels, whores and demons and pre-destined births. He made her and Henry memorize it. *"The woman fled into the wilderness to a place prepared for her by God, where she might be taken care of for 1,260 days,"* she whispers to the man, pressed close to her.

"Twelve hundred and sixty days," he says. "You've been gone almost that long. We had to make sure it was you. We've been waiting," he says. "We've kept you safe, we've been watching. Now it's almost time. You haven't forgotten, have you?"

Nora shakes her head, climbs forcibly out of the silent space he's made between them. "That's not me anymore," she says. "You have to go back and tell them. Tell them I can't—"

He grips her harder, his round, owlish eyes unavoidable. "Who's going to save us now? Who's going to take care of us now? We need you. *It has to be you.*"

"I can't—"

"Remember who made you," the man says. He presses something into her hand and slips away into the crowd, gone like a fleeting thought of death, an Annunciation: it has to be you.

The parade returns to her gradually: a pricking of her ears, the remembrance that she has responsibilities here. "Mike," she yells. "Mike Innis!" She shouts his name into the crowd, but her voice is drowned out by millions of other voices. They're belting out the "Go Cubs Go" song, tuneless and gleeful. The crowd, the city, draws its breath, then releases it down the sleek glass-walled avenues, through the immigrant neighborhoods, down into the South Side, through the trees of Grant Park, out into the expanse of the lake.

Nora looks down at the slip of paper in her hand:

When the day of the Pentecost came, they were all together in one place. Suddenly a sound like the blowing of a violent wind came from heaven and filled the whole house where they were sitting. They saw what seemed to be tongues of fire that separated and came to rest on each of them. All of them were filled with the Holy Spirit and began to speak in other tongues as the Spirit enabled them.

Below the verse is a Chicago address.

"Nora!"

"Mike!" The beefy men are returning through the crowd, bearing her patient. They set him back in his chair with astonishing gentleness. "I saw them," he says, his eyes bright and feverish. "These folks brought me all the way to the stage. I touched Jon Lester's shoe!"

Nora grabs the men's hands. "Thank you. Thank you." They bob their heads shyly, and move on through the crowd.

"Bet you never thought you'd cry over a baseball game," Mike says.

Nora touches her cheeks; they're wet. She almost lets the paper tear itself away in the wind, almost, almost—

Damascus

2008

(Twenty-five days until the world ends)

"THERE'S A NEW COUPLE I have in my sights," her father announces at the table. "He's about ready. But the problem is the wife."

Her mother listens from her usual place behind the counter. She's almost never seated when the rest of them are eating; there's always something else for her to bring, or take away.

"Bring Nora with you," her father says. Nora looks up in time to see her mother's mouth draw thin. "She knows what to do."

Her mother puts a plate down so hard it clatters and rings. "You know I don't do that kind of thing, Frank."

"You're good with the wives. Just talk to her. We need this couple."

"Get one of the other women. Get Lonnie."

"The wife doesn't trust me. She's got to see my wife, see our family. She needs to know we're good people." He rises, moves to the counter, and puts his arm around Nora's mother in a way he rarely does. Her mother pauses her scrubbing; her gaze grows distant like she's remembering something.

"Do this for me," he says.

She shakes her head, and he pulls back. "The other women on this compound are loyal. They understand I've been charged with a mission. But not my wife. No, not my wife."

"Stop it." She leans heavily on the counter, her head hanging low.

"Nora, get in the truck," her father says without looking, and she gets up, knowing the smallest hesitation will be seen as an insurrection. She can hear his voice rising as she leaves ("I thought you knew what it took to be a part of this family. I thought you understood what was needed").

Nora sits in the cold truck, watching her mother and father's heads move back and forth in the kitchen window as if they are dancing. Her mother's head shaking, no, no. Her father straight and focused as a hunting dog. She watches him advance. Her mother inclines her neck. Her father leans close and, shockingly, kisses her. There's such power in always believing in your rightness, as he always does. In an argument with him there is never the slightest doubt about who will win.

She's seen a photograph of her mother big-bellied in Indiana, her hair long and wild, her father's arm around her. They're posing in front of the old church, her father skinny and proud, his arm protective. He's grinning at the camera, but her mother is looking at him. She seems so happy. Drunk with it, a little stupid, her eyes half-closed.

Her mother blows out the front door. She gets into the truck and starts it without a word, just a jerk of her wrist, the jangle of her keys.

⁝

The couple, Beth and Rod, own a nearby junkyard that Nora has passed by many times without ever going inside. From the road, Nora has seen the high jumbles of rusting metal, the scattered yellow grass hiding abandoned cars, the burned out shells of tractors, even a rusting school bus covered with psychedelic paint. She's heard a rumor that there are strange metal statues on the property. But the rumor doesn't prepare her for the sudden appearance of what looks like a giant rebar cross, with a stick figure of metal rods crucified upon it. Beside the cross, a ten-foot human figure, the head like a birdcage, turned thoughtfully, one metal rebar foot forward, one skeletal arm raised, pulling an object over a shoulder.

"David," her mother says.

"Who?"

"It's King David. Michelangelo's David."

"You can tell just from looking at it?"

"Of course. It's the pose. David is the perfect man." Her mother shivers a little. "At least, the Bible thinks so."

A dog standing on a shifting pile of lumber begins to bark aggressively as a woman walks toward them through the rusting vehicles. She's wearing black rubber boots and a duct-taped parka, her frizzy graying hair bundled on top of her head in a tumbleweed. "I know you're not the Avon lady," she snaps. "So why don't you tell me who you are?"

Normally, Nora would immediately leave: backwoods women like this are too hard, too wily, too bitter, not worth the effort.

But her mother is hard, bitter and wily, too.

"Hush now," her mother says at the barking dog, which immediately goes quiet. "Beth?" she asks questioningly. When the woman doesn't contradict her, she continues. "We're from the church. The one up the road. We heard you needed our help and we wanted to see what we could do."

"Don't need anyone's help," Beth responds sharply.

"Forgive me," her mother says. "What I mean is, everybody needs a little help from God, from time to time."

Beth lifts her shoulders, but she doesn't turn away. "I thought you people would be after us. It's about money, isn't it? It's always about money."

Nora has never seen her try mother her hand at conversion. She wonders what method she'll use.

"It's a hard life, being a woman up here. I can tell you're worthy of it," her mother says. "You know God built women to endure almost anything."

"Almost," Beth says.

"I'm not here to ambush you. I came with my daughter, so you could see that we are real people," her mother says. "The truth is, there are a lot of women in our group, but we need more. We need practical women who know how to take care of each other. We're getting ready for the time when women will need each other."

Beth half-smiles, her eyes narrowing. "And what time is that?"

"Soon," her mother answers. "When the hard times come, the women and the children are always left wailing and forsaken. Not many words are spared for how they keep the family fed and the lights burning during the times of trouble and war. In our community, I intend to keep the women safe. The only power Christian women have ever had is when they stand together. It's the only way we survive."

Beth raises her hand to stop her. "I'm a Christian, all right," she says. "But that doesn't mean I cotton on to all your ideas. We're trying to live ordinary lives here. I've heard what you people are up to back there in the bluffs. And that's probably not the half of it. I don't go in for all of that. You all are bloody-minded."

"Pardon me," her mother says. "But are you sure you're a Christian?"

The words have their intended effect: Beth bristles. "What's that supposed to mean?"

"We're redeemed by blood. Birthed in it," her mother says. "We come from blood, we're washed in it. The wisdom of the blood redeems us."

"That's so, but—"

"I always thought faith was something you kept to yourself, that you lived with quietly. But a church that's worth the name has to be more than that, and we have to live our lives with more than that. Being a Christian requires you to live an extraordinary life. If you're going to call yourself a believer, then there's no living in the ordinary world. Excuse me for saying it, but you'll die out here. Not just your body. Not just on this earthly plane. You'll die the Great Death."

There's hesitation on Beth's face. "I think you should—"

Nora feels herself falling before she even realizes she has decided to fall. Without any protection, her knees hit the hard earth, the ground rushing up to her face. She closes her eyes. She can hear Beth stirring distantly over her head. Nora cries, "There will be a column of fire." It's an easy move, but it works just right.

Now there's a hand smoothing her back, stroking it more gently than her own mother ever did. "There now. You're all right, hon. We had a daughter," Beth says. "We lost her, a few years ago."

"What happened?" her mother asks.

The hand moves to her hair. "Car accident. She was walking home from a party, by the side of the road. These roads, they're dark at night. We always told her to wear something—white, or light—anyway, a drunk driver hit her."

Her mother murmurs, inarticulate sounds.

"We both started going to church again. That thing you said," addressing Nora, "about a column of fire. Where does that come from? Is that something you saw?"

"Fire attracts the presence of God."

Her mother adds, "Elijah went to the mountain where he called down the fire. And God came to him then, in his prayer. He called to God, *Send me grace*, and God answered."

Beth is nodding in agreement. "Rod started making these sculptures.

I don't know why but they seem to give him some measure of peace. He says each one is a prophecy."

"What gives you peace?" her mother asks.

Nora cracks one eye. This woman isn't seeking protection, she's seeking someone to protect. But she doesn't know if her mother sees it. "I hurt my leg when I fell," Nora says in a soft, whining voice, playing younger.

"I'll get a wet cloth," Beth says. When she goes into the kitchen, Nora yanks up her pant leg. She and her mother have time to quickly lock eyes. Then, in one swift movement, Nora rakes her fingernails down her own calf, drawing tracks of blood.

Beth returns. "Looks like you scraped yourself on something. This yard is a menace." She pats the fresh red wound while Nora makes small sounds of distress and comfort. When the woman is leaning close, concentrating on the angry marks on her leg, Nora whispers, "You'll see your daughter again."

There is a long silence. "I've prayed and prayed that I would," Beth finally says. She has gone back to stroking Nora's hair. "But I never get an answer."

"It isn't about praying for rain when clouds are in the sky," her mother says. "It's praying for rain when the sky is clear. When it hasn't rained in a long, long time, that's faith. Women have always known this. We keep building things, caring for each other. Families. Children. We keep making things because we know what they mean. Because God is there even when He's not."

After more talk, Beth pours a finger of golden whiskey in two glasses, and her mother drinks with her, sealing some kind of allegiance between tough women. Nora has never seen her mother drink before. Soon after, they leave the house with biscuits in a ziplock bag, and a bandage on Nora's leg. Within a month, Beth and her husband will join the church. They'll bring their metal yard, with its precious junk, including a rusting school bus that Levi works on in his spare hours, determined to get running again.

Her mother drives a little way down the road before pulling over. "I think we did it," she says.

"I think so too."

Her mother's face is heavy. "How does it feel?"

"How does what feel?"

"Your leg, girl."

"Oh." It flares with pain as the remembrance of what she's done becomes clear. She can still feel the tracks of her own nails in her skin, but the thrill overrides the sensation. "It's fine."

"Why did you do it?" her mother asks.

Nora only realizes it now: her mother has never been caught up in the excitement of the Spirit. "I had to," she says.

They should be heading back. But they keep driving down the road, the wheel sliding between her mother's fine fingers. They bypass the turnoff for home. "Do you know where this road goes?" she asks. "You've been this way before, haven't you?"

Nora nods. She has driven this way with her father on mission trips, winding up and down the peninsula, searching for their people.

"But you don't know where it leads," her mother says. "You don't know the first thing about the world, do you? I haven't taught you anything." They're still driving in the wrong direction, getting farther and farther from home.

"I know lots of things. Like how to survive if there's a cyclone, or radiation, or an earthquake—"

"When you made that woman remember her dead child," her mother interrupts, "how did you know to do that? Who even taught you that?"

Nora is surprised. "Dad. And you."

"They always blame the mother, you know, if you lie or cheat or steal. They'll blame me."

Nora doesn't know who "they" is.

"All I've done is hurt you," her mother says.

They drive for awhile in silence, the road curving and winding through the forest with no apparent direction.

"Sometimes," her mother finally says. Shakes her head. "Sometimes I wonder what made you. Who made you."

The words sit there between them. Eventually, her mother takes a turnoff that will bring them back toward home.

Chicago, December

IT'S STILL DARK OUTSIDE. Nora has a full day ahead of visiting people in pain, washing hair, changing bedsheets. She should be getting ready, but instead is spending the last minutes before dawn trolling through the ex-cult member forum, searching for her mother's presence.

[Is anyone available to de-program my kid? We'll need to kidnap her and hold her in a hotel room for a few days.]

[How do you get your MMR vaccine at 35?]

[What is a social security number?]

[If I burned my passport, can I get a new one?]

[What's the difference between a demagogue and a cult leader? Which one is T****?]

[I was born in a cabin in an anti-government cult. How do I get a birth certificate? How do I make myself exist lol]

[After leaving I was totally lost until I found Herbalife. I've got discount codes, hit me up]

A former Christian Scientist on the forum writes about how a beloved aunt was denied medical treatment, eventually dying of something curable. It's what finally made her leave, losing the rest of her family in the process.

Nora asks her "friend" CommuneKid, [Did anyone you ever knew died who shouldn't have?]

[There was someone, the last year,] he answers. [A kid had a fever that just kept getting worse. The leader said he just wasn't doing the rituals right. They stuffed him full of these herbal supplements—lavender oil, peppermint, you know. But he died. That was bad enough, but our Leader forbade anyone from mourning him. We weren't supposed to be attached to each other. His name went on the list of Banned Words.]

[We need to grieve,] Nora writes. [No one should be able to take that away from us.]

She tells CommuneKid about one of her patients, a rich old lady who lives in a stunning glass box on Michigan Avenue. The woman was once an actress; there are pictures of her with Humphrey Bogart and Cary Grant, soft-focus and inscribed with loving signatures.

This week Nora arrived at her place to a terrible smell. The woman was sitting upright in bed. She announced, "I shit myself." She corrected herself. "Shat. I shat myself."

As Nora bathed her in the shower chair, the woman sat in a deep funk, the humiliation brewing inside her. Nora soaped her wasted legs, wondering how the skinny quills of bone once floated across a stage. She recalled a speech exercise her mother once taught her, to practice her elocution. Her mother had acted in school plays, before she met her father. It was important to know the meaning of every word you said, and to speak it clearly. That was how you made people remember you.

Nora said it aloud, almost to herself: "She slits her sheets. Her sheet she slits."

There was a tiny gleam in the old woman's eye. She knew this one too. "Upon her slitted sheet she sits." Sometimes that was the work. It was being there. Listening, witnessing.

She wants to explain this to CommuneKid, show her work now is not that different from what her father did—what she once did: making sure people felt heard, that the universe cared about them. That we all exist in some fundamentally beloved state, even if that love took the form of violence.

But he is still bitter, offended by comforting stories. He writes, [They take a good feeling, any good feeling, and they dole it out to you in these tiny little portions, so you're starving all the time, grateful for any scrap. That's what I finally realized. That's what made me leave.]

[How did you?]

They've reached the question all the forum threads get around to eventually, the way former drunks need to tell how they reached rock-bottom. It's the only story that matters once whatever story you believed in is gone.

[I couldn't stop thinking about the kid who had died,] CommuneKid writes. [I was trusted to sell produce in town and I'd been doing more reading at the library and I knew that someone could have saved him. I thought, that could have been me. I could have lived my whole life on that farm and died and no one would have mourned me, I would have just disappeared in smoke, all for our Leader's pure principle. And whatever happiness our Leader said we had, it didn't seem like such a great tradeoff for love. I was afraid I'd never know what love was or be able to feel it myself. And I wanted it for myself. This one thing, just for me.]

[So what did you do?]

[There were these Chicano guys who always came by our roadside stand and bought peaches. One day I asked them where they were headed, and they said Salinas. They were looking for construction jobs. I asked if I could go with them. And I got in the truck and just—rode away. All those years, and I didn't know it would be that easy.]

[The hard part comes after,] she writes.

[How did you leave?]

The cursor blinks, a little halo of intimate light beaming out of her phone. The quiet kitchen table. There are parts of her story that she's learned are shameful even in this permissive real world.

She puts her phone in her pocket and watches the street lights switch off out the window as the dawn arrives, quiet as a prayer.

§

At Mrs. Lailami's house, Nora inserts a needle under the woman's ribs to draw away the fluid collecting around her lungs. The fluid makes it hard to breathe; it will accumulate again, but at least this will relieve the sensation they call "air hunger."

Her husband sits in a chair near the bed, stone-faced and silent. Mr. Lalami is a small, dignified man with tufts of white hair for eyebrows, and a careful way of navigating the kitchen or walking with a cup of tea. He folds the laundry in neat geometric piles and refuses Nora's help: she is there for his wife, not for household tasks. He often sings to his wife, soft melancholy tunes in Hindi.

Usually a friendly man, he uncharacteristically greeted Nora at the door today without a smile or a hello. In his silence, he appears to be mulling something over; perhaps he has finally absorbed the fact that his wife has so little time left, and that care is not the same as cure.

The last time she was here, Nora listened to him talk about when his kids were young and running around the house. "And then one day you look up, and they're gone," he said half-smiling, aware of his own cliché.

"Where are they now?" Nora asked.

"One in LA, one back in Delhi, one in London," he said. "They have their own lives. They came to see her last month. They're good kids."

After he was done talking about his family, he opened a small cabinet facing the bed, revealing an elephant God statue. He lit a stick of incense and they started to pray together, his voice strong, dark and steady, his wife's lips barely moving.

Nora got up to leave, but he raised his hand to stop her. "You don't have to go. Would you like to pray with us?"

She blushed. "I don't know the words."

"That's all right. You can just sit with us and pray however you do."

The wrathful God she knew did not have a place in this quiet room. So she sat and listened to them pray, and did not let her God enter.

Done with the needle, Nora feeds Mrs. Lailami some rice pudding, a food she will still occasionally eat. When she takes a bite, and Nora turns to share the triumph, Mr. Lailami replies angrily. "You know what you're doing, don't you," he says. "You're feeding the cancer. You're giving it the strength to kill her."

Nora lowers the spoon. "I can't prevent that. No one can prevent that from happening."

"Stop feeding her," he yells. "Stop this whole pretense. It's a sick game you doctors and nurses play, keeping people alive."

"We can't choose to stop. It's not up to us."

"Who is it up to, then?"

She says nothing, which makes Mr. Lailami even more furious. "You call yourself a nurse. But you think her life is in God's hands. What will you truly do, to ease her suffering? Nothing!" He spits the word out, full of a venom she knows doesn't belong in this gentle man.

Nora gathers her kit and her jacket. "I'd better go."

Down in the kitchen, a funny feeling makes her open her medical bag and count the supplies again. She has to know exactly what she has at all times.

A syringe and two vials of injectable Fentanyl are missing. One would have been more than enough.

She shoulders her bag and climbs the stairs slowly, one step at a time, her limbs heavy. "Mr. Lalaimi."

"What are you still doing here?" He is on the bed with his wife, holding her hand.

"I think I may have left something here. It can be very dangerous if it's not administered by a professional."

He won't look at her; a muscle pulses in his jaw. "I don't know what you're talking about."

"If it's injected incorrectly, it can cause infection, an inflated vein . . . all sorts of trouble and pain."

"Is that so."

She takes a shaky breath. "You don't want to be the one to do this."

"But who will?" He still won't look at her. "Have you checked the night table?"

Nora opens the drawer and retrieves the syringe and the vials, sparing him the indignity of a lecture. They both know what he hoped to do, and what neither of them can do. She feels for him, watching his wife die. She wants to ask him, Have you ever stood and waited for the end of the world to come? The waiting is the worst part, until the unimaginable after. But he knows that already.

⁂

It's two weeks before Christmas, and the Santa stockings are hanging in the window of the coffee shop. At the same table where they met several months before, Mike's cop friend sits across from her, bulging under a massive winter parka.

"I've got some information for you," he says. "But be warned. It's a real mess." He pulls out a manila envelope and taps out a sheaf of papers. "Like I thought, the sheriff's department up there keeps shitty records. And the county coroner is just some asshole who is elected to the position, he doesn't even have to have a medical license. A couple of federal agencies were in the middle of a massive investigation of the compound your father lived on when he died. But you knew all that already, didn't you? There was some kind of a standoff when you were there?"

Nora nods.

"Well, the ATF—that's the Bureau of Alcohol, Tobacco, and Firearms—has been trying to improve their PR after Waco and Ruby Ridge. So they've had a 'noninterventionist' policy in place in recent years. Particularly if the group in question is white and not jihadists, if you catch my drift. There are white supremacist groups armed to the teeth all over this nation, I'll tell you, and nobody is doing a thing about it."

They were lucky, Nora thinks to herself. An accident of birth, citizenship, race, and religion let them do whatever they wanted to.

"So anyway. The reports are sketchy but there was some sort of armed standoff. Shots were fired. At the end of it, your father was dead. A bunch of people were arrested. They got charged with drug manufacturing and unlicensed firearms." He shuffles his papers. "You can look through these."

He hands Nora the papers, which she flips through impatiently. This face and that one, all familiar, still eliciting the same old fear in her.

"You knew about the drug dealing?" he asks.

"I figured." She'd been stupid for so long about what the deacons were up to, but has smartened up since coming to Chicago, seeing what she has seen. It was just another of those things about the church that she was not permitted to know.

"After your father's death, it looks like the authorities decided to back off. Threat neutralized, you know. They put a lot of stock into taking down figureheads. They were probably patting themselves on the back."

"So they didn't investigate his death? Who shot him? Some cop?" Nora doesn't realize she's been tearing a paper napkin to shreds until the sweaty pieces fall into her lap. A string of bells tied to the front door keeps ringing every time someone comes in, making her jumpy. "Rudolph the Red-Nosed Reindeer" pipes through the ceiling speakers.

"Well, that's the thing. It wasn't them. His death was ruled a suicide."

"What?"

"It was a shotgun blast, close range. The gun was registered to him. One of the few guns on the whole compound under his name, actually. He was found in the woods after the fracas."

Nora struggles to speak, to block out of the ringing of the bells. "Are you sure?"

He lifts his shoulders. "They're never going to say it was anything but suicide, hon. It lets them off the hook." He slides the papers across the table as though they're something illicit. "Here's the official report, but there's nothing in it I haven't told you." He pauses for a moment. "You know, I've seen a lot of suicides, and if it's a man, it's always with a gun. They're on the rise among men your father's age. They get lonely, they get bitter, they used to have a purpose in life and people who depended on them and now they have nothing. Most of the time, those around them don't see it coming. Maybe he was backed into a corner. Maybe he saw the thing he'd built was about to blow up." He leans forward. "What was it like, growing up there?"

Something in the center of her lets out a long sigh. He's curious, just like everyone else. They all want to hear about the screams in the trees, the fires on the hill. It wasn't like that, she has had to say, again and again. But maybe it was. Maybe all those things were happening while she wandered the woods with Levi, dreaming up prophecies and basking in the glow of God's love. Maybe there really were bodies buried in the woods. She can't be sure of any part of the past anymore.

"We were brainwashed," she begins. "We were totally under his control."

She's read enough on the ex-cult forum to cobble together a good story, something that will give him his money's worth. Orgies and firewalks and drug-induced dance circles. She throws them all in for good measure. He listens, shaking his head in wonder, until he's satisfied. Then he slaps his thighs and says, "Well," and stands, the universal Midwestern goodbye. "I hope this gives you what you need. You may have to be okay with never knowing for sure," he says. "You may have to find a way to be happy with that." And with a curt, official nod, he walks out of the place, closing the door gently so the bells won't ring.

⁂

"How can you say he'll be good for us? How can you even say that?" Kiki is yelling in the living room.

When she enters the room, Nora sees that Kiki is watching TV with Sonya and Brianna, their new roommates. On the screen, the primary colors of the president-elect flash by: blue suit, red tie, vast white slice of shirt, that artificial thatch of gingery hair. In the crowd, evangelicals are waving signs saying he's blessed by God, that he's going to save America because he's going to save the unborn babies. With their matching red baseball caps, and the teary fervor on their faces, they resemble the people at the Cubs' parade.

Sonya is stretched out like a lazy dog on the couch, her feet on Brianna's lap. Brianna, from Jamaica, and Sonya, from Romania, are usually bent over their phones or doing each others' nails, with the easy intimacy some women share. "He's a strong man, he's a fucking capitalist," Sonya says, all relaxation in the face of Kiki's hot anger. "I've seen what socialists do in my country, Kiki. Don't even talk to me about that nonsense."

"He fucking hates our kind, Sonya," Kiki spits back. "Immigrants. He wants you out."

"People like *me*? Slavs and Eastern Europeans? He loves us. He married one." Sonya laughs, long and slow. "Didn't you come here for the hot dogs and the American Dream? Don't you want a truly American man with a set of balls running things?"

"He's a liar. He lies about everything, even the things that don't matter."

"Every politician lies. He just doesn't pretend that it isn't all bullshit. He knows exactly who he is, and he isn't afraid to show it."

Nora has heard this conversation repeated endlessly in different contexts since the November election: on television, in her patients' homes, in snatches of angry chatter on the L. There are the people who treat it all as sport; and then there are the people who actually have something to lose.

Kiki waves her hand, perilously close to giving Sonya the finger. Sonya does it for her.

"I have a shift." Kiki says abruptly, hurrying out of the room.

"Hey," Brianna calls to Nora. "We're going out tonight. You should come."

Normally, Brianna ignores her, but she looks bored tonight, restless and curious, her eyes moving over Nora's lean body, her slumping posture, evaluating. "You're always with Kiki," she says. "That girl doesn't know how to party. She's always working and studying. You, though—you could learn how to live a little."

Nora leans into the doorframe. The spark in Brianna's eyes seems to grab at her, pull her in. Her father sometimes spoke of women like this, the ones with the dark light inside them. They were dangerous. Not for *their* life.

"All right," she answers.

Nora bundles up in her old canvas coat and Kiki's borrowed turquoise blouse and rides north on the L with Sonya and Brianna. They're tired of South Side bars, the same old R&B, the same pick-up lines. Brianna wants hipster boys tonight, the artists, the aspiring hopeless comedians. She wants that funny mix of entitlement and privilege and naiveté, the cozy suburban childhoods you can read on their faces.

They find a place that is blasting Christmas music and sliding shot glasses of hot cider down the bar. The three of them rest their elbows on the shiny waxy wood and talk with a few skinny young guys with beards and beanies, accepting terrible eggnog drinks and pretending to love them. Nora laughs along with the other two girls, watching their eyes, their hands, their easy draped posture on their stools. Everyone is lonely tonight. She can feel it throbbing in the dark close walls of the bar, the windy arrival of each newcomer.

"Tell him where you grew up," Brianna whispers, nudging Nora in the direction of a young man who has been grinning at her for a while.

"Who would want to know about that?" Nora asks.

"God!" Brianna tosses her braids. "This girl, she needs an explanation for everything. Because it's *interesting*." She tugs on the man's sleeve. "This girl grew up in a cult."

Nora is surprised when the guy draws closer. "Like, a commune, or—"

"Christian," she says. "Sort of Pentecostal."

"I grew up Mormon," he says. "Kinda the same thing, right?"

"I guess?"

"No, really. Mormons have this clean-scrubbed vibe, they assimilate and seem mainstream. But if you really drill down into the things they believe . . ." he trails off, eyebrows climbing. "Do you ever get the feeling—" and now he's closer still, speaking into her neck so she can hear, "Do you ever feel like you're just pretending to live your regular life, when really there's another you, the spiritual you, that no one knows about?"

"Yes," Nora answers. She has to sit back and take another look at this man, with his untrimmed beard and his trendy silk scarf, his wide-eyed, childish gaze. "I feel that."

"And no one will ever know the real you," he says. "The real you is back there, with God."

She's had too much eggnog. He smells like nutmeg, sweet and strange at once. "Yes, yes."

"Come on," he says. "You and your friends, come back to me and my roommate's place."

Brianna slides in beside Nora, puts an arm around her. "You wanna go?"

The apartment is in a sleek modern high-rise on the Near North Side, forty stories up and full of industrial concrete columns. Jeff and his roommates, Kevin and Ashok, are all in advertising, Nora learns, once they're clustered around the kitchen counter together, the men hunting for booze in the cabinets. Not artists, but at least they're creatives, which is good enough for Brianna.

There are signs of male living everywhere: a lone sock on the back of the couch, a tangle of wires and video game consoles by the TV, bread crumbs dusting the kitchen counter, bowls in the sink. Nora finds it sweet the way Jeff hustles around the apartment cleaning up, trying to dart in front of her to grab random stuff off the floor wherever she walks. They down shots together. Kiki would be scolding her right now, drinking so much so late, it's a work night, you don't even know these guys, you have shifts tomorrow, you can't miss a day, not a single day.

Brianna and Sonya dance together to the Christmas songs playing on someone's phone, Kevin and Ashok watching. Kevin asks what they do, and Sonya says, "We're nurses," and everyone leaves it at that, because the truth is too sad, too much of a downer for this festive night.

Nora follows Jeff to his bedroom so they can talk some more. It's a chaos of dirty laundry, empty mugs clustered by the bedside, used tissues on the floor around the trashcan.

"When did you leave your church?" she asks. They are standing close to the floor-to-ceiling window, gazing out at the lights of the city. The Sears Tower a glittering black monolith, the lake a slice of brilliant midnight blue off to the east. She can feel the cold air radiating off the glass.

"I never officially did," Jeff says. "I tell my parents I still pray. When I go home and visit, we all go to temple together. I even keep a pair of the garments. I bring them home and send them through the laundry. You know, so my mom will think I still wear them." He smiles, shrugs; the things we do, to keep our families happy. "It's like I'm living two lives. When I'm home, I'm still their good Mormon boy. And I believe it, I really do. It's like God is really there. But when I'm here—"

". . . You're someone else."

"Yes." He leans close. She can smell the warm stickiness of sweet booze on his breath. The musky toothpaste smell of his body spray.

"But which one is the real you?" Nora asks. She needs to know. Is it the earnest Mormon boy praying with his parents, or the stranger in this dark room, sliding his hand down her leg?

"I don't know. I figure we're all just lots of people inside, you know? This one and that one—" his hand waves vaguely. He's drunker than she thought. "Who really cares which one is the real one?"

She watches him go in for a kiss in slow motion; she's too tired, or maybe too curious, to swat him away. Why not just be this person tonight, and who cares if this is the real her or if the other one is, the one who fears the devil and prays to keep her body pure of sin. That girl is boring. That girl never really existed.

They fall clumsily to the bed, kissing sloppily, their tongues too wet and too slow. He can't get enough of her breasts, caressing them frantically, sucking her firm nipples. He does the things he thinks girls like—licking her earlobe, sliding his leg between hers—and maybe he's not wrong. They breathe into each other's necks but say nothing; the room is ringing with silence compared to the laughter just outside the door. Is the devil in there with them, the way her father promised? She can't be sure. Better not to know.

When he yanks at her jeans, and fumbles with his own, she remembers the danger. "Do you have—?" she whispers hoarsely. He groans, but rolls toward his bedside drawer, opens a half-empty package. It's over quickly, a few fierce thrusts, a whimper from him, a feeling like pain lying close alongside pleasure. It's been a while. There's the feeling she's almost forgotten, like right before the voice came upon her—heat and pressure, a rising wave, a surrender, the realization that there's no turning back.

When they emerge from the bedroom, the others are lounging around the TV watching a nature documentary, the smell of weed skunky in the air. Brianna's braids are mussed, Sonya's dress one button less. "You guys have fun in there?" Brianna asks.

Nora flushes, and moves away from Jeff's outstretched hand. Now she's a little disgusted by his floppy Gumby walk across the room, the way he drinks from an open bottle of beer on the counter without asking whose it is. Her father had said, "When the good feeling passes—and it will—sin is the only thing that remains."

"Did you really grow up in a cult?" asks Ashok. "Did you have a bomb shelter? Did you think the world was going to end like, any day?"

So other people had been listening to her at the bar. "We had storage cellars. We had a lot of supplies. We were getting ready."

"How could you really believe that?" asks Kevin, pawing boredly through his phone.

"Dude. Brainwashing," Ashok says. "She was a drone. Like a worker bee. All for the hive." He buzzes his hands around the room.

She looks to Jeff to defend her, hoping for whatever fragile alliance they've formed. Or the women. Aren't they her friends? But no one speaks; Jeff leans over the counter, curious; Brianna and Sonya snuggle into their partners' arms.

Okay. Fine.

"We weren't drones," she says, speaking slowly so she can find the old rhythms of speech. "We believed in something that made a certain kind of sense. Most people think there was a beginning. There had to be. In the beginning God created the heaven and the earth. Doesn't it stand to reason that there will be an end too? Everything dies eventually. It's an observable truth. Why not be ready for it?"

"But what made you think you'd see it happen in your lousy little lifetime?" asks Kevin, sinking lower on the couch. "There have been apocalyptic groups before yours. People who climbed on top of their roofs at midnight and jumped off, thinking angels would spirit them away to heaven. They were stupid and they were humiliated." He has a sneering way of speaking.

"So they were wrong about when," she says. "We wanted to be ready."

"But this isn't like preparing for a hurricane or an earthquake. This is crazy."

"Millions of people believe Jesus is coming back," Nora says. "This country was founded on Christian principles, and that includes the belief that there will be a final day of judgment. Who knows what the future will hold? All the experts and pundits have no idea. How can we know, what the world will look like when it's near the end? Maybe it'll look just like this."

And there it is: the whiff of apocalypse is now in the room.

Ashok snorts with laughter. "Entering late-stage capitalism."

"But come on. Those people who think Jesus is coming back, don't *really* think it," says Kevin.

Nora shakes her head. "Of course they do. If you don't believe, you won't understand." She turns to Jeff. "You know what I mean."

Jeff shifts uneasily. "Well, yeah. I guess."

"You said—"

She's surprised by Ashok's laugh. "Oh damn. What did you tell her, Jeff? That you're still some good little Mormon boy?"

Jeff's lips crack into an awful grin. "Yes, well—it was true. I was raised Mormon."

"You haven't believed in that shit for years. You gotta watch out for this guy," says Ashok, putting an arm around Nora's neck. "He'll say anything to get into your pants."

Nora unhooks his arm, takes an unsteady step away. She wants to run out of the room; what would her father do if someone laughed in his face? It never happened; there's no script for this moment. So she just keeps holding her beer, smiling and and staring at her nice going-out shoes.

Brianna rises from the couch with a thump. "Time to go home." Sonya rises with her.

"Oh, come on. The night is young." Ashok reaches out for them, tugging on their hands. But Brianna is firm, hustling Nora to the door, shoving her and Sonya into their coats with quick jerks of their sleeves.

They walk together toward the L. It's late, the bars are closing, the fairy lights going out on storefronts. No one should be out alone at this hour. But there is someone—a bundled shape in a long coat, walking a half block behind them, taking the same corners they do. Brianna and Sonya don't notice him, but Nora can't help half-turning her head. He's one of her people, she's sure. Now that she knows they're watching and waiting, she sees shambling shadows in every dark alley. Is tonight the night he touches her arm, and she nods, and goes with him? She'll never understand these outsiders, and they'll never understand her. Her loneliness feels savage, dangerous. The only thing keeping her from turning to him are the two girls flanking her.

They stumble down the long staircase to the empty subway station. A full day of work tomorrow, with its accompanying disappointments and humiliations. She was so sure of herself, her power to convince with words alone. In the beginning was the Word, and the Word was with God, and the Word was God—but she was the one seduced, with just the right words to make her think she'd found a friend.

"Did you know?" she asks Brianna, who has seemed so worldly-wise all night. "Did you know he was lying to me?"

Brianna glances over at her. "You're not the first girl to be told something that wasn't true. If I had a dollar for every time a guy told me just what I wanted to hear, just so—"

Nora looks down the black tunnel of the subway, as if all her life is stretched out into that darkness, all its drudgery and compromise, and she can see the end if she leans far enough. The wind moans from the void. She thinks, suddenly, of the ventilation shaft in the mining hills, its consuming deep dark. It feels sometimes like the pit is trying to claim her, waiting for her to return.

"Did you have fun?" Sonya asks, limp and happy and drunk, hanging on Nora's arm. "Did you get what you wanted? I hope you didn't expect to fall in love or anything."

"I didn't," she says softly.

"We just go out once in a while," Sonya says. "You have to. You have to go out into the world and not care so damn much about everything." And with that she leans out over the train well and whoops, long and glorious, into the echoing tunnel, the sound so perfectly itself.

⁂

It's Christmas Eve morning. Nora opens her eyes, listening to Kiki snoring in the top bunk above her. Her mind quickly races back to the old compound, wondering what it looks like today. Is the snow already knee-high? Are people out shoveling the paths, pulling frozen strips of deer jerky out of the cold root cellars? She was always so afraid of climbing down the rickety ladders into those chambers. The smell of cold and dirt made them seem like graves.

On Christmas Day, they usually had prayer, of course, and a reading from the Gospels, the Good News. There was singing and dancing, too, and lit candles to ward the dark away. She pictures Levi lighting a candle, his face both young as the child she once knew and as adult as the last time she saw him. She pictures his hand flicking the match, cupping the flame, the serious commitment he gave to every task he ever undertook.

Who is leading the ritual now, clanging the bell? Is her mother lighting candles somewhere?

Kiki's hand floats down from above. "Hey. Church tonight?"

"I'm all right."

"You're a heathen," she says sleepily. "I'm telling my aunt you went or she'll start praying over you." Kiki thumps to the floor, stretches; her hair a fuzzy black halo around her face. She'll spend the day on the phone, talking to her mother, her father, her fiancé. She'll make the best of it, trying not to show how much she wishes she were with them.

[Merry Christmas Eve,] CommuneKid texts her. They've started messaging each other directly instead of through the forum. Just little greetings or good nights, questions about the real world that the other might know. What's the difference between a driver's license and a state ID? How do you get health insurance? What's Cheez-whiz? Will I like it?

She couldn't resist that last one. [Try it. You'll love it,] she wrote back.

Nora sits up, runs a hand through her tangled hair, and types, [Do you even celebrate Christmas? Do you know what it is?]

[Sure I know what it is. It's the Good News day. The super baby from the sky was born to a virgin, and lo, there was much dancing and rejoicing.]

She snorts with laughter, and has to pretend it's a sneeze when Kiki turns to look at her.

[That's blasphemy], she writes. [Joking about these things—]

[If you can't laugh about it,] he writes back. [Then they've still got you.]

"Who are you texting so furiously with?" Kiki asks, and before Nora can answer, Kiki snatches the phone out of her hand. "There's a lot here. Who is this, anyway?"

"Just this—guy I know."

"From where?"

Reluctantly, she tells Kiki about the forum, and CommuneKid. Kiki listens, narrow-eyed. Then she *pffts* and turns away. "You better watch out for these online friends. You think you know who this guy is, but you don't. He could be anybody."

"He's told me a lot about his life. The kinds of things you don't make up."

"Maybe so. But pretty soon you'll get a dick pic in your email. That's how it starts, you understand? This is only the beginning."

"He's not like that." Nora tries to snatch the phone back, but Kiki holds it out of her reach.

"Oh, he's not? Believe me. They tell you whatever you want to hear. They make themselves like a mirror. And before you know it, you've fallen in love with your own reflection." Kiki releases the phone, but she looks worried. "You're so easy to fool. I'm just looking out for you."

That afternoon, Nora is helping the others bake cookies. Kiki wanders by with the cell phone clamped to her ear, speaking in the patois she rarely uses here. Carols ooze from the radio, a melancholy sort of peace among the people making Christmas happen in this house instead of wherever home is.

Suddenly, her phone chimes.

[I'll be in Chicago in March,] the text reads. [A friend has some construction work for me. We could meet.]

"Nora, come help me carve," Sonya calls from the kitchen. Everyone knows she's the best when it comes to handling meat. Nora puts the phone down without answering.

They share Christmas Eve dinner, followed by the assiduous stripping of the turkey, the packing of leftovers, the saving of bones for broth, and for dessert, Kiki's triumphant great rum cake, a Barbadian Christmas delicacy with half a bottle of rum in its moist yellow crumb.

Afterward, they pile woozily around the crappy television to watch specials filled with stop-motion reindeer. Nora dozes, sliding in and out of the old dreams: walking through the woods at night, lantern lights swaying through the trees, listening to the comforting fairy tales the gospels favored of virgins and miracle children. *And the angel said unto her, Fear not, Mary: for thou hast found favour with God. And, behold, thou shalt conceive in thy womb.*

When she wakes, she's alone in the room, the TV turned down low, the flickering images strange and meaningless. Wind rattles the windowpanes. She struggles back to Chicago, to this room, this life. Kiki comes in holding her good church shoes, her hair freshly ironed, wearing her wool Sunday dress. "It's time for Midnight Mass. You could still come."

Nora shakes her head.

Kiki leans down to straighten Nora's hair, fussing and patting the way she sometimes does like a mother. "Someday you'll go back to your family, won't you," she says unexpectedly.

Nora can't tell if she means it as a good or bad thing. That there's still hope of reconciliation, or that one day she'll lose herself to them? "I'm here. Doesn't that count for something?"

Kiki says nothing, and leaves Nora alone, in front of the television's aquarium glow. Loneliness enters the room on cat paws, taking up residence.

Nora picks up her phone. [I want to know if you're real,] she writes. [Are you real?]

She waits in the darkness for an answer. Funny how modern communication can sing out to you: you're alone in a room, and the chime of a phone arrives like a presence, bringing news from another world.

[Meet me and find out.]

Apocalypse

2009

(Ten days until the world ends)

HENRY AND HER FATHER sit together at the kitchen table, the way they always do these days, ten different Bibles in three languages spread out between them, the pages dog-eared and coming apart at the bindings.

"But have we accounted for—"

"The number of generations from Adam to Christ is seventy-six. From Christ to now, it's eighty-one."

"The time has never been dictated. It's determined by human behavior, too."

They add and divide and add and divide again and again, counting the generations from Adam to Christ and onward. The day is going to be January 12th, adjusted for the Georgian and Julian calendars. They've done their calculations; they're sure. This will be the beginning of the extraordinary time, the time of unreason, when the ordinary world will fall apart, making room for heaven. 2009: the year a president takes office that a third of the country thinks is the Antichrist, the year climate scientists have predicted the world has less than a decade to reverse the damage of global warming. A time of evil and arrival. Every hour creeping closer to judgment, to angels.

Nora is happy for them, the time they've been spending together.

Henry is thirsty for the attention; he's pale and too thin in the face, his eyes always hooded. He never goes on walks with her and Levi, or hangs around the gun shed with the other teen boys, arguing about how to defend against a helicopter, a rival militia, a mob of starving outsiders. When she's in full voice in church, she often catches his straight, silent form out of the corner of her eye, staring at her, and not in the worshipful way of the others.

One day, while he is busy at the table with their father, Nora creeps into his room, looking for signs of—what, exactly? The two rifles on racks on the wall have a military neatness to them, everything stripped down and minimal, featureless and ready for use. A small Pentecostal flag hangs over his bed, next to a map of the world with tiny tick marks on it where spots of religious conflict have occurred or are likely to during the age of unreason.

She gets down on her belly and worms her way under his bed, breathing in the warm wood-smelling dust. There are a few notebooks under here that she has never seen before. The first one is an exegesis of sorts, containing his notes on Bible interpretations, flagging possible significant dates. Each note neatly labeled, cited, dated.

The second is filled with denser writing, lines close together, punctuation sometimes forgotten.

Evangelism=witnessing

Apocalypse=revelation

Witnessing is when you see God in the world and tell others about it. Revelation is when God speaks in her ear about your sins that no one else knows.

Dad says the problem is sex. Then this is crossed out, replaced by *Dad says the problem is sex=pleasure=taking pleasure from God.*

She reads further:

Why does God give us the ability to feel pleasure?

To tempt us to accept the gift.
The gift is poison. It is death.
The devil tempts us, not God.
But the devil was created by God.
Why did God create the devil?
Why does pain feel more like pleasure?
Stop the experiments. The experiments prove nothing.

A later entry, meticulously dated like the rest:

Dad says the experiments are sinful. I am trying to figure out why God tempts us to do the sinful things. Why he makes other living things capable of feeling pain but does not give them the opportunity to redeem themselves by giving them souls. Why do animals just feel pain and die and that's it.

And another:

I do the experiments so I will know the mind of God. Dad will never understand because he already knows God.

Maybe things without souls are not capable of feeling pain. They make all the sounds and actions of distress the way a human would but God has just made them this way to teach us a lesson about what pain looks like. They are our test cases to learn what not to do to other humans. They are a learning tool. They teach us to be afraid of pain because they show us what pain would feel like if it was real.

Maybe even some humans are like this, automatons with gears and responses to teach us lessons about pain. Calvin says the righteous and the damned are already decided. The only reason to treat someone as human is because you can't always tell who is damned and who is saved.

The only real humans are the ones who will be saved. That is the only reason God would condemn the others. They can't be real.

How can you tell who is human?

The next day, in the rain barrel outside where they burn trash and deer bones, Nora sees the skeletons of creatures they don't eat: rats, mice, the feathered spine of a snake, squirrels. One looks like a cat. All the little long-nosed skulls gazing at her empty-eyed from the ashy pile.

⁂

There are more recruiting trips, to round up souls and resources. Nora hardly knows what time it is, with her father rolling her out of bed at all hours and pulling her into the truck for long drives across the state. This churchyard, this night market, that revivalist meeting where people come sweating out of the holy roller tent into the freezing night air, breathing clouds of vapor into the dark. She prays over them and weeps for the coming days of judgment, then gets back into the truck and prays again and weeps again and then they are in the truck again. When they return home she is a zombie, glassy-eyed; it is hard to speak or blink, her eyes burning from so many tears. Her mother sobs that he has no right to take her this way, that they are on a mad path.

One night, after Nora has retreated to her bedroom, she hears her mother say, "That's not my daughter."

"She's not yours or mine," her father replies. "She belongs to the church. She's the church militant. Isn't that what you used to say? She's on the march."

"A girl can't be a church."

A long silence follows, and then her mother speaks again, her voice now plaintive and soft: "You have Henry. Boys belong to their fathers, I know that. I knew that as soon as I gave birth to him, I knew he wasn't mine. Go run this compound the way you want, make your deals. I know what goes on here, I know the things you do. But she was supposed to be mine."

After their next recruiting trip, her father drives home slowly through a long wooded stretch of country. The snow creates white walls on either side of the road; whole houses are half-buried and hidden among the trees, their extra-tall mailboxes poking out of white mounds. The heater isn't working right so both hunch close to the one vent that is blowing hot air, his large hand covering hers. She will always be here, she will always be safe, her hands covered by his.

He turns down a snow plowed side road, and pulls close to the edge of the lake, which is covered with a sheet of ice. They watch the sun set over the water in silence, and then night falls, as black as any she has ever seen. And then her eyes adjust, and the stars become visible, glittering and close.

"It's beautiful here," he says. "I'm glad you were raised where you could see the stars."

"What's going to happen? Really?" Nora asks.

In the dark she can't see his face. "There will be angels, and we will see the whole sky in diamonds. We will rest."

It sounds beautiful, like it is almost enough as a reward for all their effort. A better daughter would be satisfied with this answer. But she grabs his arm, shakes it like a baby throwing a tantrum. "It's not fair," she says. "Why would He—"

He shakes his head. "Maybe not even He can stop it. It's the nature of things to end."

They drive home. Before going inside, he leads her to the lakeshore, holding a flashlight as they walk quietly down the forest paths, avoiding the sentries. He climbs down the sandy cliff face and helps her down after, and they walk to one of the caves carved into the shore. In the narrow beam of the flashlight she sees a canoe shoved back into the blackness, rocking in a few inches of icy water.

"I've prepared for our family," he says. "Just us. If something goes wrong, we'll escape."

He shows Nora what he's saved: tucked in waterproof bags under the seats are spare clothes and blankets, cans of food, flashlights, batteries, camping fuel, hunting knives, a paper roll of gold coins, sacks of walnuts. Everything they need, hoarded away. Ready.

"Only the family can know about this," he says.

"But everyone is family. The church is family," Nora says. It's sinful to keep something just for yourself.

His arm comes around and presses her close. "This is only if all else fails."

⁝

Nora wakes, feeling hot and bruised all over. She is in her bed and it is late, judging by the moon's position high in her window. Her mother is there, patting her forehead with a damp rag.

"What happened?" Her voice comes out blurry. She tastes a coppery dullness in her mouth: old blood. She must have bitten her tongue.

"You passed out," her mother says. "When you were speaking in church. You've been out a few hours." Her pats are ungentle, neither of them accustomed to tenderness with each other.

The night trickles back slowly to Nora. A thumping, ferocious church meeting where her father called that the devil was near, and then a spirit of awful malice entered her, and she was speaking for him, hissing and writhing and cackling and seizing. It took all the prayers of the congregation to drive him out of her.

"Is he gone?" she asks.

"Yes," her mother says. "I told him you've done enough for one day. Enough for the Goddamned year."

Nora means the devil, not her father, but she doesn't correct her mother. Just closes her eyes as the cool rag flattens her hair, bringing herself slowly back to her own body. It's a relief to let the world drift away for a bit, like a rowboat at the end of its mooring. Be nothing, think nothing, host nothing, for a little while. The owl calling outside her window wants nothing of her, has nothing of God or the devil in its solitary voice.

"You don't have to do this, you know," her mother says. "You could stop. You could tell him it's too hard on you."

Nora wants to say, I'm the kid, you're the mother, you could tell him too. Save me.

But she doesn't, of course.

"What did I look like?" she asks.

"You were in—a trance," her mother says. "That's what I'd call it. You were in God's hands."

A part of her life, whole minutes and hours, ticked by without belonging to her. In the morning, she'll do an inventory of her body, discovering new bruises, sore places, scratches and abrasions that she has no memory of. She'll worry over each spot with her fingers, trying to puzzle out their origins, getting nowhere. She'll point out the bruises to her mother and ask urgently, What happened to me here? And here? But her mother will shake her head, saying, I don't know, and I can't. I can't.

§

The last day.

It's still too dark to see anything but her shape, haloed by the gray false dawn in the window. "Nora, baby."

"What?" Nora replies, startled out of a deep sleep. This can't be her mother, who has never called her "baby" in her life.

"Listen. Remember that whatever happens, I couldn't prevent it. I tried, but I couldn't."

Nora is puzzled. Still trying to climb out of the pit of sleep, she says, "No one can prevent it, Ma."

On her knees by the bed, her mother is as small and penitent as a child. "I can't take you," she whispers. "He'd never let me." She kisses Nora hard on the forehead, and slips something under her pillow. Then she's just a creaking step, a smell of birchbark and bread dough, a look back at the door—and then—nothing.

Nora wakes properly a few hours later. Engines roar and saws growl outside her window. She trails out the front door, where everything is in frantic motion—people hauling bales of hay and pallets of canned food, rolling fifty-gallon drums of cooking oil and gasoline through the yard. It's ten below, cold enough to freeze the animals' water troughs, but not cold enough to piss and lean on it, as the deacons say. The roar of snowmobiles makes her teeth ache. The deacons crash through the brush, dragging loaded sledges. Someone's pickup won't start, and a group of men are gathered around the open hood, arguing.

Nora needs to tell somebody what's happened, though she isn't even fully sure what has. She needs to find her father. Hannah says she saw him at first light at one of the grain silos. One of the deacons saw him heading to town for some last-minute supplies. No one seems to know where he is now.

When Nora brings an armload of blankets to Levi at a storage cellar, she gives him a look—eyes to the side twice, their secret signal. He peels away from the other men and the two of them slip into the trees.

She tells him they have to find her father, but not why. This is a family matter.

Levi follows her through the woods as they search for new boot prints in the crusty snow. Their breath huffing, the dull groan and crack of ice shifting on the lake. Crows call to each other from the bare branches of the trees, and it seems like a portent: three in a row means the devil is taking a soul. Nora is suddenly furious. Let her go, let her leave us here. Good riddance.

For some reason, she leads them to the peninsula near their little private island. No chance of meeting her father here. Nora leans out, testing the ice with her boot. Before this latest arctic snap they had a week of unseasonably warm weather, and now the lake ice is mortally wounded, threatening to break up in spots. "We can't go out there," Levi says. "It won't hold us."

Nora's thinking, What do you do with your last day? How do you not waste it? She should be searching for her father. But not yet.

"We can make it, if we do what the bears do. Remember," she says. They once watched a brown bear cross a frozen pond by lying down on its belly and inching across, splaying its body flat against the ice. Nora slides down onto the ice on her belly, starfishing her arms and legs. "Come on, like this."

Levi sways on the shore. "Nora, no." But she's too far out, pushing her way into the white expanse.

Her heart jumps at every creak and click of the ice as she moves forward. She concentrates on her breath; the great bowl of the winter sky rests overhead, the trees on the shore a brushy periphery. Breathe and move. Slide your hips. She's swimming in whiteness, slowly pedaling across the sky. Maybe this is what heaven will be like.

Then, a sickening crack: a shifting beneath her body, as if the world has tilted and the water is leaking out. She's sinking, water pooling into her jeans. She has seconds before the ice gives way, and if she lunges and scrabbles, more will break off around her, sealing off her way back.

"Nora!" Levi's voice is distant. She frog-kicks forward, reaching for the next safe panel of ice. It's becoming slush underneath her, sinking each time she pulls herself forward. The cold is a painful pulse in her feet, slowing her down. The island is so far away. Why did she think she could make it? Maybe she knew she couldn't. Maybe she wanted to see if someone would save her, if she's as blessed as everyone says. She's sinking into the blue black of the water, the roaring, clacking sound of ice knocking against itself in her ears.

Suddenly she's up, gasping for breath. Levi has his hands under her armpits and he's hauling her out of the water. Braced on a floating log, he has just enough purchase to drag her to solid ice.

Once they crawl onto the snowy shore, they lie down exhausted, drawing in the air in cold gasps. Her wet pants are stiffening on her legs, starting to freeze. The world is slowly returning. She feels the length of Levi's body alongside hers, touching at the shoulder and elbow and knee, the points of their contact electric and exact. "Stupid, that was stupid," he says. "Why did you come here? What did you want to find?"

With an effort she rolls toward him, swinging an arm onto his chest. "I just wanted—" she says, and stops and kisses him clumsily, her forehead bumping his, their lips cold and cracked.

He doesn't move at first. Then he opens his mouth a little and the warmth of his tongue seems to reach through her icy outer layers and grab her. So this is what the fuss is about, the danger, the temptation: it's a full-body ache that grows deeper the longer Levi's lips stay on hers.

"We can't," he whispers, turning away. Sweet Levi, with his mind only on devotion.

"Why can't we?" It's the last day. They've worked so hard, been so good. All their lives have been in service to something they can't feel or taste or touch.

But he just frowns, serious and ashamed all at once.

Nora rocks upright onto her heels. He's seen through her, he knows what's in her. Was this what her father meant when he talked about the devil on your back, whispering in your ear?

Levi stands up and walks to the island's edge, as the cold returns to her body. She studies his lean boy shape, alert as a deer. For a moment she sees the pure loveliness of his form, his youth, his bright-eyed love, and wonders why any sort of God would choose to end him, now, when he is so complete. It doesn't make any sense. And all the other things that will be destroyed: birds calling in the brush and the feel of air on your skin—just that, air—and people singing together. How can that not be good? How can it not continue on? It's not fair. But fairness has nothing to do with it. They live in a universe where the strong survive and the weak perish, where wolves eat fawns and lynxes eat their own young, no matter how much they are loved.

Levi is gathering kindling and brush. Before they make their way back, he'll build a fire to warm them and melt the ice off their clothes. She watches him collect what he needs, skillfully assembling a little nest of brush and wood and dry moss, depressing his thumb in the middle to make a home for the burn. He applies a match, which he always carries in a little waterproof tin. In silence, they watch the flame come to life and grow hungry. The warmth eases the hurt in her bones just a little. Levi crouches beside her, watching the fire, intent.

"They'll be missing us," she says.

People are moving in little bunches and processions to the barn, carrying lanterns. They speak in low voices, following the high-walled paths through the snow they've been shoveling since November. She's gone the whole day without seeing her father, but there he is now, ushering the others inside. Soon the prayers and songs will begin.

When Henry walks past, she grabs his arm. "Have you seen Ma?"

He pauses. "Not today."

"Not this morning? She didn't come talk to you, early?"

He looks confused. "I—I don't know."

"Well, no one's seen her, then." Nora turns away, kicks at a pile of snow. This is bad. When her father finds out—

"Go back home and see if she's there," Henry says, quickly figuring it out. "I'll stall." He jogs to the door to join their father.

Nora runs back along the path. It's dark now and all she has is her bobbing flashlight, but she knows every step. Maybe her mother is praying at home, as she has been known to do. She has always liked her privacy. Maybe—maybe—

The kitchen is cold: everything neat, the counter swept, the table bare. You can tell when a house is empty; there's something expectant in the air. Nora walks from room to room, calling for her mother.

She should rush back. Everyone will need to know. When her father finds out, his anger will be like something she's never seen. The deacons will be sent in pursuit. Friends of the church in town will be alerted. Still, Nora has had all day to tell someone, and for some reason hasn't. By now, her mother could have taken the ferry across the lake or crossed the bridge downstate. She could have gone farther still. She's traveling away from them, away from her children, her family. She is out of their realm of control.

Nora enters her bedroom. She feels for whatever her mother slid under the pillow: it's a battered prayer card, depicting St. Anthony, patron saint of lost things. It's so worn that the lamination has begun peeling away, the corners rounded and floppy. How many times has this card been passed from hand to hand, slipped into a pocket or pressed into someone's warm palm? Her mother would give it to women who needed help.

On the End of the World that Didn't Come

First will come the fire, you told us, then the flood; then disease and famine and war. All the signs of human ruin. If we survive these times of hell, then we'll get to glimpse heaven on the other side of it: angels, resurrection.

We lit candles in a circle around us to protect our dark barn, our home, our family, our armed and frightened little community. The power of the Jealous One would be at its strongest now, but we in our walled-off corner of the world would be safe. We linked arms, leaned close. We felt the rightness of being here, now, together. We waited, our breath clouding the frozen darkness. We were certain some sign would be delivered to us—a comet, a line of fire through the trees, news of cities collapsing in on themselves like dying stars. The radio crackled. Some of us wept. We held each other like lovers and in that moment we forgot our own names.

Midnight came. The local news purred on: the weather, the latest talks at the UN, the crime rates in Detroit. That was the first time we began to wonder if a mistake might have been made. We looked at each other, hoping for a sign. You said, with a hint of desperation in your voice, even now, the cracks in the tectonic plates were surely spreading.

Doubt began to spread, filling the room like an odorless gas. Maybe all our sacrifices, maybe everything we believed, maybe it was all . . .

That was when she opened her mouth. Her body began to shake. She moaned and seized, curled into a tiny ball and clutched her face and sobbed. "You left us!" she cried. "Why did you abandon us?"

Something unpredicted had happened. God was warning us, something wasn't right. "My wife—" you said, in a coldly furious voice. "She has abandoned her children. The devil is here tonight."

We couldn't believe it at first. What kind of woman would abandon her children? Only a woman who had invited the devil into her heart.

You recited from Revelation about the coming of the ruler of heaven: You have persevered and have endured hardships for my name, and have not grown weary. Yet I hold this against you: You have forsaken the love you had at first. Consider how far you have fallen! Repent and do the things you did at first.

And you said, if the time has not come, it is because we are not worthy of it.

We prayed with all we had. The kind of prayers that you save down in your heart and hope to never use. Something inhuman had taken possession of us all, prevented the age of righteousness from surging forth, let liars and vipers into our midst. While she sobbed and hissed and growled, we prayed. Together we drove the devil back into the night.

When it was over, the night felt like a gift: another chance to make ourselves right. The world was still here, we were breathing and our hearts still beat blood. There was still so much more work to do, to make ourselves worthy. You promised us it could be done. We'd been granted a reprieve; but the evil parts of us would have to be singed away.

We walked home that night singing the Battle Hymn of the Republic, feeling Godlike in our power.

He has sounded forth the trumpet that shall never call retreat;
He is sifting out the hearts of men before His judgment seat;
Oh, be swift, my soul, to answer Him; be jubilant, my feet!

PART II

Chicago, March

IN THE GREASY SPOON where they've agreed to meet, Emily opens a tiny flask from her purse and pours a bit into her cup. "Runs in the family," she says when she sees Nora looking. "But you knew that already."

"He's mentioned it." Now that she thinks about it, there's no booze anywhere in the house, not even beer in the fridge or old whiskey in a high cabinet.

Emily is middle-aged, square-jawed, her dye job a determined chestnut, her wool coat shapeless and sensible. She has her father's soft, wide mouth. None of the humor in his eyes, though. "It's just a shock," she says. "He wouldn't have told me he was sick, I had to hear it from a neighbor. I wouldn't have known until the obit came." She laughs, a rough bark. "Just what is it you called me for? You in the habit of trying to solve your patients' family problems?" Her gaze is direct and unblinking.

"No—I'm just here to take care of Mike. And I'm here for the family as well. I thought you might want to talk."

"Well." Emily shifts her gaze away. "Tell me how long he's got left."

"He is getting progressively weaker, and the paralysis will spread. You'd have to ask his doctor—"

"I don't trust doctors. They never tell the truth," Emily says bluntly.

"They leave people like you to do that."

Nora sighs. "I honestly don't know. It depends on how the tumor grows. Once it encroaches on his brain, and the part that controls his breathing, then—" Her throat is hollow. She can't believe how unprofessional she's being, collapsing at the prospect of saying the words: *Then he'll die.* "We'll take good care of him," is all she can manage.

"I know what you're thinking," Emily says.

"What?"

"Don't try to deny it. You're thinking I'm some sort of monster." She drains her cup and sets it carefully down. "You come in when he's a helpless old man. A charmer, too. He always could charm people when he had the inclination. You're thinking, How could she be so cold? His own daughter?" She continues before Nora can respond. "Look. You don't know the half of what he was like as a father. Out at bars every night. My mother agonizing at home, calling me a difficult child. I blamed her for a long time. Her wondering if she'd have to get his paychecks signed over to her so he wouldn't spend it all. Sometimes he'd get all contrite, he'd turn on the charm, tell me I was his special girl, he loved me, that he'd quit the booze for me. I fell for it every time." She laughs emptily: the grief is still there, but it's been hollowed out by time and memory. "I moved out as soon as I could, I only spoke to my mother on the phone, and that was that."

Nora listens in silence. Sometimes people need to get out their rage at a dying person. When they realize it can no longer be directed at its intended target, or that soon they'll have no one living left to blame, they're furious. If she can be a vessel for this woman's anger, she'll spare Mike. It's comforting, calling upon her old talents, the things that kept her alive.

"He never hit me," Emily adds. "It wasn't that kind of thing. I just needed him to be a father for me. And he just couldn't do it. He tried, I know." Her eyes are on Nora's, probing for her reaction. "Does that mean he gets some kind of prize? I have to hold his hand and wipe his ass now? Is that what I have to do, be a good daughter?"

"You have to decide what's right for you. I'm not making any judgments."

"Oh yes you are. I see that prim little holier-than-thou face you've got. You go into these houses, you sum up a family's life, you think you know everything. It's why you called me in the first place. You think I owe him something."

"I don't think that."

"What was your relationship with your father like, growing up?" Emily asks abruptly. "You one of the lucky people not fucked up by their parents?"

There's nothing and everything to say. Nora settles on the truth: "My father was my whole world."

"He's dead now?"

"Yes."

Emily plays with the handle of her empty cup. There's still so much anger in the tense movements of her hands. She could hurl the cup across the room, or slap Nora in the face. "I bet he loved you very much. I bet he'd do anything for you." Her voice is precise and bitter.

Nora stands up, shoving herself back from the table so the plates rattle. "I have to go."

"Wait."

She turns, but won't sit back down.

"I'm sorry," Emily says. "I'm just upset. I hate that I'm still hoping for something different. I'm so used to being angry at him, I don't know how to feel anything else."

Is this what fathers give their daughters? This anger so close to the bone, this vengeful love? Maybe there are other daughters out there, loving and hating, destroying themselves with the tug of war inside them. Maybe the only way to survive is to surrender to it.

"You're lucky," Nora says. "You still have a chance to tell him how you really feel."

She watches undertakers edge gurneys down narrow staircases with their black-bagged cargo.

She changes the IV of a woman who is in deep, frantic denial about her impending death. *I just signed the hospice papers because they wouldn't let me go home otherwise. I'm going to beat this. My sister had the same thing and look at her now. Don't you hover over me like that, you're all vultures, just waiting for me to kick off, but I won't. I won't.*

Nora wants to grab her by the shoulders and say, *Prepare yourself.* But of course, she doesn't. She thinks about the bookshelf in the kitchen at home, lined with nubby paperbacks on death and dying. Titles like, *One Foot in Heaven. God Needs More Angels. The Well-Lived Death. Finding Yourself in Hospice.* The nurses are supposed to offer them to patients and their families. But Nora and the rest of the nurses hate them. They are filled with saccharine little sayings about the meaning and joy that can come from the time of dying; cozy visions of the "better place" that awaits. No acknowledgment of the terror and pain, the loathing you'll feel about your disintegrating body, the reality that you will lose dignity, agency, control.

If she ever wrote a book on death, Nora decides she'd tell the truth. How it's going to hurt. How nothing the body goes through in this life happens without pain. She would want people to know that, so that they could move on from their dread and denial. She'd write, If the world was ending, what would you do? And leave the rest of the pages blank.

Nora stands under the stone angel at Union Station, as they agreed.

Sweat drenches her armpits, sliding down between her thighs. She watches faces glide past her in safe unrecognition until there he is: a head taller than a crowd of young women poring over a city map, his bearded, amiable face, identical to his online photo, appearing like a wild animal above a stand of brush. She raises her arm: he's seen her too, and wades through the crowd as though it's water. He stops, too close; she has to step back to look up into his face.

"Hello." His voice is surprisingly soft.

"Hello." She laughs, nervously. "Alder. Hi. What does everybody say? That you're just like your picture?" She sent him a poorly lit shot that Kiki had taken on her birthday, her face wary and dark above a ring of candles.

They sit at a cafe table, hunched close. The station may be safe in its busyness but it's also difficult for them to hear one another. Nora struggles to focus on his words instead of the hard blue diamonds of his eyes, uncomfortably familiar, the restless way he touches everything on the table, tearing the sugar packets into tiny gritty scraps. "I'm new," he says. "I left last year. I still don't know—" he waves a hand—"I still don't know much. Do you like Chicago? What's it like? What was it like when you first got here?"

"It's—" she's not sure how to explain. The crazy jumble of the city, everything countered by something else. Midwestern friendliness and rampant gun violence. Legendary corruption and gangster romance. Stunning architecture and weedy vacant lots filled with shopping carts. The sparkling lake and the rattling, rusting L. "It's complicated. So much more complicated than my old life."

"And mine." He smiles, but the smile quickly morphs into a grimace. "Everything's hard. Just being in this crowd, I get jumpy, there are too many strangers. People don't understand half the things I talk about. All

I know is spiritual stuff, or peaches and oranges. I could talk about them all day, how to make them grow, what makes them sick."

"I could tell you how to strip a deer," Nora says. "Or start a fire ten different ways. But nobody wants to hear about that." In her old life, just meeting a man like this would have been forbidden. She is aware of the V of her sweater exposing her neck, the snug seat of her jeans.

"I know!" He half lunges over the table in his excitement.

"Tell me what makes an orange sick," she asks.

"Well," he says, relaxing a little. "There's Citrus Canker. And Grease Spot. And Sooty Mold."

She responds with the things she learned: how the grain silo was built, the way rabbit and squirrel and sandhill crane tracks look in snow or sand or mud, how to boil pine needles for protein. She tells him about rituals and prayers that others would not understand: the bonfires and the late night singing to drive the devil out. Every word feels like another dangerous step back home.

Alder listens without pity or judgment in his eyes. No disgust when she describes the bitter taste of a raw rabbit kidney (copper, ammonia, blood). And she listens when he describes the great Mother Earth goddess and the soul's alpha wave power and the hours-long chanting circles where they manifested their inner auras and projected them peacefully across the world to prevent nuclear war. How all his life he believed they were the only thing keeping the world safe from Armageddon. How he was told the boundaries of identity were what kept us all from our true selves—even the boundaries made by labels such as *mother, father,* and *child.* The two of them speak with the urgency of spies bringing back vital secrets from across enemy lines. And neither of them, she can tell, are totally free of their former beliefs.

Between the Greek columns in the station, a bride and groom are taking wedding photos. The groom dips the bride low and kisses her red sunburnt shoulders, evidence of the bachelorette party in Cancun or someplace tropical still left in the white bathing suit strap marks on her skin. She looks dizzy and elated. An Amish family settles in a wooden bench and watches the couple, their expressions secret behind their bonnets.

"Our leader was an orphan, I found out later," Alder says. "Given up for adoption and shuffled around foster homes. I think he found mothers the most threatening of all. He tried to punish anyone who had a bond he couldn't share or control. He told the mothers their love was a poison." He shakes his head. "I still don't understand how the mothers stayed. How could a mother stay in a life like that?"

Nora looks down at her hands. "I wouldn't know. My mother left when I was fourteen."

Alder chews on his lip. "Maybe it was her one chance to get out."

"But to leave your children behind?"

"Maybe she had to."

Nora shrugs. "Maybe she just never loved us enough to want us along."

"I doubt that."

"You don't know. You didn't know her." She can't help snapping. The thought still makes her angry.

"I'm sorry," Alder says. "I'm just jealous, I guess. That she was yours for a while."

She swallows. "What do you mean?"

"Well, I told you about how we weren't allowed to know who our mothers were. They all wore these red headscarves so they looked the same. I had my suspicions, but you never knew for sure." He shifts in his chair; they're both uncomfortable, this conversation is too fraught for a first meeting. But he plows on. "The kids said that before you were weaned and taken away, the mothers left secret marks on the babies so they'd know which one was theirs. I used to search all over my body for something—a scar, a tattoo. But there was nothing."

"You weren't allowed any relationships at all?"

"Not exactly. You could have sex all you wanted, as long as you didn't get attached. There was a girl I spent a lot of time with. We'd pretend we hated each other when we were in public, and we got by like that for a while. But somehow we were found out. We'd have these detachment ceremonies. I had to stand there in front of everyone and say I don't love you, your love is poison, you are poison to me, while she wept. Our leader told me I needed to learn that lesson if I was going to reach my full human potential." Alder's stare is fixed on the table, his hands tearing at the scraps of sugar packet. "The funny thing was—the words made it true. I didn't love her anymore after that. I felt nothing when I saw her picking peaches. She was just—one of a blur of people in the fields. They killed her for me."

His hands clench and unclench; Nora rests her own hands on top of his. "You can't get so emotional here."

"Why?"

"People will stare."

"So?"

Nora sighs; there's so much nuance to teach him. He's so innocent, he feels things unabashedly, in a way she doesn't dare to.

"Was there anyone like that? For you?" he asks.

"Well, there was this boy—"

"And he loved you?" He leans eagerly across the table.

"Well—" she stops. "That's what no one ever really knows, is it?"

Alder is silent; his eyes look disappointed, as if he's come for a guide, someone who can help him navigate the real world, but all she can tell him is that there is so much uncertainty out here, such a cold blowing wind of doubt.

"Did you love him?" he asks.

"Yes, I did," she says. And knows, for the first time, that it's true. Why else would she spend her last day on Earth sneaking away to kiss him, hoping he would kiss her back? Why else would everything that followed have happened?

Over the next few weeks, they circle each other, meeting in busy, crowded cafes, chains mostly, with stale croissants and ceaseless pop music on loop. The places seem safely generic to her, so bland he'd never be able to find her again if she slipped away mid-sentence.

After several meetings like this, though, Alder grows impatient. He wants to know something about the city, he tells her, and what it has to offer; he's hungry to see the real world. And she's only showing him the most featureless parts.

"Take me somewhere secret," he begs her. "Someplace only you know."

After some thought, she takes him to the Chapel in the Sky, the highest place of worship in the western hemisphere. They take an elevator to the top floor of the Chicago Temple Building, where a cheerful middle-aged woman in a purple cardigan guides them and a group of tourists through a hall of Methodist history. Methodists, their tour guide explains primly, believe in sanctification. The effect of faith on the soul is profound; faith transforms us into holy beings. Early Methodist groups encountered violent resistance from the Church of England. They were seen as dangerous fanatics, and their leader, John Wesley, was treated as if he were the head of a cult. A prominent leader in the group, George Bell, began to preach that the end of the world was nigh, and that they had to prepare. But Wesley broke away from this contingent, striking out a path for respectability. "Methodists believe in the possibility of perfection through divine love," the guide concludes.

"That love is there, for anyone willing to reach up for it. It's not too late. Even for you miserable sinners."

The group laughs, and the guide inclines her head gracefully. Her knowledge is clear and masterful; she is not imposing or preachy, but it's obvious to Nora that she's a believer, not just a historian. "We are justified by faith," she says. "It's why we live and breathe: to believe. Faith produces 'inward and outward holiness.' We hope you'll feel a little of that in our chapel today."

The chapel is so small that only a few people can visit it at a time. When it's Nora and Alder's turn, they climb a tight spiral staircase into a dark wooden room lit only by lines of rose-colored recessed lights. Several rows of pews fan out before the altar. A massive Bible is open on the lectern, its purple ribbon stirring gently in the breeze of a cracked window. The stained glass encircling the room depicts canonical scenes: Adam and Eve leaving the garden; Moses parting the sea; Jesus on the cross, his mother reaching to accept his body. But beyond that are scenes of industry: the first railroad, the riverboats and factories that made the city, the destruction in the wake of the great fire. In a gold-stamped fresco before the altar, the new city rises, a modernist splendor of glittering spires, and Jesus rears over it all on some high mount that exists nowhere in the Midwest. It's odd, it's kitsch, a mismatch of image and story, Moses and Montgomery Ward, but it delights Nora for reasons she can't explain. She's swept up in it the way an outsider can be, this love for bumptious, ambitious, industrial, insufferable, earnest, always rising Chicago.

"This is a sacred place," Alder says with a kind of question in his voice.

Nora nods. Poor man, he's missed out on all the signs and symbols of this culture, the words and prayers and the special qualities of light that make something holy. She has to teach him or he'll be lost. "If we were churchgoers, we'd walk down this aisle, while the music plays, and the service would begin with a hymn, and then a reading from the Bible."

Together they walk down the aisle and she glances at the open page in the giant book:

Set me as a seal upon thine heart, as a seal upon thine arm: for love is strong as death.

She feels Alder's breath on her neck as he stoops to read the same words. She looks away, her face hot, and says too loudly, "The tour guide said this chapel is used for weddings."

He smiles at her. "I'd like to see a wedding."

They're twenty-three stories above the city. Through the open window, she can see out onto the gorgeous silver expanse of Lake Michigan. The updraft from the window tugs at their clothes.

"Let's go," she says.

"Where?"

"Just come with me."

Maybe Nora knew the day would take this direction. Why else would she have picked this meeting time, when Kiki is away visiting her aunt, and everyone else is on call, the whole house empty?

She shows him where to leave his shoes. The dishwasher hums. She stands at the kitchen window, looking at the kids playing in the street. She watches him prowl around the living room, inspecting the way normal people live. He flips through the hospice books, turns on the TV. This time of day there are preachers on three different channels. He watches for a few minutes, fascinated, until she reaches around him and turns it off.

"How do you sleep?" he asks. "I'm used to being in this big communal bed."

"It was hard at first. I didn't sleep much, the first year." She kept expecting a deacon with a semi-automatic to come barreling through the door, or to touch her shoulder in a crowded train station. *Come on home now.* "You get used to sleeping alone."

"How do you live like that?"

"Plenty of people are lonely. What's harder is all the uncertainty. No one out here *knows* anything." The words pass between them with a small thud.

Alder shakes his head. "I can't figure it out. All these people walking around without an organizing principle. Without knowing who they are."

"People don't think about it that way. You just kind of—muddle along. You build a life. You find a way to be happy."

"How?"

"Jesus, I can't tell you that." She plucks his hand away from the hospice books; there will be no answers there. "That's what everyone's trying to figure out."

Suddenly, the crunch of tires in the driveway. "Quick, upstairs," Nora says, hustling him up the narrow stairway into the hall. She hurries him into her bedroom, where they listen to a door slam, followed by Sonya and Masha's bright arguing voices in the kitchen. Nora presses her back to the bedroom door, while Alder looks around at the plain little ornaments she brought with her from the UP: a carved wooden horse and a string of her mother's beads, hanging on a nail. The boisterous jumble of photos Kiki has tacked to her stretch of the wall, compared to the stark blankness of hers.

Finally the voices retreat and the downstairs door closes. They're alone again. Nora remains with her back pressed against the door, watching Alder move through the room, touching everything. He has yet to learn about personal boundaries. "It doesn't feel real," he says, holding her mother's warped prayer card. "None of it does." He thumbs the fraying card stock. The two sides are coming apart. Nora snatches it out of his hand before he can damage it further.

"Don't touch that."

He looks at her, puzzled. "What is it?"

"Just something my mother gave me." She finds herself wondering, if he stood naked before her, could she find the secret mark his mother might have left? If she made an inventory of her own body, what secret marks would she find that her mother had left?

Maybe all this around her would come to the fore, this life would become fully hers, if he touched her. Maybe they could make it real for each other. A pact, believe in me and I'll believe in you. Like all things, it comes down to faith. At some point you have to believe in this world more than the other.

She reaches past him and switches off the light. In the darkness she feels her way to the lower bunk and lies down.

She can hear him breathing. At night, men turn into bears, her mother once said. But her mother was a liar; bears are bears and men are men. She listens to the huff of his breath, the drag of his feet on the floor as he approaches. "Nora?"

"Come here," she says, pulling him down to her. She guides his mouth, his hands. She has to be careful. He is not inexperienced, but he's childlike, clumsy. "Do you want me to—" he asks, and she presses her lips to his, can't say what she wants. He moves his mouth down her neck, the exposed V of her chest. She catches the shine of his eyes in the dark and looks away. Puts his hands in the places she doesn't have names for.

Maybe it's natural to think of the other people you've been with when you're fucking somebody, but Levi comes to mind. Levi with the lean watchful body and the dreamy eyes. An incorporeal beauty, a feeling that you could never really reach something he kept deep inside.

Levi had a touch of the divine, but Alder is earthly, all weight and warmth. They're sinking together on the flimsy mattress, creaking down toward the floor. They're going to break something if they're not careful. She laughs at the idea of it, sinking into the floor with him, down and down and down. He is real, he is here because she asked him to come, and no prophecy predicted him.

"You have to go," she suddenly whispers in his ear. "You're not supposed to be here." They are breaking so many rules, house rules and forum rules.

He struggles to his feet. Her mattress will never be the same. "When can I see you?"

"Soon. But now, you've got to go." She pushes him to the door, listens for other people, then shoves him into the hallway.

"I want to see you again. Tell me the truth. Tell me you want to see me too."

"I do."

His eyes are bright, his mouth moving. She's afraid that he'll say he loves her. He doesn't understand what that word means out here. She puts a finger to his lips. "Don't."

"Don't what?"

"Just—don't." She pushes him the rest of the way to the stairs.

She doesn't breathe until she hears him tromping out the front door, and then she lets the air out slowly, sinking down the wall, trying to savor the feeling. Waiting for shame to come, the expected feeling, and surprised when it doesn't. She'll never stop waiting for that thunderbolt of judgment. *Prepare to meet thy God—*

Lamentations

2013

(1,710 days since the world ended)

Nora arrives home, night falling fast in the October chill, to find her father sitting on the porch, a shotgun across his lap. He sits there after dinner sometimes, watching for enemies, cleaning the gun, oiling the parts. "Where were you?" he asks. "I was about to send the night watch."

She's nineteen now, gawky and muscled in odd places. Almost five years since her mother left, and no sign of her in all that time.

"Just by the shore. With Levi." This is acceptable, though still frivolous. She's always careful when she goes to Rachel's, crossing the barbed wire fence when the night watch is changing shifts. She knows that Rachel set her up that one time, sending her to meet with Roy, but she keeps going back. There's something thrilling about returning to the witch's house again and again. "We followed the tracks of the deer that's been eating the garden," she says. "Didn't get her, though."

Her father doesn't answer right away, just keeps turning the gun in his hands. "If you went to town, or somewhere else, I'd know," he finally says, matter-of-factly, as though he's just musing on an interesting hypothetical. "Anywhere you went, I'd know. God knows already what you're going to do." He never misses a chance to remind her that women are suspect, that they need monitoring to stay on the path. She's only realized recently that it's a buried assumption in everything he preaches.

Nora brushes past him without responding. Such a tiny rebellion, but it's the only kind she's capable of.

In the first few days after the world was supposed to end, the church members wandered about the compound, aimless, guns on their shoulders. Some of them opened the cans of tomatoes and jams and peas that were supposed to be saved for end times and ate the food while standing around, digging their fingers into the containers. Others refused to eat entirely. Her father stood at the living room window for several hours each day, waiting for news from the people he had sent out, waiting for her mother's return, waiting for the world to shrug and tremble and heave itself upside down.

Whole days went by without church meetings. The night watch skipped three nights; the front gate was left unchained and swinging open, until her father called a church meeting about laxity in these dangerous times.

During the meeting, they did a roll call, and discovered that ten members had slipped away, emptying their trailers. They have doubted, which is the greatest sin, her father declared. We are being tested, and they have failed. They will regret it for the rest of their lives. He tore the leg off of a chair and lit it on fire to use as a torch, then marched out of the barn, leading them all to the trailer of the first deserter. When they got there, her father instructed the deacons to pour gasoline and pile kindling. He touched his torch to the pile and set it alight. Soon the others were gathering branches and old deck chairs, whatever they could find, adding to the growing pile, watching the flames climb higher. No one spoke. While the first trailer was still burning they went on to the next one, and the next one. The fire burned all night, and the blackened hulls of the trailers smoked for weeks afterward, filling the air with the awful smell of burnt plastic, rubber, and fiberglass.

Afterward, everyone went back to their old jobs, calmly and with new commitment. The little prayer cards her mother had handed out to the other women disappeared from kitchen windows.

Over the next few months, the rules changed gradually. Higher chain link fences and more patrols. Night drills. Deacons sweeping through the compound at all hours. New rules for where people congregated, who could leave and when. Any place where two or three were gathered was reason for suspicion.

A new group, Morality Watch, was formed, asking questions about who the members had been talking to in town, as well as searching people's homes. "You wouldn't believe the things they're hiding," Levi, who was part of the group, told Nora one day. "Some of those who we thought were good church people. The things we've confiscated—"

"Like what?"

He shakes his head. "I can't tell you."

When he and his father were out working, Nora wandered into Levi's yard one day, unlocking the tool shed with the key he kept under a stone. Inside was a dusty milk crate filled with romance novels, women's fashion magazines, and magazines with pictures of naked women, the pages rippled and faded with age. Nora flipped through one carefully, taking her time. The funny cat-eyed women with their glossy highlighted hair; their tight, firm skin and dazzling teeth. They looked inhuman, not like the women she knew. Whores, her father would say, a term he used more and more to refer to almost any woman who displeased him.

Nora slid the magazine to the very edge of her vision, said a quick prayer, then looked away. If you see something by mistake, it's not really a sin, is it?

What was there to look at? What's so dangerous, really, about looking? Nora edged the magazine closer and closer to the center of her vision. Her eyes met the eyes of a woman sitting on a plain wooden chair, her legs spread wide, her hands on her knees. She was leaning forward as if with anticipation, the dark spot between her legs the exact midpoint of the photograph, her face commanding and unashamed. Go ahead, look here, she was saying. The woman's body was burnished in a fake bronze color, slick and gleaming like a fish. Suddenly, a crow called outside like a warning and Nora shoved the magazines back into their crate.

The next time she passed Levi's place, he was tending a bonfire in the yard, the magazines curling into ash.

Nora was standing in front of her house one late afternoon almost a year after the world was supposed to end, looking into the dark haze of the trees that surrounded the property, when she felt her father's fingers closing tight around the small plane of her shoulder. She'd seen him put his hands on members like this before, right before he took them into the forest.

"Where's she gone?" he asked. He hadn't spoken to her for a week.

Nora didn't turn around, didn't ask *who*. "I don't know."

"You're her daughter," her father said. "I've seen you together. She'd have told you. She'd have let slip something, given you some sign."

The grip tightened. Nora finally turned, to prove she was honest by meeting his eyes. "She didn't tell me anything. She just—left." Her throat hollowed, and tears stung the corners of her eyes.

He let her go. "I guess she never trusted any of us," he said.

She watched her father crunch away through the snow, back toward the house. It was blisteringly cold but she was angry, too angry just to shrug and follow him inside. Angry at her. "She was doing all sorts of things you didn't know about," she called after him. "She was giving medicines to the other women. Forbidden things."

He paused and turned to look at her. "And you never told me. You never said a word."

She was left momentarily speechless. "I'm saying it now," she croaked, finally. She remembered what his hand had just felt like on her shoulder, and how she had once been grateful for his touch.

"Anyone whose name is not found written in the book of life will be thrown into the lake of fire," he said. And went into the house.

A week later, Nora was tipping a pan of dirty water out in the back yard when she saw Henry standing in the muddy snow by the woodpile. His footprints showed that he'd been circling around and around, grinding down a track into the frozen grass.

Nora hugged herself in her flimsy coat. "What are you doing out here?"

"Just looking for something." He was touching each piece of wood, shifting it slightly, peering underneath.

"For what?"

He glanced back at her impatiently. "For a message," he said. "A sign. I thought she would have left something."

"You think she's coming back?"

He shook his head. He had the axe handle in one hand and was spinning it slowly on its head. "She's not coming back."

"How do you know for sure?"

"I heard them talking about you one night," he said. "She was saying to him, You've turned her into some kind of monster." His gaze raked across her face, hungry for her reaction.

"You're lying," Nora said, but without conviction. Sometimes Henry lied, and sometimes he didn't. There was no logic to when he chose to tell the truth.

"You're why she left," he said. "You know that, right?"

There seemed to be nothing to do but walk away from him, so she did, retreating into the dark empty house. For a long time after she heard the methodical *chock chock* of the axe. He was splitting every piece of wood, searching for a hidden message.

⁂

Time passes, weeks, months, a year, then another.

One morning, when Nora is scrubbing the oatmeal pot in the kitchen, her father waves to her from the front door. "Come on," he beckons. Wordlessly, she puts down the pot and goes for her boots. She thinks they're off on another mission trip, but outside in the early morning cold, he doesn't head for the truck. Instead he leads her to the locked gun shed behind the house.

He stands in front of the neat row of weapons. "If this compound were under attack, which one would you take?" he asks.

Nora considers the virtues of each. The semi-automatic holds the largest magazine and shoots the fastest. She points to it, but he shakes his head. "I asked which one *you* should take," he says. "That one's too heavy for you, and you're not familiar with it. The best gun is the one you can shoot."

She takes down her old deer rifle instead. They call it a girl's gun because it's so light, a nice starter gun for your daughter is how they market it in shops. They head over to the shooting range, a rocky bare hill where the deacons gather in the evenings with beer and Christian rock blasting on pocket radios, practicing their aim.

"Let's see how you do," he says.

He stands behind her while she settles into her crouch, lining up the shot on the black paper cutout of the stag, its head and tail up in an alert pose. She's done this many times before; she knows how to aim for the neck in order to save the good meat. But her father puts a hand on her shoulder. "What if you wanted to kill without saving the meat," he says. "What would you aim for?"

"The neck or head are still good choices."

"But harder to hit. What if he was charging at you?"

"Well—then anywhere that would bring it down. The torso, the heart."

"Could you line up your shot when it was leaping right at you? When your own heart was pounding like crazy? When you knew you were going to die if you missed?"

"I'm a good shot. I could do it."

He walks to the target, removes the paper deer and clips on a new target—the black silhouette of a man.

"How about now?" he calls to her. "What will you aim for?"

She stares at the silhouetted figure, standing there with its hands on its hips, a broad, easily recognizable shape, her father beside it mimicking the pose.

"Still, the heart," she answers.

"Show me."

"I'm not going to shoot with you right there."

"God doesn't ask us to do easy things," he says. "When the day comes, you won't get a nice clean shot with no one else around. You won't have time to line it up just how you like. You'll have to not hesitate. If you're so sure you're a good shot, go ahead and take it."

She takes a deep breath, tries to let it out smoothly, but it stutters past her lips. Her hands were steady before.

He shakes his head. "You're taking too long. " Then he adds, "You're soft."

She swings the gun into position and fires rapidly three times, two in the head, one in the heart. Neat and pretty as a poem.

He descends the hill grim and satisfied. "You have to do it that fast every time. You can't fail, don't you get that? This is about survival. You get one chance. One. You can say one thing for your mother. She wouldn't have hesitated," he says.

Nora jams the safety of the gun on, turning away. She'll do anything to please him, diligently serve his higher plan, and still he is a stranger to her, as unknown, as empty, as that black outline on the target paper. He'll never explain why he does the things he does, he'll offer only the part of himself that makes her love or fear him.

⁂

Henry operates the smoke machine outside the barn windows. The new attendees, invited to sit right in front, are surrounded by a phalanx of members so that they can't easily slip away if something makes them uncomfortable; her father has been using more "hellfire" in his services to try and attract new members. There will be music, too, and long tables of food the women have been making all day, hot venison pot pies and berry tarts and barbecued chicken, whatever draws people in. The food is covered and congealing in the cool autumn air. As usual, Nora's performance will be the climax.

The singing starts. Nora is supposed to walk down the aisle to the stage, let her throat swell, her nerves flood, open herself up the way she's done countless times before. Her body tenses, a deep sense memory of falling, of pain.

Her father is not on the stage, or in the audience. Instead of walking to the front, Nora slips out the side door. She passes Henry, jiggering the smoke machine to stream through the windows, lips pursed in concentration. There are a couple of women guarding the food from the dogs, exchanging murmured conversation and soft laughter. And farther away, near the tree line, her father stands in the small cone of a truck's headlights. A few of the younger deacons are with him: Matty and Bill and their crowd, the ones who wear tactical vests and ride their ATVs ceaselessly across the compound with their guns pointed in the air.

She slowly approaches the group, keeping the truck between them. "We can make the order this week if we have the deposit," Matty says. "It's a lot of money." Her father's voice is low.

Matty spits impatiently on the ground. The other men shift lightly, restive and observant, looking from one to the other. "You pay for two things, quality and discretion," he says. "We're saving money on the bulk buy. No names, no registrations on anything. Enough long guns and semis for every man."

"Enough for every man to have two," her father corrects. "We're already armed. We're not sitting ducks here."

"You said it yourself, preacher. When the enemy is at the gates, some farmer's shotgun isn't going to stop anybody. If you want to be ready for war, you have to stop playing games."

"But what kind of war are we getting ready to fight?" her father asks. His voice is weary and deadly at once. The men shift back on their heels. They fear God and the devil, and her father. He could touch their foreheads and strike them down. Nora wishes he would.

But he just nods. Matty climbs in his truck and drives away, while the other men return to the service. Nora can hear the singers reaching the last verse of "The King is Coming": *I just heard the trumpets sounding and now his face I see.* That's her cue. They'll miss her soon. She's got to get back.

But she stands in the cold night air, watching her father tilt his head back. She doesn't know if he's looking at the eaves, where the wood-pigeons build their nests and sing mournfully, or the stars, remembering the angels and diamonds he promised five years ago. The night draws close around them. Nora watches him a moment longer, past the point of safety or reason.

⁏

Later that night, when everything is over, Nora is counting a stack of rumpled bills that her father gave her to sort and put in the lockbox he keeps buried under the house. Henry studies at the table beside her. It's a cold night, wind whistling through the cracks in the floorboards. They both wear their coats in the house because no one is home during the day to keep the stove going.

Nora is exhausted, bruised and weary from another session of speaking in tongues. She counts the cash in silence, making quick little flicks with her thumbs.

"You didn't get all that from donations, did you," Henry says without looking up from his book.

"No. We got hardly anything." The people they attract these days bring muscle, restless energy, and cans of gasoline and flak jackets, but not much money.

"So where do you think it all comes from?"

The cash slows in her hand. "I don't know."

"Don't you wonder how they got it?"

"It's not our job to wonder."

Henry snorts. He gazes at her over his crooked glasses, which he got when he was a child and are now too small for his face. "There are so many things going on here that you don't have the slightest idea about," he says.

Nora flushes, trying to find her place again, but the fives and ones keep blurring together. "Don't try to scare me. I'm not a little kid anymore."

Henry shrugs. "If you're sure you don't want to know."

The bills flash past, but she can no longer make her brain count them. "I've talked with people who left," she says. It comes out as a whisper. A tree branch lashes against the window like a knock on the door.

"So?"

"They told me about the stuff that goes on here."

"You mean that guy who almost kidnapped you," Henry says. "What did he tell you?"

"It was years ago. He was just a sad, lonely man." Suddenly she feels protective of Roy.

Henry turns a page. "Well, people who leave don't tend to live long," he says.

"What?"

"Just that. Defectors have a way of disappearing." Henry has always known things. When the neighbor kids back in Indiana pushed him into rain gutters, he always knew the Bible verse that would curse them best. It's his only weapon in a dangerous world.

"What happens to them?" she demands. She thinks about Rachel.

Henry shrugs and goes back to studying. Nora wishes that they could speak the way they used to; she wonders, suddenly, where the mural of the Noah's Ark animals they worked on so happily so many years ago has gone to. She wants to ask him, but then her father blows in the door with the wind, wet and cold and looking for coffee.

Nora rises without being asked and puts the kettle on for him.

⁂

In the years since the world was supposed to end, her father and Henry have spent countless evenings at the kitchen table, arguing about this or that point of doctrine. Tonight, Nora tries to join them, picking up a book she hasn't noticed before, *The Varieties of Religious Experience*. She opens it at random and tries to read, but the writing is dense and academic. Hypnagogy, mystification, transmogrification—she mouths the words uncertainly, afraid to mispronounce them.

"There are ways that people experience God," her father says, looking up from his spread of books. "There's a rational dimension, and an existential dimension, and a moral dimension. The rational dimension is when we look at all the evidence and can prove God exists, and so we believe. The existential dimension is when we realize we could not be without the creation of God, and so we believe. The moral dimension is when we look at the inherent morality of humankind, and we cannot deny that only God could have made us desire to be good."

"But there are so few people who *are* good," Nora says. "Why does God make so many people bad?"

Henry sighs and pushes up from his chair. "I'm going out for some fresh air."

Their father ignores him. "Now you're talking about the problem of evil," he continues. "The fundamental Kierkegaardian question."

She likes listening to the sound of his voice. It has been a long time since the two of them have been together like this, just talking.

"If there is no creator, then our existence is meaningless," he says. "If no one made us, then why do we care that we have been made? Without a God to create us, there is no morality, with no inherent value of good or evil. Everything is permitted in a Godless universe. Dostoevsky said that. Without acknowledging God's role in every dimension of ourselves, we're empty. We talk to the darkness, and only the darkness echoes back."

"But how do we know what's good and what's not?" Nora is trying to rise to the challenge of his knowledge, showing him that she's been thinking these things through. "The Bible tells us to do some things that we don't do. It contradicts itself."

"You're thinking about human culture. Eat this, don't touch that, wash this way. Human civilizations have always been our best attempts to make cities and tribes and governments that function in a fallen world. You have to think eschatologically."

"Eschata—"

"End times. In the final age of man, we'll be expected to purify ourselves in preparation for the final sacrament. When the earth is sanctified again, and all corruption is washed away. The final stage is when the true church is made manifest on earth."

"The church militant and the church triumphant," Nora says.

Her father frowns. These are Catholic terms, and they both knew where she got them from. "Until that time comes, we live in the shadow of the devil," he says. "This—" he waves his arm—"is his world."

"All of the world?"

"There's no place he can't reach," he says. "I used to think there were places where we were safe. But nowhere is safe. For anything to make sense, the devil has to be everywhere. If you recognize the presence of evil in our world, then you admit the existence of God, because the concept of value has no meaning in a Godless universe. Who's going to decide what's good and what's bad? Are you?" He puts a hand on her shoulder. "Most people don't understand this. It took your mother leaving to make me finally see. The presence of evil *proves* God exists, and that the church triumphant is on its way. The devil is God's gift to us—and his warning. The devil is the bellwether."

It's hard to imagine that this safe, protected place has been infiltrated. That all this time, they've been overrun. "If this is the devil's world," Nora says slowly, "Why doesn't he just take us all down to hell? How can we win?"

"You really can't see, can you?" her father snaps. "This is a war." He pulls the notebook from his pocket that he always carries for making plans and drawing diagrams, and turns to a clean page. "Look, this is how I explained it to Henry. There's a math problem. A thought experiment." He draws a grid on the blank, creamy page, filling the paper with squares. "Imagine a grid, like a checkerboard stretched across a coordinate plane. The game board is infinite, and there are only two players: a man, and the devil. The man is on the board—" he draws a small stick figure in one square—"and the devil is everywhere."

"The devil can light any single square on fire. And all the man can do is run." He scratches out one square, and then another. "How many squares would the man need to move in each turn in order to stay alive, so that the devil can never trap him in a ring of fire?" He sketches the little man one square over. "What do you think? If he moves just one square with each turn, can he escape?"

Nora stares at the grid, trying to imagine the devil lighting one square at a time, the man moving in this desperate cat-and-mouse game. Beyond learning arithmetic, she has barely been sat down for math lessons; while Henry did mental math drills, she was usually with their mother, learning how to make tinctures of willow bark to prevent fever. "I don't know," she says.

"He can't," her father says impatiently. "If he only moves one square with each turn, the devil has him every time. Does he need to be able to move a hundred squares in one leap? A thousand? No one knew the answer to the question for years, but finally the problem was solved. If the man can move just two squares per turn—just two! In all that infinite space, then the devil can never catch him."

"So what does that mean for us?" she asks.

He claps shut the notebook. "Just two steps, you see? One we take. The other is in God's hand. If we try to walk alone, one square at a time, the devil wins the game. With God, we escape. Man alone is nothing."

She is upset with herself. Always too slow to understand, always behind. "What are we doing, then?" she asks. "What am I?"

He looks at her tolerantly. "You're the magician's lovely assistant. You're a demonstration, a prop. We cut you in half and put you back together again."

⁑

Her father is in full voice today, praying with his eyes closed, reciting the favorite verses: "*Do not prostitute thy daughter, to cause her to be a whore; lest the land fall to whoredom, and the land become full of wickedness.*" There's a feeling growing like a hot ball of jelly in Nora's chest, squeezing out the space for her lungs. Together, the congregation holds its breath.

"There have been some investigations in town," her father announces. "Outsiders snooping around, assuming we're up to no good. We have to watch who we talk to and what we say. There are so many out there who don't understand what we're here to do. They want to tear us apart and turn us against each other. They want you to lose your trust in me."

The congregation murmurs its dark dissent.

"I've been given a vision," he continues. "There are vipers out there, people who once were righteous. Apostates and heretics poisoning the water. Someone will betray us."

An uneasy silence laps through the barn. "I should have known better," he says, tragically. "But I did not see. They fooled us. We weren't ready, five years ago, but we're getting close now. The prophecies are coming true."

After the crowd has filed out, Nora remains standing in the front row, clenching and unclenching her fists. "What did you see?" she asks her father. "Who's going to betray us?"

He's looking over her shoulder at a cluster of men waiting for him. "I don't have time for this now, Nora. There's a lot to do."

"Who's the betrayer?" Is he talking about Rachel? Have her visits been found out?

He shakes his head and quotes Lamentations: "*The adversary hath spread out his hand upon all her pleasant things: for she hath seen that the heathen entered into her sanctuary, whom thou didst command that they should not enter into thy congregation.*"

"Tell me," Nora insists, but he eases her aside, still quoting: "*She hath none to comfort her: all her friends have dealt treacherously with her, they have become her enemies.*"

As Nora undresses for bed that night, she stares at her naked body. Her arms and hands, pocked and ashy with scars from the jumping sparks of campfires, the grabbing pecks of chickens, old scabby blisters from carrying heavy loads or swinging an ax handle, the wood shaft sliding repeatedly in the groove between finger and thumb. She gazes at the rest of herself; ugly, marked-up, nothing like the smooth bronze sameness of the naked woman in the magazine. Her body wants things she can't understand. It wants to fill itself with more than just the voice of God.

She pulls her nightshirt on and claws her hair slowly out of its oily braid. The house is quiet, her father and Henry off on church business, the games men play. There is no one to see her put on her mother's old coat, which has been hanging in the back of the closet, the only thing of her mother's that Nora was able to hide before her father pulled the rest out into the yard and burned it one day, smoking a cigarette and staring silently into the flames. She drapes the coat around herself, loses herself in the familiar smells of woodsmoke and lavender. Her mother used to sew little muslin pouches of dried flowers and stuff them in the pockets of clothes. Nora digs in the pocket and finds one now, and presses it to her nose, breathes the smell in.

What does this body want from her? What would it cost to find out?

⁝

Rachel perches on a high kitchen stool, cigarette in mouth, sketching.

"Have you noticed anything—strange, lately?" Nora asks her. "People watching you in town? Somebody following you?"

Rachel's gaze slides to her. "I've seen the investigators in town. Federal agents, I think. FBI? Or ATF? You can tell, they wear those silk jackets."

"What about our people watching you?"

"Am I in danger? Are you warning me about something?"

"No—no." Nora rubs her forehead. "I don't know."

"I haven't said anything," Rachel says. "I mind my own business. But there are other defectors out there who aren't happy. You know, people who think you're planning the next world war."

Not planning a war, Nora thinks, just planning *for* one. She changes the subject. "Levi and I were hunted by a wolf the other day."

"Yeah?"

"We walked for hours along one of the trails. When the sun was low we turned back, following our own footprints in the snow. Along the way, we began to see the huge paw prints of a wolf, like a dog's but much bigger, treading between our boot prints, tracking us. We looked all around, but there was no sign of the wolf."

Rachel nods, cocks her head and looks at Nora the way she sometimes does, sad and sharp. "Who's hunting you, Nora?"

She isn't sure. She studies Rachel, the thin hunched shape under her shapeless flannel, the long dusty braid. Are there the same tiger stripes she saw on Roy's arm under that shirt? Were you punished, Rachel? Is that why you left? But maybe it's also why you stay?

"Do you think about why people join your group in the first place?" Rachel asks. "Is it fear? Maybe that's what gets their attention. But it's loneliness that keeps them, isn't it. I think people are just looking for a little contact. Some human comfort."

"You can't keep anyone forever without love," Nora says. She's not sure who she heard that from. Maybe her mother?

It's getting dark out, the light in the window going blue. "Time for you to hit the road, kid," Rachel says, stretching up from her stool.

"No one will notice if I stay for a little longer." She doesn't want to leave the warm quiet of Rachel's kitchen quite yet. "Who's talking to the feds about us? Who's the betrayer?"

Rachel looks out the window. "Like I said, time for you to go," she says.

When she's halfway across the meadow, Nora turns back: someone is pulling into Rachel's yard. In the darkness she can only see the outline of a pickup with one headlight out. A figure steps down from the truck, a skinny rectangular shape of a man. Rachel is standing in the yard, waiting for him; they talk for a moment, Rachel hiding her arms in her sweater. He touches her head, strokes her hair, and Rachel turns to his hand, leans into it like a cat. They go inside.

Maybe Rachel is not as alone as she appears to be.

Nora uses the jouncing flashlight beam to guide her home in the dark. When she reaches a straight, orderly stretch of trees, she knows she is in the Run. They call it that because the poplars here grow in a long straight line as though planted by hand.

She follows the trees farther than she normally does, until they've petered out among the wild pines. Her flashlight catches the corner of an old shed, hidden among the trees, that she has never noticed before. It doesn't look like one of the newer storage sheds the deacons are always putting up; its wooden sides are weathered and raw, the edges mouse-nibbled. She moves the light over its mossy corners. She understands that she should let some things go unnoticed, but curiosity can only be tamped down so far, for so long.

Nora approaches the shed—there's a rusty padlock on the handle, but it's hanging loose—and opens the door. She casts the flashlight about in the blackness. It looks like a regular gardening shed. Tools lined up against the wall, hoses coiled in neat loops, ropes hanging from hooks in the ceiling. Dust drifts down in the flashlight's beam. The light catches a rickety folding chair placed in the middle of the room. A hose nearby, dripping, as if recently used. Next to it, a large chain, puddled on the floor. Nora scatters the loose sawdust with her boot: underneath, dark stains that look like recently dried blood. She kicks some more sawdust, uncovering older, faded stains.

She sits in the chair. Across, on the wall, is a rack of wrenches and snub-nosed pliers. Her light climbs the wall, higher, higher. Painted above the door in white letters: ONLY FEAR OF THE LORD WILL REDEEM ME.

The early prisons in America, her father told her once, were designed as spiritual places for moral reflection. That's where we got the word *penitentiary*: a place for the penitent. Solitary confinement was considered a way to be closer to God, alone with your creator and your sin.

Nora wonders how long people have been left here, alone with their sins.

On How He Does His Work

He can take the form of someone we love. A father. He can torture with kindness, with the withholding or offering of what we crave. He can strike a blow without raising a hand. He can kill, slowly, with words: *don't disappoint me. I do this because I love you.*

We wonder sometimes, when we're standing in the darkness by a bonfire, or walking in the woods and seeing wolf prints in the snow, patiently tracking us, and suddenly we feel afraid—if the devil was made by God, is he still his servant, carrying out his orders? Maybe the devil's work is Godly work, too.

When you took us to the shooting range, asked us to look down the sight, you said it was a test, to see if we were fast enough and brave enough, if we could make the right decision. Sometimes when we're lying awake at night, we think about the test again and wonder if we passed. Or whether it was more of a dare. Then, the devil is very close. We know he's sitting on the end of our beds in the darkness, waiting for us to acknowledge him. His eyes are black featureless lakes. His chest is a gaping wound, where his heart was torn away when he fell from heaven. He whispers the things about ourselves that we fear the most. He tells us to do things. We try to close our ears, to drown out the sound of his voice, but it's coming from inside our own heads.

Chicago, April

NORA IS STANDING WITH her back to Kiki, rooting in her drawer for a pair of stockings. Kiki says, "Don't tell me how you got those. I already know."

Nora turns her head. Kiki is staring at the long reddish scars that stripe the backs of her calves. "You don't know everything," Nora snaps back.

"I know what lash marks look like. Those didn't heal right. Your father made those, didn't he?"

Nora says nothing. She grabs the stockings from the drawer and pulls them on over the old purple marks. She has locked that night so far away that it hardly means anything anymore. It's just one of the many scars that mark her body: knife slips and campfire burns, dog teeth, fishhook pricks in the pads of her fingers. The lumpy cartilaginous tissue along her spine from so many hours writhing on the bare boards of the barn floor. Her body is tattooed with its own story.

Kiki puts up a hand. "Look at you, you're forgiving him again."

"I didn't—"

"You don't have to *say* anything. You can't blame him for one blessed thing." Kiki slams a drawer shut, tugs her blouse into place with a jerk. "If you're going to keep forgiving him, you can stop coming to me for help. Y'all lost your mind. There's no other way to say it."

"We weren't all crazy." She's tired of being a fool in Kiki's eyes. "I was talking to God. And I was good at it. It was wonderful."

Kiki's look softens. "You're good at plenty of other things. Like putting up with the worst patients, for one."

"Not lately." Nora sits down on the bed with a thump. "I used to be able to make people *believe* in things."

"And take their money, and make them terrified for their earthly souls." Kiki won't let her get away with gauzy memories. "That's what your father made you do. It wasn't what you were good at. It was what you were good *for*." She touches Nora's shoulder, a quick, tender gesture. "The things your father did, Nora—I keep trying to tell you. They're not what other fathers do. They're not what people do to the people they love."

Nora looks up at her. Something is stuck in her throat, forcing her to speak. "What if he didn't commit suicide?"

"You think he didn't?"

"I don't know. I just don't think he would do that. He wouldn't do it to his family." It still seems impossible. He was so bent on survival, on them all making it together. He wanted them to all see the sun rise over the tilting planet on the last day of creation, to walk the plain of Golgotha and fight in the final battle. What could have turned him away from that dream? Maybe the loss of a daughter, after the loss of a wife? Maybe without her, he was helpless. "When you left Barbados, did you feel guilty for leaving your family behind?"

"I came here to help take care of them."

"You didn't just come here to be the good daughter. You wanted to come."

Kiki sighs, flattens her hair with one hand. "Maybe you're right. I wanted to do something, just one thing, for me."

They finish dressing in silence, and spend a long time winding their scarves at the door, bracing for that first step into the chilly spring air. It's so rare for girls like them, girls expected to serve, to be allowed to want things. It's dangerous. Girls like them have to learn to put the want away, to sigh so quietly no one else hears.

"One of these days, you're going to realize how angry you are," Kiki says. "And then—oh girl. I hope I'm not around to see it."

⁞

During the day, Alder works on a construction site downtown, while Nora has her patients, so it's only during the evenings that they get to explore the city. The blues clubs and bars are too loud and packed for them, so they go to the museums that are open late—the Museum of Science and Industry; the luminous drifting jellies at the Shedd Aquarium; Degas' ballerinas curtsying at the Art Institute. They pore over every informational plaque in a state of intellectual starvation.

One night, in the whisper chamber of the Museum of Science and Industry, where two plastic barriers shaped like giant parentheses funnel sound intimately across the room, Nora watches Alder chat for several minutes with a stranger he never actually sees, their backs to each other, Alder's eyes alight with warmth and sympathy. "What did you talk about?" she asks afterward, and he shakes his head, smiling. "Nothing important. Just life."

"How do you do that?" she asks. "Strangers don't open up to me the way they do to you."

"You always have this wary look," he says. "It's your 'are-you-fucking-with-me?' face."

She catches sight of herself in the reflective glass of a building. Her mouth is a flat, questioning line, her eyes darting and suspicious. Back in the UP, this look kept her safe, preventing her father from knowing she was thinking any unsanctioned thought.

In the Fields Natural History Museum, they walk hand in hand down the Hall of Indigenous Peoples, studying the shards of pottery and bits of ancient dried corn. They're alone in the exhibit; Alder draws closer, presses his arm around her waist, while Nora breathes the cool, regulated air, glancing behind her to see if someone is following them.

"I want to ask you something," he says.

She turns to look at him. In the dark exhibit space, his face is eerily lit from beneath, as though they're around a campfire in the woods telling ghost stories.

"You were the one calling all the shots, weren't you."

"What? No. That was my father."

"Sure, he started it. But you said you were the prophet. That's where the power lies. You were the one making people believe."

She leans away. "Yes, but—I was doing what I was told. Like everyone else."

"Come on. You and I know there are two kinds of people in a cult, leaders and followers. There are the people who want to believe in something, and the people whose job it is to engineer that belief."

She starts to walk away from him, fast.

"Nora!" He hurries to catch up. "I'm sorry, okay? I'm just so tired of bullshit. I feel like I have this new chance—this one chance—to live without all the lies. Promise me you won't lie to me. I don't care what you did, as long as you don't lie about it."

She stops walking. She can't hide the quaver in her voice when she says, "I just had to speak, let it come through me. It was real to me."

"They do that. They take the best part of you." He folds his arm around her again, hungry and unashamed.

They're in front of a giant Mayan sculpture of the underworld, with Quetzalcoatl the feathered serpent, the creator and destroyer, twined around the king in a deathly embrace. *The Mayan calendar ends in 2012, a placard explains, but some scholars believe this date represented a rebirth rather than an ending.*

She wonders what would have happened to their civilization if the conquistadors had not swaggered their way onshore. If the federal agents hadn't driven up to the gates with their warrant. If there is a way to live on, past the ending.

⋮

Nora creeps into her room late that evening to find Kiki in bed, flipping through a magazine, her hair in a ruby-colored wrap. "Out with him again," she says crossly.

"Yes." Nora sits on the edge of the bottom bunk and unrolls her tights slowly down her thighs. Hides the new runs with her hand. "What's wrong with that? Weren't you the one who said I needed to go out and find a man?" She hears the irritated turn of a page over her head.

"You just better hope he is who you think he is."

"I don't know yet," Nora says, feeling a small flush of pleasure: she doesn't know. There's no map for where this is going.

"Hey, Nora."

"Yeah?"

Above her, Kiki's arm drops languidly. "You know what I realized today?"

"What?"

"No one's coming for me." She laughs, but it's not her normal laugh, not any sound Nora has ever heard her make before.

"Kiki, what happened?"

"Vincent's not coming. He kept promising and promising and asking for more time and more money. I don't know what took me so long to see it. But today I finally knew. I said, "You're not coming, are you?" And he said he just didn't know how to tell me. He's in love with this girl back home."

"Oh, Kiki." Nora stands and reaches out to Kiki, who rolls away from her.

"I *know* her. We were *friends*. He said it's different when you're with a person every day. He said he hardly remembers who I am."

She has never seen Kiki cry; she does so like a little girl, whole-heartedly, all her grief in each wrack of her body. "All this time I had a dream of what would happen. I had this plan for my life. But he was lying to me all along."

As Nora's eyes adjust to the dark room, she sees the mess around her. The dresser drawers are open, clothes trailing out. A suitcase is on the floor, half-full. "I'm going back," Kiki whispers. "They've all forgotten me. I have to go back and make things right."

Nora grabs Kiki's arm, holds it tight. "You can't. He's not worth it. You have a life here now."

"No. I can't do this anymore. I've decided."

"But you're happy here."

"It's too hard," she sobs. "I've given up too much."

Nora climbs into the top bunk with Kiki. "If he returned the money you sent him, you could do what you've always wanted." It would be enough for her to go to school for her full nursing certification. Then she could work in a hospital, have the career she's always told Nora she wanted when they are in their beds, too tired to sleep, exhausted from their work.

"I can't get that back now," Kiki says.

"But you can't just—"

"Nora, no. It's gone, all right?" She collapses into sobs again. She has always seemed so calm and resilient. But take one joist away, and then another, and everything falls. Nora knows that well enough. She hugs her friend tightly. *Vincent. You messed with the wrong girl,* she thinks to herself. Nora still remembers what it's like to be a weapon of God.

⁝

When Kiki is in the bathroom the next morning, Nora picks up her cell on the night stand, scrolls to Vincent's number, and copies it into her own phone.

She doesn't have a plan. Just the number burning in her pocket as she makes her regular rounds that day, only half-listening as patients complain about their discomforts. Even Mike has to wave a hand in front of her face to get her attention. "Hey, you there?" he asks.

"Yes, sorry. How are you feeling?"

"Okay." He's lying in bed in the pressed-back way that's become his regular position. When her patients are too weak even to raise their heads, they get a helpless, infant look. Both trusting and suspicious. Most of the functions of life are now out of their hands.

"Listen," he says. "You've seen it happen more than I have. Tell me what it's going to be like. When it ends."

Nora opens her mouth, then pauses. There are answers she could give: the peaceful one, the clinical one, the mystical one. They all have their own kind of truth. She has to remember, there is more than one way to experience the truth. "Are you sure you want to know?"

"Yes."

"Well, I don't think you'll know that much about it. Consciousness is funny. You'll become kind of detached. No matter how lucid you are, you won't be all there. Most of us assume we'll be thinking about everything we'll miss, but the dying stop missing things."

223

"But what will it feel like?"

"Nobody knows that. I think—" she looks away — "I think it might feel like when pleasure and pain run together. The brain experiences them in nearly the same way. I think it will be just—an opening up. Like breathing out one long breath that never ends."

He smiles. "Like a great, cosmic sneeze."

Her favorite patients don't lose their sense of humor, not even at the end.

She holds up Mike's catheter bag in his cramped bathroom and in the light from the small window, it glows the same way the porcupine bladder did, all those years ago: something both natural and defiled about it, soiled and saintly at once. It's startling how time shrugs up against itself. That day is still hers, all the blood and gold of it. Men were always underestimating the life and death women held in their hands. They always forgot the things women saw, caring for the dying, the being born. All of it is bloodsport.

When her time with Mike is done, she finds excuses to sweep up around the kitchen, plump the pillows behind his head. She doesn't want to leave yet. She can tell he doesn't have much time left, and she promised him he wouldn't go alone. But she can't wait here forever, standing in the doorway zipping up her coat. She's not his daughter. She listens to the hum of his ancient mint-colored fridge, like a ringing deep inside her own ears. Like the feeling of electricity in the air before a storm, back in the woods, when the birds would all go quiet. Her father would raise his head and look into the distance, watching the clouds gather over the surface of the lake.

That night, when Kiki is out of the house on a late shift, Nora dials Vincent's number. The air between her ears is heavy. She should put the phone down and go to sleep. She should let this go.

"Hello?"

"Hello," she answers. Only the voice that comes out of her is not her own. It's the old voice that used to visit her, purring and smoky and sweet.

"Who is this?" There's a warmth to his voice, the Bajan accent so musical, each fine note distinct. She can see Kiki falling in love with this voice. Being sustained by it, even through the waiting and the lies.

"A friend, darling," she says, because sometimes Kiki calls him that. "Is the weather fine? How is your girl? Is she happy you're keeping Kiki's money?"

There's a pause on the line. "I don't know what game you're playing," he says. His voice suddenly sounds stiffer, more formal.

"You think this is some sort of game?" Her father's favorite retort, throwing someone's words back at them. "Foolish, foolish man," she says. "I know what you did. You played and played her. I know your sins, I know all of them. And you think you got away with it. You think you're going to walk out of her life and no one will ever know the sin in your heart." She knows that Vincent, like Kiki, is religious. He believes in angels and demons. Kiki has told her if three crows land on the road, he takes three steps back to ward off death. He says a rosary before going on a journey. She can work with this. The old engines are creaking to life inside her.

"You have only heard her side," he says, hesitantly. "It's complicated. Love always is."

To listen to what a person says and hear the unsaid things, her father told her, is a talent: a calling. She can hear the longing and guilt in Vincent's voice. And something else: fear. He's afraid of what he's done, the way the universe has let him get away with it.

"Love?" she lets herself laugh, leaning into the slow, syrupy sound. "You think this was ever about love?"

"It was love," he insists. "We loved each other. Things just changed between us, that's all. You can't help these things sometimes. It just went bad between us, it's no one's fault."

Nora laughs again. Allows a grudging admiration to rise in the phantom space between them. As one manipulator to another, she can see the moves he's made, stringing Kiki along for each dollar. If she lets Kiki go back, she will bankrupt herself to this man before it's over. Only she can save her.

"You don't have to pretend with me, darling," she murmurs. "I know. In my world, everything is permitted."

"Who are you, anyway?" Vincent demands.

"I'm a *duppy*," she says. She's picked up a few Bajan words and expressions: a *duppy* is a bad spirit. "You know it." This voice coming out of her is uncanny and cruel, full of malice, of sleepless, ancient threat. "You held the light for the devil to see by. And if you want to be free of me, there's only one thing you can do. If you don't, I'll never, ever let you go." She releases a shriek into the phone, wild and otherwordly, the kind of inhuman sound that used to come out of her and make men and women believe the devil was among them, heavy on their backs. She's almost forgotten the joyous release of it.

By the huff of Vincent's breath, she knows he's hers. She eases the phone down from her ear, waiting a long moment before hanging up.

Her body doesn't cease trembling for hours afterward.

Nora is sipping coffee at the kitchen table a few days later when Kiki walks in, a fistful of mail in one hand. She flips through the junk, putting aside the letters for the other women. Then her hand stops. "What's this?" Kiki's nail slides down the envelope, tearing it delicately. She asks again, softer, "What's this?"

"What?"

The envelope is unmarked except for her address. Inside, there is a scribbled note, and a check from a Barbadian bank. Tiny little crosses in the memo line, to ward off the evil eye.

"He says don't bother coming," Kiki says.

"Guess you don't have to go," Nora says. But she says it too quickly. Kiki's stunned gaze shifts from the check to her.

"You knew about this?"

"I—"

"You did," Kiki says, and it's not a question. "You talked to him, didn't you. You—you did something."

"I just spoke to him once—"

Kiki drops the envelope on the table in front of her. "Goddamn it, Nora!"

"What?"

"You went behind my back. When I asked you to leave it alone. How could you. How could you?"

"I just—"

"No." Kiki scatters the pile of mail to the floor. "You used your old tricks. I *told* you not to get involved. You *promised.*"

"I got your money back!" Nora exclaims. "This was my chance to do something for you."

"I didn't want the money. I wanted my old life back."

"You can't have it," Nora says raggedly. She can't make every miracle, after all. "He doesn't love you. Now you don't have to go and find that out down the road, after he's taken more of your money. I know how people like him operate. He'd take and take from you. He'd take things forever, and you'd let him." The things she's saying are so cruel. She should have said them to her father's people long ago. "Now you don't have to go."

"You think I can take this money?" Kiki says softly. She doesn't sound angry anymore, just tired. "You don't understand the first fucking thing about relationships, Nora. Or about friendship."

"I helped you! Isn't that what friends do, help each other?"

Kiki takes the check. And then she's tearing it, smaller and smaller, into tiny bits. "You didn't care what I wanted. I didn't ask you to save me. All those people you thought you were saving, you never thought about *their* lives. What *they* wanted. Did you?"

Nora is silent to that.

"Just leave me alone," says Kiki. "Figure out your own messed-up life. When are you going to stop running away from everything? You don't even belong here. What are you *doing* here?"

"I'm trying—" She tries to draw a breath but the kitchen is shrinking around her, the air gone.

"You're afraid of what you might do," Kiki says. "And here you are, doing it. You still think you're some kind of prophet. Maybe it's time you admit what you really are."

Nora finally chokes out, "And what is that?"

Kiki stares at her, eerily calm, her face stone cold. "You're nothing. You're nobody. You haven't been allowed to form a personality. I'd pity you, if I had the time." She bends to pick up her medical bag, a gesture Nora has seen her do a hundred times, but her straight sturdy body is suddenly old, crooked with grief. "I've had enough," she says. "All your bullshit. Maybe we should both go back where we belong."

❖

Nora is sitting on the stoop of Alder's row house. She's clutching her medical bag, her feet numb in her flimsy nursing shoes.

Alder's tall shape stops at the corner, then hurries up the steps when he sees her. "Hey there, Michigan girl," he says, all worried charm. He fumbles one-handed with his keys, the other arm around her, rubbing life and self back into her body.

In his bare-walled studio he pumps up the space heater and gets a kettle going. He wraps Nora in a giant rough horse blanket, and holds her in the warmth of his body. He only asks what happened when she has stopped shivering.

"I did something bad. I betrayed her. My friend." But then nothing else comes. She can't tell Alder what she's done. It's too shameful. "I tried to help her," she says, vaguely. "I went behind her back."

"Well," he says. "You thought you were helping."

"But she told me she didn't want me to interfere."

"So why did you?" he asks bluntly.

Nora curls up tighter under the blanket. It's only sinking in now, the depth of her violation. A hot nausea swarms in her belly. "I wanted to see if I could," she says quietly. She can hear an argument in the apartment next door, voices rising and falling in familiar complaint.

"What will you do?" Alder asks.

"I don't know." Her only friend, betrayed. Maybe this life doesn't hold as much promise for her as she hoped. There's a clock that has been ticking in her mind since she received that letter in the mail. Prepare yourself. "What would you do?" she asks him, "if you knew the world was going to end?"

"Like, imminently?"

"Yes."

He presses the mug of tea between his hands, thoughtful. "I'd go back," he says. "I'd want to know who my mother was. I'd want to ask her why we were there. I'd want to talk to her about a lot of things."

Nora absorbs this, looking around his small room. The space is entirely bare of decoration, like her own. No pictures on the white-washed industrial walls, a patched mattress on the floor, an open, upside down paperback beside it. No table lamps or piles of clothes, no magnets on the fridge. It's only a temporary space, but he has staked no claim to it at all. Like her, Alder doesn't know how to live in a world of possessions. They barely know how to possess themselves.

He embraces her. "It'll be all right," he says. "You will be forgiven." Nora doesn't know if he means by Kiki, or her vengeful God. He pulls her to the mattress. He takes his time warming her cold body with his hands and lips. She touches every part of him as if it is for the last time. She didn't know sex could feel like grieving, like letting something go.

When he is asleep, her hand creeps out from under the sheet, moving to her coat, rustling around in there almost of its own volition. Finds her pocket. The slip of paper thrust in her hand at the parade, the address. She's memorized it by now, but the feel of the paper is reassuring.

When her phone rings, she jumps, and silences it without looking at the number. She looks at Alder's wristwatch on the floor instead, listening to its tiny ticking through the night.

"So what now?" Alder asks. He's shirtless and sprawled on the mattress beside her, curled around her compact shape.

"So—nothing. I go to work. You go to work." It's early morning, the birds starting to call outside his small garden-level window.

"I mean, what happens next for us?"

"You go back to California." His job ends in two weeks.

"What if I stayed?"

Her throat feels hollow. There is no room for him here. No time left to find out what they might be together. "I don't think that's a good idea."

"Why? I could get my job extended here. I could join the union, work my way up. That's what people do, don't they? They build a life."

"We barely know each other," she says, sitting up. "You can't upend your life for a stranger."

"There's nothing for me back in California. Couldn't we get to know each other?"

She looks around the room, her eyes resting on a ceramic dish on the counter piled with cash and loose coins. "You're a mess. You don't even know how to live yet."

He's silent. Good, let him retreat, realize she's a cruel bitch.

"You're still in contact with them, aren't you," he says.

Her body suddenly feels heavy. "You don't know—"

"That's the number one thing. *The* thing we can't do. Are you still making promises to them? Have you been telling them about the end of the world?"

"Just stop. You don't know what you're talking about, okay?"

"At some point you're going to have to admit," Alder says slowly, "that it was you doing the talking. It was you collecting the money. It was you telling people to sell their houses and cut ties with their families. *You* were the one telling them. And they believed you. They loved you. They changed their lives because of you."

"I was a kid. A kid who wanted to please my father."

"You were what, eighteen, nineteen at the end? People vote at that age. People go to war. You could have thought for yourself."

"You forget that I was a believer. You were one too, you know what that's like. You're not thinking for yourself, that's exactly the point. You give yourself over. You surrender everything you have."

"I want to show you something," he says abruptly. He reaches for his phone. "Have you seen this?" He starts playing a video on the small screen, fuzzy and VHS quality. As best as she can tell, someone is filming a garden patio, with two people sitting in lawn chairs, stiff and elbowy and awkward, hands folded in their laps. They have matching bowl haircuts, so it's hard to tell at first that one is a man and one is a woman. The woman begins speaking in a frail, soft voice, the voice women sometimes put on when they're expected to sound girlish and shy. "We just want you to know that what we're doing, it's entirely of our own choice," she says. "You'll see the vehicles that we leave behind. You won't understand—people won't understand."

"What is this?" Nora asks. She's too tired and confused to figure out what she's looking at.

"It's the video the members of Heaven's Gate made," Alder says. "They filmed themselves, went to Disney World, got matching haircuts and matching Nike sneakers and then committed suicide. Thirty-nine of them."

The woman looks steadily at whoever is holding the camera. Nora recognizes the stunned, tranquil look on her face. It's her mother's look in that old photograph, when she gazed up at her father.

"What do you want me to say, Alder?" She feels strangely irritable. "It's disturbing. It's creepy as hell, okay?"

Alder has stopped the video, but is still staring at the frozen frame, the man and woman smiling in their plastic chairs. "Do you think *he's* holding the camera? Marshall Applewhite?" he asks her. "They called him 'Do', like 'Do Re Mi.' He told them he was their father, and that he was the first note of creation and God and Jesus and the Buddha and everyone rolled into one. Do you think that's who she's looking at? Do you think she loves him? Is that why she goes through with it?"

Nora says quietly, "We were a family." Then her phone rings, a work number. She rolls away to answer it even as Alter is whispering, "You can't make promises to them forever. You can't promise to belong to them."

"Nora. There you are. It's Masha. We tried to call you last night, but you didn't answer."

"I had an emergency." It's still early; her shift doesn't start for an hour. "What is it?"

"It's your patient. Michael Innis. He died last night."

Acts

2013

(1,730 days since the world ended)

HER FATHER IS SITTING in the chair by the window, examining some papers, squinting under the dim light of the reading lamp.

"I want to ask you something," Nora calls out from the sink, where she is doing the dishes.

Her father looks up, expectant.

She's not even sure how to describe it, why she felt such an ominous feeling when she was inside the shed. It just could be a place where animals are slaughtered or meat is prepared for smoking. "What happens in that shed on the run?"

"Are you sure you want to know?"

"Yes," she says. Her voice is high and frightened.

He says nothing, laughs, and turns back to his papers.

She marches over to him, and yanks the papers out of his hand. They fall to the floor.

He looks up, too surprised to be angry. "You have to understand, Nora," he says. "Everything that is done here is done willingly. People need to feel that they belong. Sometimes, that means being reminded of how we need each other to survive."

He bends down to pick the papers off the floor. That's all the explanation he believes she is entitled to.

Nora returns to the sink, feeling the soapy dishes in her hands. "That's not good enough," she mutters. "We have rules. All my life you've told me we live by God's laws here."

He sets his pencil down, stands up slowly, and walks across the room toward her. One of the dishes, trembling, slips from her hands and shatters on the floor. He stares at her silently for several seconds. His eyes flint. Then he returns to the table.

Nora gets a broom and sweeps up the broken pieces. She'll have to work extra hard to earn his forgiveness for this slight.

The next morning, Nora stands in the doorway and watches her father get in his truck and bump away down the drive. He won't be back until late. She feels old, standing there with her apron on. As he makes a turn, she can see that one of his headlights, the left one, is broken and hanging out of its socket.

Nora is still standing there when Levi walks into the yard. He looks her up and down, but doesn't say anything; he knows her moods. He opens the door of the other truck and roots under the seat cushion for the keys.

"Where are you going?" she asks.

"Town," he says. "Your dad wants me to make some flyers to hand out."

Looking at him, she can feel herself coming to a decision. "Take me with you."

Levi keeps his eyes on the road, his posture straight, hands at ten and two. He doesn't have a license, but lots of people in this part of the UP have expired licenses or no plates or missing bumpers. It is warm today for late fall, so he is wearing a t-shirt, which clings to his back. She knows the hollow of the small of his back so well, the deep channel of his spine, the freckles on his collarbone. The silly untrimmed wisps of hair at his neck. Once she saw him unbraid his rattail: the long strands of chestnut hair floated around his shoulders. She laughed, "You look like a girl." The next day, the rattail was gone, buzzed roughly off.

"People have checked us out before," she says. "Remember those social workers, making sure we were getting our vitamins?"

"Not like this. Someone in town has been trying to stir up trouble about us, get an investigation going. The deacons think that person called the Feds. Now it's a mess. They're watching us."

The truck eases onto Main Street. The local kids are hanging out in the parking lot in front of the DQ. Nora stares out the window at the girls with their hands in the kangaroo pouches of their sweatshirts, talking about who knows what.

"Do you ever hang out with the kids from town?" she asks. "When you're getting supplies?"

Levi's eyes flick to her, then back to the road. "Nah."

"Why not?"

He flips through the channels on the radio, searching for the Christian station. You can always tell the music that has God in it within a few bars: something pounding and hopeful about the chord progressions. "They'd never talk to me," he says.

"What do you mean?"

"They can tell I'm different from a mile off. Even back in Indiana when we were little, nobody would talk to me. I'd just go to church every day to help out the minister. When there was nothing for me to do there, I would sit at home and look out the window at the kids playing in the street."

She touches his arm. It's astonishing to her that he could still have secrets he has never shared with her.

"I told myself they knew I was special, and that they were jealous." He tries to smile, but it comes out more like a grimace.

At the copy shop, Nora leans her face toward the beam of light that slices along the scanning tray while Levi copies flyers to hand out to potential recruits. When she is done, she presses the warm copies to her chest and approaches the counter, where the pimply teenaged girl at the counter rings her up. "That'll be $8.50." The girl flips her dark blond ponytail behind her back. The gesture calls up something for Nora—that round freckled face, hazel eyes. Before Nora can put it all together, the girl blurts out, "Hey, I know you. You're that kid from the compound."

"You're—"

"It's Vicky. We've met before. You remember my mom, Sally, from the RV park? And Roy?"

"Yeah, of course," Nora answers.

"Wow, funny," the girl says. "How's things?"

"Good, good." And then, because that word does not tell the truth about what her life is really like, she adds, "—you know." She rolls her eyes the way she's seen the other girls do in town, the way she could never in front of her father. *Ugh, life.*

"Yeah," Vicky says, and grins. A door has been opened. The strangeness of their earlier meeting has given them an unexpected intimacy. Vicky leans over the counter, snaps her gum. "My mom's back in rehab."

"Oh, Jesus!" Nora means it as a prayer, but Vicky nods, rolling her eyes. "Yeah, well, at least she's in it, you know? She's relapsed before. Shit was getting dark. And with Roy and all, she was in a bad place."

"What about Roy?"

"You didn't hear?" Vicky's eyes move over Nora's face, probing, curious. "I mean, it just happened, why would you."

"What?"

"He killed himself," she says. "A few months ago. They found him in the woods with a rope around his neck."

"Oh my God. I didn't—" There's a quivering in her hands that spreads to her wrists, her shoulders. Nora jams her hands in the pockets of her jeans. Roy with the loose, happy way he flopped his body when he prayed. Roy with the fervent gaze. Roy walking alone into the snow-covered woods. In despair. The terrible loneliness of living without the love of God. Then the thoughts come, unwelcome. Roy not walking into the woods alone. A man with a gun. Or two of them. Her father would never have forgotten how he'd briefly taken her from them. She remembers his dark promise: *the enemies of the faith will not survive this war*. What is the difference, really, between a prophecy and a promise? Before she found that shed on the run, she would never have thought it possible. But all that's certain now is how much she doesn't know.

"Hey, sorry I brought it up," Vicky says. "I thought you knew. People from that compound are always drifting around town. Seems like they know everything that goes on here." She flips her hair again. "Listen. Do you want to come out tonight? There's a bunch of us going to—a thing. You should come." It's like she's forgotten that Nora is not one of her kind, that they don't belong together smoking in the parking lot of the DQ or singing summer camp songs in somebody's backyard. Nora looks down at Vicky's hand on the counter, her chipped black nail polish, her plastic skull ring, the kind you get out of a vending machine. Maybe this is what she's been looking for.

"Yeah, okay," she answers.

Before they get back in the truck, Nora tells Levi. "It's just hanging out with some kids from town. I need you to cover for me. Please."

"You're crazy." His foot freezes on the running board before he gets into the driver's seat. "Your dad would never allow it."

"I know he wouldn't." She kicks a tire. "It's just one stupid night. Just talking with normal kids for once. Just talking." There aren't many people their age left on the compound, after the departures when the world didn't end. The ones that remain smell like deer piss and gunpowder and won't talk about anything but battle readiness.

"This is how it starts," Levi murmurs.

"How what starts?"

"Just—"

"Just what? The devil? You think the devil's going to get me tonight?" It feels good to just say his name the way outsiders do. *Before the devil knows you're dead. You'll catch the devil.* Not with that charged and ominous light. Just a word like any other word.

Levi winces. "Don't, Nora. Your dad—"

"Shut up about my dad, okay?" She shoves away Levi's offered hand. More gently she says, "You can come too." Maybe it would be all right to have him there, his serious unwavering gaze. She looks at the little line of shops and gas stations, the lights of the diner and the bar coming on, car headlights floating above the darkening road, Wisconsin one way, across the bridge downstate Michigan the other. The only major road, the only town she's known for more than a decade, the rest of the world a blank. There is so, so much she hasn't seen. They could see it together.

But Levi shakes his head. "I've been with outside people. Normal people. I know what it's like. And you don't want that, Nora."

She pictures the boy sitting in a dark house, watching children play outside.

He knows he can't stop her. "Promise me you'll be back before—" he checks his watch—"ten."

"I'll get a ride to Big Bay Road, and meet you at the turnoff," she promises.

Vicky greets Nora in the parking lot, jingling the keys to her red truck in one hand. "You sure you're not going to, like, get in trouble?"

Nora shrugs, with the studied indifference she's seen in other girls, her face blank. "I can handle it."

Vicky grins. "If you say so." They get in. The truck jolts and races on its way, the radio blasting one of the forbidden stations, Vicky singing along, tilting her chin back, something lightening in her. Deer raise their heads among the trees, startled and curious, watching them fly past.

"You know what I'm going to do when I graduate?" she says. "I'm moving to Green Bay. And then once I've saved up some money, Chicago. I swear, if I'm still living in this town a year from now, you can send your goons to shoot me." Her mouth crooks wickedly.

"It's a deal," Nora says.

They park near a public-access path into the woods, lace their fingers into two six packs of beer and head into the trees. Somewhere in the dark Nora can hear voices rippling with laughter. A branch cracks. "Halt! Who goes there?" someone shouts.

"It's Vicky."

"I know not of whom you speak!"

Vicky rolls her eyes at Nora. "It is your high priestess of the moon, returned from her questing to the north."

A teenage boy emerges from the trees, dressed like a wizard— long black cape and a pointy hat spangled with stars. "You didn't wear a costume," he says, disappointed, his voice small and normal, a wash of freckles over his round nose, his ears emerging large and pink from under the hat.

"I had to come straight from work, Jesse," says Vicky.

Nora has caught his attention. "Who's this?"

"This is Nora. My friend."

"You don't have any friends we don't know," Jesse says. Nora feels goosebumps on the back of her neck. How long did she think she could pretend to belong? She shrugs under the direct beam of his gaze.

"I'm from the church property, up the road," she says.

Jesse leans in, and a few other kids who have wandered through the trees draw close. "You mean that—militia group? With all the guns and shit?"

Her father has always told her to tell the truth, until you can't anymore. "Yeah."

"So you came to hang out with us," he says. "The Godless heathens. For our spell circle."

There's a long, beating silence. How strange she must be to all of them, these kids living ordinary lives. "Vicky didn't tell me about a spell circle," Nora says, her voice loud in her ears. "But why the hell not?"

Someone starts laughing. And then they're all laughing. Nora feels a grin creeping over her face, sheepish and defiant. "As long as you don't try to convert us," Jesse says. "We're all lost causes."

"Fair enough," Nora replies, and they walk on together to the campfire.

The kids gather in a circle. Someone jets a thin stream of lighter fluid on the fire, which explodes with a dull *whumpf* of heat into their faces. The trees close in the way they always do at night, bearing silent witness. "We call upon you, Satan," Jesse roars. "Oh Lord of Darkness, hear us!" The kids all smile, clasping each other's hands. Vicky holds out her hand, but Nora hesitates. It's all just a joke, isn't it? The devil has better things to do with his time than to show up at this campfire.

Before she can decide, Jesse grabs her hand. His eyes are black and brilliant in the firelight, his cheeks round and shiny. He's secreting something in his palm: poppers, the tiny fireworks you throw at the ground to make sparks. He's got an illusion of some kind up his sleeve. Nora knows all the tricks, the smoke machines and hand buzzers, the white ribbons that turn magically red to symbolize Christ's blood. Sometimes, people just need to see a miracle.

"Don't be scared," he whispers to her.

As if this boy could scare her, with his shabby little tricks.

"*E pluribus unum ad nauseum,*" he intones. "Oh Lord of Darkness, tell us if the Packers will win the Super Bowl."

The circle stares hopefully into the fire, which crackles and flares steadily. "Guess not," says one kid. "Packers suck!" yells another.

"Ask if we're going to graduate," says Vicky.

"Oh, great and powerful Lord of Darkness, will we all graduate?"

There's a crack and a pop of blue light; the fire hisses. "Yes, if you study for the bio final," Jesse says, and everyone whoops.

"Ask if Greg Johnson will stop kicking the shit out of me," a skinny boy with a long wobbly neck and a black eye says from the circle.

Jesse bows and asks the question. Again there's a crack and a flash, and the flames dance purple. "There will come a time when you are free from Greg Johnson," he says.

The mood is mellow. The kids sip their beer and stare into the flames. There's something hypnotic about a fire, the way it consumes without having substance itself, hovering in the air like it's imaginary, a trick of the light. Vicky's head falls to Jesse's shoulder. In the darkness, you could almost miss the fact that she's crying. His hand comes to her face and strokes it absentmindedly, a gesture full of casual tenderness.

These are not the golden high schoolers Nora's seen playing football or hanging off the backs of expensive cars. She should have known that there is more than one kind of normal; these are the kids who argue about polymers and *The Neverending Story,* who wonder what's at the center of a black hole. They're outsiders of their own sort, but they've found each other, and formed an alliance. The circle folds protectively in on itself, walling off the forces trying to get in. Nora's knees press against other knees. She tilts back her chin, looks at the stars clearing above the trees. They're all lifting a few inches off the ground, hovering in the cold night.

"Would you like to ask a question?" Jesse asks her.

Nora gazes into the fire. She wants to ask, *What's going to become of me?* Instead, she shakes her head no.

It's well past ten when Vicky drops her off on Big Bay Road. She's missed her meetup with Levi, and there's beer on her breath. And she's not sure why, but she doesn't care.

She walks down the road to the compound, finding an unguarded spot in the barbed wire to slip through. Snags her shirt on a barb and laughs to herself as it tears free. In the morning, things will be different.

There's the house up ahead, the lights out, just one glowing bead of red brilliance somewhere in the black. She'll have to come up with a good story—

The porch light clicks on. He is there, sitting with his shotgun across his lap.

"Welcome home," her father says.

Rapture

2013

(1,730 days since the world ended)

HER FATHER'S FACE IS dark. All Nora can see is the outline of his lean, familiar shape, the gun in his lap, the grill beside him on the porch glowing red with banked coals.

"I ask God every day what He wants me to do with my life," he says. "I say, God, put me in your hands. Make me an instrument of your will. And every day, He reminds me what I'm here for. My purpose is to keep his people together, and keep them safe."

He pounds his fist on the armrest on *safe*, making Nora jump. "Do you ask God that? Are you listening to the voices, the things God says through you? Or are you just some holy fool?"

He waits for her answer.

"Yes," she finally whispers. "I'm listening."

"Are you really?" he asks, stretching out the last word slow as a rubber band. "I come home, and my daughter is gone. Gone. And I find out she's out partying with a bunch of hooligans. Doing God knows what." He grabs her shirt collar, hauling her up to meet his gaze. His eyes have a cold blue fire she has never seen before. "I thought you had left like your damned bitch of a mother."

"I didn't. I was coming back!" she cries. She wrenches her collar from his grip, stumbles back.

"Don't lie to me, Nora," he says, his voice dangerous. "Don't you understand that people need you here? Everything depends on you." He presses a knuckled fist straight into her cheek, lets her feel the hard bone, how it would feel if he came at her with all his power. "If you'd been born a boy," he says, "It would be different. A girl has to be empty. Empty mind. Untouched. A repository for the Lord. Clean as a glass bottle. Don't you get that by now? Don't you see?"

Oh, she thinks. Oh. This is what it means to be a girl, what is required of her.

He picks up something that's been sitting on the coals. A long switch, burning red at the tip like a cigarette. She knows the cleansing power of fire, the way it strips old veneer off a piece of wood, turns sins into scars. "You have *responsibilities*," he says. "These people love you. They need you to be good. They need to see that goodness is possible. Does that mean anything to you?"

He cools the burning switch a little by waving it into the air, so that the burn on the backs of her legs won't quite sear her skin. She can see there's no preventing it, there never was. Her father is a man who believes in predetermination, in destiny, and this moment between them has been ordained. After he lashes her, he'll cup her chin in his hand, swipe the tears in dirty streaks from her face. He'll tell her that she shouldn't blame him for this. There was nothing he could do, they are both locked in this story, she the sinner, he the punishment. There's a cleanness that comes, after violence.

A new feeling, cold and silvery, slides through her veins, helps her bear the pain as the switch bites: anger. She won't look at him. Sinks to her knees, and turns her head away.

Nora is in bed later that night, on her stomach with wet rags on the backs of her legs, gritting her teeth through the white-hot pain, when she hears a scratching at the window, light as squirrels in the attic. She doesn't get up; she is concentrating on keeping the pain penned to a small part of her mind. She drills it down to a tiny point, dropping it down a ventilation shaft so that it gets more and more distant, falling forever.

When the scratching comes again, she rises, and shuffles to the window. "You all right?" Levi whispers.

"You told him. You told him everything," she hisses.

"I'm sorry, Nora. When he asked where you were, I had to tell him."

"Whose side are you on? His or mine?"

"Why do I have to be on different sides? Can't you come out so we can talk?"

She wants to scream at him, but she eases her jeans over her sore legs, grabs her mother's old coat, and slips outside into the night.

They walk quickly and silently through the trees until they're a safe distance from the house.

"I waited at the road like you said, but you didn't come," Levi tells her. "And then your father drove by. He knew I'd be there, I don't know how. I had to tell him where you were."

She pounds her fist into his chest as hard as she can, but she's weak with pain. He sways back but holds. "Why couldn't you just lie for me? Why couldn't you lie, just once?"

"Nora, I can't. Lying lets the devil in."

These things they say, their charms and protections, never sounded so inadequate. She strikes him again, but her heart isn't in it. "Why couldn't you be loyal to me? Don't we mean something to each other?"

"We do."

They're so exposed here, out among the trees. He leads her to one of the dry goods sheds scattered across the compound. This one is filled with chains of drying onions. The smell is sharp and earthy, surprisingly sweet. He shakes her shoulders urgently. "Why did you have to go? Why can't you just be good?"

She's crying now. "I just wanted to see," she gasps. "I just wanted to see what normal people—"

"You didn't just want to see," Levi says. "You wanted to be one of them. You always have." He kisses her ferociously, so that blood runs from her lip. Time wallows. They might have been standing like this for hours. They might have been kissing like this all their lives. If her punishment was predetermined, then this is too. He lays her down on the dusty floor of the shed. Onions and drying apples giving off their ripe stink. "I'll be loyal," he promises in between each kiss, each gasp for breath. "I'll be loyal."

The sex is not like wolverines shrieking in the woods. It's quiet, fumbling. You have to know what you're doing, it turns out. And both of them are so dumb. Eventually, though, the place she has no name for is named. A wave of feeling drowns her. Her body loosens, time still windless. Levi cries a little. It's almost funny, how ordinary it all is. Will people really lose their place in heaven for this? When they're done, she holds him, bruised and grateful and sorry.

"We have to get back," she says gently. But they stay for a while longer, waiting for hellfire, a lightning bolt to strike them down, a voice promising damnation. Levi butts his head tenderly into her chest. An owl calls; a damp flutter of wings tells them he's caught his mouse.

⁂

Strangers keep showing up at the gates of the compound, asking if they can attend services. They wear puffy nylon jackets and big aviator sunglasses that hide their eyes. When a deacon asks who sent them, how they heard about the church, they don't have an answer. Her father turns them away. Nora still sees them around town, sitting in the cabs of pickup trucks, taking up space in parking lots, congregating in packs. Levi told her he has spoken to a few of them, but he wouldn't tell her what was said. Just stay away from them, he warns her.

Since that night in the shed, there has been another night, and another. Always furtive and rushed, half-dressed, their breath misting the cold air. And then, leaving separately, guilt red and livid on their faces.

Nora pulls the prayer card her mother left out of its hidden place at the back of a drawer. It's battered from being handled. She stares at the soft-focus drawing of St. Anthony on one side, a bald, solemn monk holding his small holy child. On the other side, text explaining that St. Anthony is the patron saint of lost things, and that if you have lost something, you should pray for it in his name.

She imagines her mother traveling away, sitting on a bus, maybe, or driving at night, watching the yellow lines on the road, a little freer each mile she gets from her monstrous child. Nora grips the card in two hands and tries to tear it down the middle, but the plastic lamination won't give.

She feels slow and strange, like she's walking under water. Gathering wood or kneading bread dough, everything's a fog. She's quiet in church; the voices won't speak. But everyone is too anxious to notice, with the strangers circling the compound. Unmarked vans have been seen parked at the mouth of the road. A sympathetic neighbor came by to tell her father that people had been to his house asking questions. They want to know what her father preaches, and whether he's making any plans for violence. The deacons step up their patrols, reporting on hunters moving through the woods in orange vests but not picking up any kills.

Riding in the truck with Henry and her father, Nora listens to them argue about tactics. This is the sort of conversation not usually for her ears, but they're both agitated these days, their arguments spilling out into car rides and dinner conversations.

"The younger guys, the deacons, want some kind of action," Henry says. "They don't want to sit around and let our guns get taken away."

"We came here to survive," their father responds. "Not to burn up in some standoff. Surviving means using common sense, waiting out a conflict instead of letting it all blow up."

"They came here because they believed in something, and they thought we'd all stand together if our principles were tested."

"We will. But our fight isn't with some po-dunk sheriff's department. It's not with the FBI either. It's with principalities. With spiritual forces—"

"—In heavenly places. I know," Henry finishes the verse for him. "You told me to learn the book, and I've learned it. You've primed us to prepare for a war. Isn't this what we've been waiting for?"

"You want to launch a crusade? Bring everyone in this community down with you?" their father says. Suddenly, his hand slaps the back of Henry's head, driving him forward. There's more force behind it than usual. Nora notices for the first time how his neck softened an instant before their father's hand struck. From long habit, Henry knew the blow was coming, and how to prepare for it.

Her mother once pointed her to a line in Genesis about "the way of women." The way of women was what made them unclean. "They're talking about your period," she said in that frank, sardonic way she sometimes spoke when her father wasn't present. "When men talk about it, this is what they say. But it's nothing to be ashamed of. It's just a clock. It's the way our bodies keep time. When the clock stops, it means another one is starting inside. You understand?"

At night, Nora lies in bed in the dark and waits for her clock to start ticking, but it won't. She's been late before, living this hardscrabble life, in the lean winter months when they were low on meat and had to boil the marrow out of deer bones to thicken their miserable turnip soups.

The world is holding its breath, waiting.

⁂

Nora has to wait until dawn, when the changeover of the night watch happens, to dash through the woods to Rachel's. She hasn't been back since she saw the pickup truck pull up after she left.

Rachel opens the door. She's wearing a flannel nightgown, squinting, a coffee mug in hand. "It's so early."

"Am I a whore?" Nora asks abruptly. She figures another one would know.

Rachel freezes, the cup to her lip. "Nora. What's happened?"

"I—I'm—"

"Did someone hurt you?"

"No." Her voice is nothing but a whisper. "I wanted it. But now I'm—"

Rachel's eyes narrow with understanding.

"Am I a whore?" Nora asks again.

Rachel stares at her for a long time. "We're all whores," she finally says. "You, me, all the girls out there. Anybody who ever did something because they liked it. Anybody who ever stole a little pleasure from God." She pulls Nora inside, plucks her jacket from its hook on the wall. "The first thing is to get a test. Then we'll figure out what to do."

"I can't go to town."

"What?"

250

"I'm not allowed. All of us, we're on lockdown. And somebody would see me. It's never been so secure before."

"Stay here, then. I'll get the test." She keeps muttering while she laces her boots. "I knew this would happen. If you would just—" On her way out the door, she says, "Did you know, my name isn't even Rachel? Your father named me that. He said I needed a good Biblical name for my new righteous life." She closes the door.

Nora is alone. She sits down on a chair, admires Rachel's drawings on the walls. She didn't understand what might happen, and she did. She knew the consequences, but she didn't really believe. She knew the universe liked its angels and emissaries pure. She thought she was one of those. Blessed; lucky; whatever you want to call it.

Nora yanks up her pants and returns to the kitchen, and together they stare at the result. Rachel gives a short, angry shake of the head. "So, what are you going to do, Nora?"

Silence opens up between them, stretches in the room.

More than anything, she wants her mother. But she knows what her mother would say: I thought you knew what it took to survive in this place. It's always been the same. Whenever you seek purity, there has to be a purge. This has always been the math.

"I'm not going to tell you what to do." Rachel's voice is unexpectedly gentle. "But I'll help, if you want me to. You have to decide. No one can do it for you."

Levi is waiting outside the house when Nora returns. "Where were you?"

"Nowhere. Just walking around."

"You shouldn't go wandering off alone. It's not safe." Levi has his .22 slung over his back, the way all the men carry their guns around these days, looking over their shoulders, hunting for noises in every stand of brush. She hadn't noticed before how tall he has become, but still too thin, his cheeks hollowed, his wrists bony.

"I always used to walk alone," she says. It's a dumb answer, but she doesn't know what else to say. She wants to embrace him, feel his warm cracked lips on her lips, on her neck, her earlobe. She feels loose and open and strange, like something has already started turning lights on inside her, barging into rooms where it doesn't belong. If she could get a moment alone, she'd tell him. And then, together, they'd know what to do. Levi always knows what to do. The plan he's laid out for his life is so clear, every sentence is already written.

She turns and wretches into a bush. When she rises, wiping her mouth, Levi is staring. "I'm scared," she says, by way of explanation. He puts his arm around her. If she asks, he'll protect her. She's sure of it.

"Meet me tonight," she says. "Our place."

His eyes dart. "There's a church meeting tonight. About the investigators."

"Tomorrow night, then. I need to talk to you."

He nods.

※

The church meeting is frayed and tense. Old-timers shout questions at her father and Henry. How many feds are watching them right now, and what are they planning to do? "The worst thing we could do is panic," her father says. "We can't fail the first real test the Lord has given us. There will be harder times before it's all over."

The deacons are excited, pacing at the back of the room, outfitted in their tactical armor and black market bullet-proof vests, semis strapped to their backs. They're ready for war. Her father has to shout to make himself heard over their arguing.

"When the end comes," he declares, "It's not going to be in the form of federal agents and law and order. It's not going to be over permit issues and property taxes. There will be angels and demons, believe you me."

"But the devil comes in worldly ways, too," someone shouts. "He doesn't always bear a sword. Sometimes he has a clipboard and a gun."

"Quiet!" When her father's voice goes iron-hard, the room obeys. "I know we're facing a threat, maybe the greatest threat we've ever faced as a group before," he says. "But we must be sober-minded and watchful. *Your adversary the devil prowls around like a roaring lion, seeking someone to devour.* I've received a message. I know what's going to happen."

He looks out over his ragged, restless congregation. Nora can tell that he's about to say something momentous. She knows his every mood.

"We know that in the end times, there will be certain signs," he begins. His voice is strangely hoarse, rough with emotion. "A special woman touched by God will give birth to a child, and this child will signal the beginning of the long war. The book of Revelation tells us this. We've been waiting for the sign, and my friends, now we know. The woman is among us, and she will give birth to the child."

A long, shocked silence follows. Nora listens to the beating of the blood in her ears.

"We should have known all along who it would be," he says. "Only our girl could be the one. Our vessel of the Spirit."

His eyes flick to her. And so do everyone else's. They are all staring, the way they always do when she begins to speak in tongues. But now she wishes she were invisible. She wants to burn up in a column of holy fire.

Her father bows his head, intones the lines from Acts:

'And it shall come to pass in the last days, says God,
That I will pour out of My Spirit on all flesh;
Your sons and your daughters shall prophesy,
Your young men shall see visions,
Your old men shall dream dreams.

They don't say anything on the short walk home. No one turns on a light when they shuffle back into the house. Henry mumbles something about how late it is and vanishes down the hall. It's just the two of them standing in the dark.

"How did you know?" she asks in a small voice.

"I know everything that goes on here," he replies.

She opens her mouth, to beg his forgiveness. But he speaks first. "Nothing happens without my permission. Everything is part of the plan. Haven't you figured that out?"

An understanding is finally coming to her, arriving from the end of a long fuzzy corridor, but she doesn't want to look straight at it, to see what he's trying to tell her.

"This is going to bring us together again. We were losing our purpose, our vision. This will hold us together." His hand startles her in the darkness, rough on her shoulder. "Levi will take good care of you."

They have always been the perfect team. The way they drove all night on winding forest roads, searching for souls to save. The way they could work a crowd, the call and response, picking up where the other left mystery. She should have remembered how he saw the birth of his own children as a sign from God. It stuns her now, her stupidity: for her whole life, he's been pulling the strings just so, building things she can scarcely imagine. She wonders if Levi ever really loved her, or liked her, even. If all this time, he's been carrying out his orders, the ever loyal Levi.

She bites her lip, tasting blood in the dark. He touches her hair. Then he walks away from her into the private corners of his house.

⁝

Nora can see her breath in the early morning chill, the fog lying heavy on the trees, the sound of the lake a steady purr as she runs along the secret paths only she and Levi know. She is carrying a rifle; if anyone asks her where she was, she can say she was out hunting.

She waited by the shore for him, growing cold and damp as the night went on, the nocturnal animals rustling noisily; several times, she risked calling out for him, in case he was searching and couldn't find her. But he didn't come. By the time the sky turned blue black with the approaching dawn, she knew he wouldn't appear; she could hear the deacons, and what sounded like people gathering by the front gate. She should have prayed then, asking for guidance; surely she would have been given a sign. But she didn't. She waited another hour, hoping, and then slowly letting go of that hope, realizing she was alone, and that no one would tell her what to do.

She ducks under the barbed wire at the border of the property and then she's home free, running across the meadow of feral wheat. The little house rears up alone in the grass; when she knocks, Rachel is quickly at the door, her hair morning wild.

"I need your help," Nora says, still panting. "Please."

In the kitchen, she's expecting Rachel to prepare something in her mortar and pestle, or perhaps boil bitter herbs on the stove, the way her mother used to. But instead she produces a rumpled paper pharmacy bag. "What, you thought I was going to brew some potion for you?" she snaps, seeing the surprised look on Nora's face when she shows her the bag. "You're in the wrong century." Her tone quickly softens. "You always have been."

There's an orange bottle in the bag with two pills rattling inside it. "Take the first one now, and the other one in three hours," Rachel instructs her.

"And it'll be—done?"

"This will be." Rachel tilts her head. "But what then?"

"Then? It will be okay again." She'll pray and prophesy the way she always has, and life will go on, its rituals intact. She takes a swig of water from a glass on the kitchen table and swallows the first pill.

There's a breeze coming through an open window, fluttering the sketches pinned everywhere of birds, deer, a fox with a mouse in its grinning jaws. In the next room, a twin bed with a homemade quilt. For a moment, Rachel's life presents itself to Nora in all its solitude. She is not a fairy tale witch or a devil in disguise—she is a woman living according to her own plan, with all the freedom and compromise that entails.

Rachel nods at Nora. "Go on, then. For God's sake, don't let them catch you." She touches the top of her head, a blessing or a warning, or a goodbye.

The woods are quiet, everything so still that Nora can hear the tiny *tic, tic, tic* of leaves falling to the ground. Like the ticking of a clock.

Three hours. The lone white pill rests in her deepest inner pocket—she is scared to be caught with the orange bottle on her. She can already feel her stomach turning uneasily, the beginning of a deep muscular ache in her back and belly.

I couldn't give you much of a home. I couldn't give you any kind of life. There is barely enough room here for me to breathe.

As she gets close to home, Nora hears the sound of ATVs roaring;

voices drift down the path. There is a group of people near the front gate to the compound, milling around in an uneasy scrum.

If I let you survive, then I won't.

When she was young and didn't know any better, Nora would ask her father questions about the things that didn't make sense to her. Why was Lot's wife turned into a pillar of salt, simply for looking back? By looking back, he explained, she showed longing for the sinful city they were leaving behind. She was doubting the justice and rightness of God's plan for them. She had the audacity to want a different fate for herself. Nora pictures this unnamed woman, fleeing the burning city, her husband tugging her through the sand. Wiping tears from her eyes as she gives up the only life she's known. *Just one look back—*

On the other side of the gate, a cluster of vans, and men in navy jackets and black baseball caps, some armed, some wearing military style boots and bulletproof vests. A tall, stocky woman with a long ponytail and a pistol at her hip is at the front, speaking to her father. The two of them seem calm, their gazes direct and challenging. It's not yet a standoff, just a conversation. Still, the police and the church members clustered on either side of the fence are tense, playing with the holsters of their guns. Her father is telling his usual story about their community, the safety and privacy they seek here. But the woman cuts him off with a raised hand. "Mr. Delaney, I don't care about your worship or your beliefs. We're just here to make sure no laws are being broken."

"I respect that."

"But you see, we have a problem." The woman shifts her weight, draws her hands back onto her hips, showing off her gun in its holster, her bullet-proof vest, the shield emblazoned on her jacket. "We have a warrant here to investigate your property on suspicion of illegal substances being manufactured and sold, and of illegal arms purchases. But I need my people to be safe before we can enter. And you've got a contingent of heavily armed individuals here. We're going to need you to disarm. And we're going to have to check the permits on all of your weapons."

Her father doesn't back down. "I need my people to feel safe, too. They're a certain type that doesn't like being separated from their protection. They know their rights."

The woman does not seem surprised. They've sent their expert today, the person who knows how to keep things calm. "With a warrant, we have the right to enter this property and search it, Mr. Delaney. Stalling now won't do a thing."

Her father catches sight of Nora at the edge of the crowd, waves her over. She walks hesitantly toward him; once she is close enough, he grabs her arm, pulling her into his grip. "I got my kids here. This is my daughter. We're a family here, officer. We've got nothing to hide but a heck of a lot to protect."

She's not a kid anymore, not by anyone's guess. But her father is determined to play the old games. Suddenly, her stomach cramps and she doubles over.

"What's wrong with you?" he mutters out the side of his mouth.

"I feel sick."

"Well quit acting like it or it'll be another excuse for them to barge in here. They'll call child protective services."

"I'm nineteen," she says loudly, so that even the woman on the other side of the gate can hear. "They don't call CPS for nineteen-year-olds."

He's silent for a moment, scanning her face.

"Mr. Delaney, everyone I deal with has a family," the woman says. "I'm not going to wait much longer before we open this gate by force."

There's a loud *snick* of metal as someone cocks his gun.

Nora pulls away and runs through the crowd, pushing people aside, stumbling her way to the nearest line of trees. She runs past the meadow. Someone is burning a bonfire on the hill, tossing things into it—sheaves of paper, an old computer. Another person is running in and out of one of the buried arms bunkers, passing guns to a line of waiting, nervous young men. The door of a trailer is wide open and the person inside is throwing things out unto the ground to be added to a burning pile in their yard. It's past time, the hour is late, and all their worry and preparations have not been enough.

Nora is nauseous but she has to keep going. It's past morning now and the mist is rising from the trees, as if the ground is steaming. She digs in her pocket for the second pill and swallows it dry.

She stumbles deeper into the woods, searching for a place where no one can find her. She slides into a shallow ravine ankle-deep in fallen leaves, the damp loam soaking her shoes. *Warning, Danger* reads a sign on an old sawhorse with weather-chipped paint. The old mine shaft where she and Levi stared down into the darkness is nearby. She creeps nearer, stumbling in the brush, the pain in her belly coming in pulses. She reaches out for the reassuring solidity of a tree and slips to her knees, eases her pants down her trembling legs. *Dear Jesus Christ, have mercy on me, a sinner. Dear Jesus Christ*

A crow calls like a warning. Far away the sound of a gunshot rips through the air.

The pain stabs deeper now, makes her dig her knuckles into the harsh bark of the tree. God, she knew, will not abide love that He does not own. Far above, a crow settles on a branch to watch her. In the quiet she hears it ruffle its feathers. She feels a strange kinship; it seems to be waiting out the pain with her.

Then a gushing warmth, hot sticky blood on her thigh. A torrent. She's crying with relief. It'll be all right now, everything can go on the way it always has. "I'm sorry," she breathes, and does not know who or what she is speaking to: the little life seeping out of her now, her father,

God. She cannot be what any of them need her to be.

Nora waits until the bleeding eases a little. Her underwear is gory. She hikes up her old canvas pants slowly, leaning on the tree to steady herself. The rifle she's been carrying all day is lying in the brush, and she re-shoulders it shakily. She has to get moving. She has the animal instinct not to linger where blood is in the air.

"There you are."

She jumps and whirls; the voice sounds like her father. But it's only Henry, standing a little distance away. He's wearing his raccoon tail cap, a shotgun dangling loose in the fingers of one hand. "Everyone's looking for you."

"What's happened?" Nora asks, a little breathless.

"It's started," he says, and his voice is exhilarated. "Someone fired a warning shot. We're not sure who did it—them or us. They fell back but they're regrouping. No one's backing down. Dad needs you to talk to everyone."

She shudders. The thought of speaking in tongues now, praying to God, seems impossible. "What can I do?"

"Prepare them," he says. "Tell them what's going to happen. Give them a prophecy. Remind them they have to protect you." He steps closer, peering into her face. "Just make up something the way you always do."

"I don't just make it up."

"Of course you do." Henry's gaze is flat and direct. "You and Dad play your game. You play it real well." His voice slides down the word *real*, his hand slides down the barrel of the gun. "The two of you turned this story around, didn't you? Everyone's forgotten what you really are."

"Stop it, Henry."

"And they said, 'Should he deal with our sister as with a whore?'" he chants softly. The gun in his hand tilts up toward her.

"What are you doing?" She takes a step back. Her rifle is difficult to reach, slung on her back. *But he has a shotgun, I have a rifle,* she says to herself. It seems important but she doesn't remember why.

Henry takes another step. "Fuck you, Nora. I'm so tired of you having your way. The golden child. The chosen one. Whatever you think you are. I know the truth. I do the work. I read the books. I'm the one who knows what all this means."

He's close enough to touch the muzzle of his gun to her chest. He half-raises it, aims somewhere between her legs. She feels another wet trickle of blood as if in response. "What does all this mean, then?"

"This is all going to end," he says. "Maybe right now. And I know you're not special, I'm not like all the others who think you're going to save us. You're a whore."

"Maybe you're right," she says. Poor, unloved brother, doesn't even know what he knows. She thought she could return to the house and everything would be all right. But it won't be, and maybe she knew that when she took the pill; when she got in Vicky's truck; when she knocked on Rachel's door. She feels sorry for Henry, all those long years in a dim room with one book, just one book, memorizing all those theories about destruction. What does he want from her? The gun keeps rising, now pointing at her chest. Their father taught them both the same lesson: never point a gun anywhere except where you intend to shoot.

Then the gun stops. "What's—that?" Henry is staring at the blood-spattered earth, the leaves still dripping. It's obvious some violence has been done here. He might understand, he might figure it all out.

She shoves him hard into the leaves and runs and runs. Past men lining up rifles and women burning things on the hill. Past secret buried bunkers filled with gasoline and tinned peaches and maps and board games and bibles, their entrances marked by planted clover. The community is streaming to the front gate. The standoff is behind her, deacons are patrolling the borders on either side; there's nowhere to go but the lake. She can hear Henry thrashing through the brush behind her. If he catches her—she doesn't know what will happen. She doesn't know who her brother is, or what he's capable of. The gun thumps on her back. *He has the shotgun, I have the rifle* repeats in her head.

She staggers to a halt on the cliff edge. Fifteen feet below is the rocky beach, the lake in its foaming advance along the shore. And lining the cliff edge are the caves. They're all dead ends. But one! Where her father has hidden the canoe. A last-ditch escape plan, a final preparation underneath all the other preparations. *If our family should need to escape—*

"Nora!" Henry is callinf for her, his voice terrifyingly close.

She eases herself down the cliff face, trying not to hurry, remembering her previous fall. She slips and scrabbles at the iron-red soil. Finally touching the shore, she runs to one cave mouth and then the next. There's a long row of these little pockmarks in the stony cliffs; if she picks the wrong one—

"Nora!"

He's so close. But he can't see her below the cliff edge until he's right on it. She stumbles forward, into one cave and then out again—was it this one? This one? It was so long ago that her father wrapped the canoe up in oilcloth and lashed it to a metal spike deep inside one of these dark holes in the earth. She remembers a narrow entrance with a bottleneck halfway through, almost like an hourglass.

"You filthy whore!"

His voice. She dives into one of the caves. The water is up to her calves. She sloshes in the darkness, praying that she's chosen the right one. *Jesus Christ, have mercy on me, a sinner. Jesus Christ, have mercy on me*

There. Tucked away at the back, bobbing gently on the water. A long canvas shape, covered in pine needles and lakeweed. She tears the canvas off; the canoe looks all right, it's still floating. She unwinds it free of its mooring and eases it through the dark. There's a moment where it gets stuck in the hourglass and she struggles with it. If Henry gets to the opening, there'll be no way out. She hauls the canoe with all her strength. And then it's moving, and she is outside, the canoe with her, heavy and dragging on the shore.

Henry is still descending the cliff face, maybe fifty yards away. She crouches behind the beached canoe and shoulders her rifle. Her breathing stills, her shoulders are steady. She has time to line up the shot just the way her father taught her, her quarry in the crosshairs. This is why it mattered, that she has the rifle and he the shotgun; hers is the long-range weapon. If she can keep him at a distance, she'll be in control.

"Don't move," she shouts.

Henry takes the last step down the cliff face. He turns, slowly. He can see her there, just a face behind the canoe, the rifle trained and steady.

"Please," he says, and the old, haughty tone is back in his voice. "I'm your brother."

Neither of them move. She doesn't know what to do. She knows only that she is a fierce and dangerous thing, half-wild, half-blessed, glory and retribution at her fingertips. The power to forgive and to destroy. Death in the woods is no great event. It happens every day. The animal part of her understands this, and it will do anything to survive. She can feel it as a liquid certainty, pumping through her body.

"I never wanted to hurt you," he says. "I just wanted him to love me."

Nora lowers the rifle. For the first time she wonders how it was for him to lose their mother. How she might have been the last wall of protection between Henry and their father.

She knows she can't go back.

"Don't come after me," she calls to him.

She eases the canoe into the water, feels it buck and bob, impatient in its natural medium. She clambers in and starts to paddle. It's too far to cross the lake; that was always a ridiculous dream. But she can paddle parallel to the shore until she's beyond the compound's borders. She can make it to town, catch a ride with a trucker or tourist going downstate, keep driving. This canoe has clean clothes, a little money, a little food, a chance at survival. She can't think past that. Can't think about the moment when her father, when Levi, discover she's gone. "Tell them—" she calls to Henry.

She passes close enough to be in the range of his shotgun. He could wound her badly, or sink her fragile little escape vehicle. But he doesn't raise his gun. He just watches as she glides past, and then he's growing smaller on the red coast, her brother at first, then just a boy she thinks she knows, then a stranger, then a shape; then nothing.

On Recognizing Him in our Midst

There was that time you called me into your den when I was seven or eight years old, and you announced to me that the devil was awake and active in our world and that it was up to us to stop him. You told me you'd need all my strength and all my knowledge, and I felt so proud that you called upon me, that you needed me. I asked how we'd know the devil—by sight? By looking at his feet? Or maybe we should ask every suspect person to recite the Lord's Prayer, which the devil cannot do without making a mistake.

You asked me, Are you stupid? You can't recognize him with a silly trick. He's in your heart. In the things you do.

That I do?

Yes. He's in you just like everyone else. The only question is if you'll listen to him, or if you'll listen to me. I'm not holding out much hope. If you're slow, he'll always be a step ahead.

But I'm your—

Then act like it. The saved are special. Show me you're special.

Then you sent me away, and you called her in. I sat with my back to the closed door and I listened to you tell her that you'd need her, all her God-given grace, and that she had something inside her that no one else had, and it was going to save them all when the time came. I listened, and felt the cool hard wood of the door against my spine, and the scrape of the carpet on the bare soles of my feet, and listened to the buzzing in my ears that could have been cicadas or it might have been something else entirely, because the buzzing never really left. It's a droning in my ear, like someone is whispering very very softly, telling me why I'm the way I am, telling me what to do and who to blame, if only I could hear it.

It's been with me all this time.

Chicago, April

NORA KNOCKS ON THE door and Emily answers. She's wearing a black dress and stockings, her hair drawn back, doing her best Irishwoman in mourning. Her mouth draws to a thin line. "Oh. It's you, after all."

"I just heard. I'm so, so sorry."

"When I called last night," she says, one hand on the door, blocking Nora from entering, "they said his regular nurse wasn't available. Some stranger had to come instead."

Nora tries to still the trembling in her lips, her hands. "I'm so sorry I wasn't able to be there. I hope it was peaceful."

"Well, I think it was." Now it's Emily who struggles to master herself. "I tried to do what you said—with the lollipops, and the new pain patch every few hours. I don't think he suffered." She finally lowers her arm from the door. "I guess you'll want to come in." She turns and walks into the house, letting Nora follow.

Nora passes through each room, seeing it as if for the first time. There is the spot by the bay window, with the ancient television, the ratty armchair; there is the sitting room crowded with knickknacks, baseballs, photographs on the mantle; there is the kitchen table where she fed him spoonfuls of soup when his hands were numb; there is the back window where he looked out on his weedy little garden overrun with tenacious nettles. Emily is talking busily on his cordless phone, making arrangements. There are always so many people to call. Where were they when he was dying?

Nora trails upstairs to the bedroom. His body is on a gurney beside the bed, covered in a white sheet, about to be wrapped like a mummy with a neat bow over the face. Then his sheeted form will go inside the black zip bag. The funeral director, a tall morose man she's worked with before, nods. "Quiet?" he asks, as he always does.

"I don't know," Nora answers. Her throat burns, her eyes burn. She touches the white robed figure on the gurney lightly. He wouldn't want any empty promises of the afterlife, or reassurances of heaven. There's nothing she can say now, nothing that will absolve her.

Emily is in the doorway. "Are you finished?"

Nora turns. "Can I ask—are you planning a church service?"

"Of course I am." She's still holding the phone; she has plenty to do. "Why?"

"It's just that—he told me he didn't want a service, or a wake. He didn't want a religious ceremony. He was very clear on that."

Emily glares at her. "His *family* wants a service. There are rituals you do, things you say. How can you possibly know better than his family?"

"His family never came in all the months he was sick," she says, and regrets it instantly. But it's true; she was the one there for the late nights, for the long painful days, the steady waiting. If that is a measure of devotion, then she was devoted.

"This is none of your business." Emily puts a hand on one hip. "He wasn't your father. You really had me going there for a minute. I thought you cared about him a little. But when the time came, where were you?"

Nora takes a step back. "I'm sorry." *Afterward*, Kiki taught her, *You go, quick and quiet. Now the family turns in to itself. Now they have to figure out how to grieve, and you can't help them do it.*

Nora returns to the house to gather a few things: her clothes, minus her uniforms; the few small possessions she's accumulated. Her mother's prayer card, the small battered knife she carried with her in the early Chicago days and nights, when she slept in train stations. It's midday; the house is empty, the cold spring wind whooshing outside.

She pauses to open the pocket-sized, black dog-eared bible she carried with her from the canoe's emergency cache, that is always on her night table. She's returned to it diligently over the years, revisiting verses that feel like old friends. Once, a woman patient looked at her and asked, "What's going to happen to me? Have I been good enough? Who's going to love me?"

Nora went home and opened the bible, searching for old comforts. But the more she searched for affirmation, the more she found that women were portrayed as betrayers, profiteers, pleasure seekers. She started going through the bible with a pen, careful and thorough, searching for passages about whores:

Genesis 38:24   *And it came to pass about three months after, that it was told Judah, saying, Tamar thy daughter in law hath played the harlot; and also, behold, she is with child by whoredom. And Judah said, Bring her forth, and let her be burnt.*

Leviticus 19:29   *Do not prostitute thy daughter, to cause her to be a whore; lest the land fall to whoredom, and the land become full of wickedness.*

Leviticus 21:9   *And the daughter of any priest, if she profane herself by playing the whore, she profaneth her father: she shall be burnt with fire.*

Judges 19:2   *And his concubine played the whore against him, and went away from him unto her father's house to Bethlehemjudah, and was there four whole months.*

Proverbs 23:27   *For a whore is a deep ditch; and a strange woman is a narrow pit.*

Ezekiel 16:28   *Thou hast played the whore also with the Assyrians, because thou wast unsatiable; yea, thou hast played the harlot with them, and yet couldest not be satisfied.*

Ezekiel 23:43   *Then said I unto her that was old in adulteries, Will they now commit whoredoms with her, and she with them?*

Hosea 2:4   *And I will not have mercy upon her children; for they be the children of whoredoms.*

Revelation 17:16   *And the ten horns which thou sawest upon the beast, these shall hate the whore, and shall make her desolate and naked, and shall eat her flesh, and burn her with fire.*

And so on.

Nora adds to this what she thinks she knows, now, her father would say: a whore is a woman who destroys a family.

She imagines great flocks of whores moving through the Abrahamic landscape like herds of wild bison, as common a sight as plagues of locusts. She pictures them walking down the streets, arm in arm the way girlfriends loop arms and laugh and stumble together after a night out in Chicago. She sees them swaying to whatever music was played back then—pipes from animal horns, goatskin drums. She sees them flashing the bare skin of their ankles and arms and not caring. Letting their hair flow loose and knotty and wild. Dancing together because righteous men will not touch them, and are aghast at their carefree joy. Drinking more than they should. Carrying the exhaustion of such public, relentless shame like a child on a hip. Crying sometimes— whores weep like women do. Laughing at the men warding them off with garlic and charmed oils and goat sacrifice. Opening a side door for those same men, waving the regulars in. Having sex for fun. Having sex for money. Regretting nothing. Regretting some things. Praying to God. Believing and feeling redeemed by belief. In their private moments, hoping for things that no God will ever give them. Paying the price for their lives, again and again, willingly, with the full measure of their devotion. Saying to no one in particular the phrase reserved only for Gods, *I am that I am.*

She wonders when she joined their company. If she traces the line back through her life, she can't find a moment when she wasn't one of them. All the women she knows in the outside world, they're part of it, too. They'd fold her in if she asked, welcome her the way a church opens its doors, the way a mother loves her monstrous child.

She lays out the shirt she borrowed from Kiki, the turquoise one with the hearts on the sleeves, along with her nursing bag, and lets herself out.

That evening, Nora tries to describe her day to Alder, Mike's body, Emily, her leaving her house and nursing. As she speaks, she notices he won't look at her, his eyes sliding away when she tries to meet his gaze. "What is it?" she finally has to ask.

A sheepish, cringing smile comes over his face. "I met this guy today, on my lunch break," he begins. "The guy was in a bind. He said he was on his way to deposit his paycheck, but that he'd been mugged. Gunpoint, couple of teenagers, broad daylight, can you believe it? His month's rent, gone." He goes on to tell her that the guy claimed he knew Joe, who he said was one of Alder's coworkers, and that Joe would vouch for him. He was good for the money, of course he was: just write down your address, your email, he told him. You'll get it back in the mail. Swear to God.

Alder walked with him to the nearest ATM, withdrew $400, and handed it over. "Only now I think I didn't write my email address right."

"Jesus," she says.

"What?"

"Just think for a second. Did you ask for Joe's last name? Did you ask to see his pay stub, or anything else? Did you ask him if he'd gone to the police?" She stops, because there's no point in grilling him further. "You lost your money, Alder."

"He seemed like he really needed it. He promised he'd pay me back. He gave me his phone number."

"Try calling it." She shakes her head. He's so poorly equipped for life outside the cloistered world he grew up in. He can't possibly understand the complexity of what she's trying to tell him—care and family and the demands of hospice, privacy and personal boundaries. There's simply no way they could make this work like normal people.

"What's wrong?" he asks, noticing a faraway look on her face.

"You can't even see how you've gotten scammed. You're still a child." Last night, while she lay unsleeping on his mattress under the heavy weight of his arm, she reached out to the warped spiral notebook he keeps by the bed. Flipping though it, she found page after page with a single line:

To whom it may concern (my mother),

Dear biological mother,
Dear mother figure
Dear miss
Dear "mother"
I think you may be my
Are you my mother?

He is so thoroughly fucked up. They both are. By their mothers, and their fathers, and the things they've done. She thought they could figure out a way to be together in the outside world, but the outside world is more challenging than she thought. Deceit is everywhere. The country is coming apart, fragment by fragment, family by family; the warring factions have found their sides and dug in, as her father predicted. Both sides hungry for the cataclysm. The war is here.

She sits on the edge of the mattress and he rubs her shoulders, but she doesn't relax. Her heart is pounding. "What are you doing here? What are we doing?"

"We're just being here. We're together. Isn't that something?"

"You heard everybody on the forum. We shouldn't be doing this."

He's rubbing gently in widening circles. Her body, against its will, finally begins to ease. She shouldn't—she should keep her guard up.

"I want to stay in Chicago," he says into her hair. "Should I?"

She's afraid to speak. Love of anything, even in small doses, threatens love of God. And she has never really stopped believing that there is a plan for her, even with all the lies and deceptions.

"I have to tell you what I did, Alder," she says. "To Kiki." Better to be honest now, to find out what he really thinks.

"What?"

She tells him: the demon voices, Vincent, the money.

When she is done, he sinks back into the mattress. She absorbs the hurt on his face.

"You went back to lying, and manipulating people," he says, suddenly standing so that he is looking down at her. "You're one of them."

"I just needed—I wanted—"

"You don't get it, do you," he says. "It's people like you who came along and broke people like me." He sighs, draws himself up; he is searching for something to say, some way to forgive when she doesn't deserve it. "You still think it's a gift, don't you. But it'll kill you."

She looks down at the floor. "Well, it doesn't matter. You shouldn't be around me. I just hurt people."

"That's not true. Why are you saying this?" His face changes. "Nora—"

"What?"

"I'm scared you'll go back."

"You're being ridiculous."

"Don't lie to me. You think you have to go back. It's Pentecost, isn't it? You think it's important. I've heard you talking about it."

She's gets up and runs to the door. "Listen, Alder. I just have to know—"

"What are they planning, Nora? Do you even know? You could get there and find that they've whipped up a batch of Kool-Aid."

"Don't even joke about that."

"You think I'm joking?" He picks up the black bible she's brought back with her and hurls it across the room. The pages flutter crazily as it settles to the floor. "You and I know what they're capable of," he says quietly, chest heaving. "They want power over life and death. That's the power they want over you. They want to bring you down with them."

"Goddamn it, Alder." She's sobbing now; seeing the book fly across the room like any dead weight has opened something in her. She can't stop, all these useless tears streaming out of her. She feels his hand on her shoulder, struggles to compose herself.

"There's only one thing I'm good at, Alder. They need me." She has to find a way to make him see. "They're my family."

"They've been lusting after the end of the world for your whole life," he says. "You can't save them from what they believe."

"But I'm the one who made them," she insists, doggedly. "I told them to believe, and they did."

He grabs her arm. "I won't let you go." But she shakes him off. He can't understand that she belongs to these people as surely as they belong to her. They made vows to each other, as solemnly as in a marriage. And it wasn't all bad. It was quiet. It was the undefiled smells of pine resin and gunpowder, it was birds singing in the trees, every one of which she could name. Small, scrappy wild strawberries, nothing like the watery things in supermarkets, as sweet as candy. Deer and otter and bear, the certainty of the woods, every life, every death, in its appointed place. Silence on Sundays and her father's hand on her head. The kind of life that kept you safe.

Pentecost

IT'S RAINING WHEN NORA gets off the L. She hurries down the street with her hood up. The address on the heavily creased slip of paper leads her to a grassy lot, surrounded by a chain link fence, a FOR SALE sign teetering by the curb. Inside the fence is a small, steepled chapel splashed with mud and rain. Nora has seen churches like this all her life. They dot the landscape of the Midwest, crumbling, dilapidated, stony or clapboard or aluminum sided, their walls washed with silt and iron-red soil. Letter boards with old signs still making dire pronouncements, or else re-arranged into obscene messages.

Light shines from the back windows. Cars are parked in the grass. An old school bus with the lettering scratched off is camped in the drenched weeds. Nora slows. A figure is coming out of a side door, hunched into an old canvas coat. She watches him try to light a cigarette in the rain. She knows the shape of him so well. He didn't used to smoke, but since she saw him last, he must have picked up the habit.

She could still run away, but she keeps looking, drinking him in. He's thinner; the cigarette illuminates deep hollows in his cheekbones, a wispy beard climbing high up his cheeks. He's like one of those miners from old photographs of the UP, aged into another era.

Then he's seen her. He tosses the cigarette to the ground and stands there, hands in his pockets. Nora steps closer, taking in his damp campfire smell. He's brought the woods with him: pine resin, camphor, coppery dirt.

"I knew you'd come," Levi says formally. His voice is hoarser but still, it's him. His arms come around her hesitantly. She can feel bones when she presses against his body.

"Who's here?" she asks. Faint singing has started up behind him, warbly and familiar.

"Most everybody," he answers.

He leads her to the old school bus. They shake the rain off their jackets and sit facing each other in a row of brown vinyl seats. His face is shockingly hollowed out; she's seen that look in her patients, when the flesh starts to melt off them. He hasn't been taking care of himself, or there's no one to worry about him. His eyes gleam out of their deep pits. "Everyone will want to see you," he says. "We all knew you'd come back to us."

Part of her expected to see her father waiting for her here, with that old look on his face of mute fury. But of course, he isn't here. There's only Levi. "What have you been doing all this time?" she asks.

He inclines his head. "Some people left. I sent a few others to find you. Once they did, they stayed here, to make sure you were safe. I remained back on the compound. I've made sure everything is in working order. Kept the lights on, stocked the cellars, so that we'd be ready for your return. I've dug five new bunkers. They're so hidden, you'll never find them. There's more gasoline buried under the hill, and two new generators. You can do a lot when you have a lot of time on your hands." A cracked smile, like he's forgotten how. His jumpy hands—like he doesn't seem to know what to do with them anymore. He seems part feral, like those solitary men of the woods they occasionally encountered in the UP. Bearded, skinny, suspicious men with mysterious back stories, crumbling houses and basements full of tin cans and guns, men in full retreat from the world.

She reaches for his arm. "It must have been lonely. Levi, I'm sorry I left you. All of you."

His arm tenses under her touch, then slowly relaxes. "It's all right. I knew you'd come back, eventually. And solitude, you know, it's not so bad. It brings a person closer to God. After everything that happened, I needed the time to get right again." He half-closes his eyes.

She wants to press her forehead to his, calm the wild animal out of him. "What happened the day the agents came? What happened to my father?"

He draws a long breath; this will take care and effort, and Levi has never been one for storytelling. "You saw how it began. There was a standoff in the woods. They had us surrounded. They weren't just at the gate, they had people on three sides. They were working with our neighbors. We were so stupid, thinking we were prepared. Somebody shot first, I don't know who. They just came pouring in. We tried to fall back to our defensive position, but a lot of our people just ran into the woods." He clenches his fists. "They were cowards. The first sign of a fight, and—" he doesn't finish, just turns his head to the church outside the bus window, the little lights in the rainy grayness. "I'm glad they got arrested. The people who are left, they're the real faithful. I'm just happy you got out of there. You must have been given a sign to leave."

"But what happened to my father? The reports say suicide, but he would never—" He loved himself too much.

"Of course the reports would say that. They wouldn't want to take the blame. It makes things nice and neat for them, doesn't it? The crazy cult collapses in on itself." Levi has lost a few teeth; there is a black gap in his mouth's ivory line.

"So it was a cover-up? They killed him?"

He's staring at his boots. "That's what everyone in there believes," he says, jerking his chin toward the church. "Wouldn't you like to believe that, too? It's a good story. It's kept us together. We all need a common enemy. The devil worked against us just like we always thought he would."

The offer presents itself; believe the story her father would like her to believe, make him a martyr to the sinister forces he first withdrew from twenty years ago. Somehow past his death he's still holding out his hand, demanding something of her.

She shakes her head. "I need to know, Levi. The truth."

He draws a deep breath. "It was Henry."

"What?"

"We were running, in the woods," he says. "Your father and me. Trying to get to the bunker. When the shots started, people started scattering, and most of us got separated. I thought we were going to regroup. It seemed like our only option. I thought we could still make it out if we just stuck to the plan.

"But your father said we needed to find you and then get away if we wanted to survive. He said we'd been betrayed and there was no trusting anyone anymore. He told me he had some sort of escape plan and we had to get to the lake. Then we ran into Henry. Your father told him we were going to escape together, him and me and you, and that we'd all make it out of this.

"Henry told us you were gone. He was very calm. He looked . . . decided. He had a shotgun. He waved me out of the way. I started to charge at him, I knew he was about to—and then he fired. He shot your father, Nora, and then he turned the gun on himself."

There's a ringing in her ears, like the low-pressure blaring that comes before a cyclone. "What?" is all she can say at first. And then, after a few moments, "That's not what the report said. There was nothing about Henry."

Levi leans forward in the close, humid air of the bus. Rain is drumming on the windows. "No one else knows."

"No one—"

"I didn't want the rest to think that the plan had gone so wrong. They could lose their faith. It's better for them to think the government got him, Nora. And that the traitors who told on us were the real enemies."

"Levi—" she can barely speak, but she presses on, she has to know. "Levi, what did you do?"

"I dragged him a ways. It wasn't too hard. He was light. We were already close."

"Close to what?"

"The ventilation shaft," he says.

In her mind, she walks through the woods, pushes the WARNING and KEEP OUT signs aside. She leans over the edge and peers down into that black slit in the earth. She can smell the air coming up at her, full of old iron, quicklime.

To think, Henry has been down there all this time.

Levi is still talking, explaining what happened next—arrests of the deacons, investigations of the property, trailers repossessed, mass defections—but Nora doesn't want to hear anymore. A memory rises, just one out of any number her mind could have selected: Henry looking at her one night over his glasses at the kitchen table, his face illuminated by the little cone of light made by the lanterns they used to conserve power. He swipes his eyes to her, and she swipes hers back. The two of them allowing themselves a tiny, conspiratorial glance, in the old language they once spoke. Like *who are we, anyway?* And *what is this place? Is this our lives?*

If one of them had spoken, they might have been able to save each other. To get out together.

Then the memory is gone, and she is left thinking there is so much she doesn't know about her brother: not just all the things he learned in books, but all the stories that made up his life. The small circular track of his existence. All the loneliness and rage.

"Nora," says Levi.

"What?" She drags herself back to the bus, the vinyl sticking to her damp jeans, Levi leaning urgently toward her, his knees touching her.

"There was supposed to be a baby," he says, tentatively. "We thought you ran away to protect it, like the verse says. *A great sign appeared in heaven. She was pregnant and cried out in pain.* Was there—"

Her voice is a whisper. "There's no baby."

"No one blames you, for how things turned out. The enemies came sooner than we thought." He's speaking quickly, almost to himself, in a low murmur. "It's almost Pentecost, and you're here. We'll be together, and there will be a baby, and after the war comes, everything on earth will be as it is in heaven."

She's staring at his arm, at the bare weather-scarred skin she can see in his loose-sleeved coat. A series of tiger stripes, old and reddened, are traveling up into shadow. "What did you do wrong?" she asks. "You never disobeyed. Never. Why were you punished?"

Levi shakes his head. "You still don't understand. All are punished."

"My father told you to fuck me, didn't he," she says. "You never really—"

He clasps her hands between his, aggrieved at her vulgarity. "He explained to me that it was a necessary sin. We were going to be vessels. We'd be making a miracle."

She can see how, through long observation and steady devotion, he's picked up a thing or two from her father. That same bright, fervent gaze, the tendency toward poetry. It's these things, she suspects, that first drew her mother in, made her fall in love. There's a promise men like them make that feels like the difference between an ordinary and an extraordinary life.

Nora feels for the creased prayer card in her pocket, the small protection she's carried with her for so long. This time, when she feels the gapping folds, she realizes the two layers are barely holding; something has been put between them, the pieces stuck back together. She pulls them slowly apart. It's a lock of hair. Just a curl or two of baby hair, mousy brown, delicate with age.

She can finally see what a small miracle it was that her mother was able to escape. And why she had to disappear so completely from her and Henry's lives. There's something appropriately biblical in it, a mother abandoning her children. Maybe there was some kind of loving in it as well, in the spaces between the prayers, in the tiny breath she always left between May the Lord save you—and keep you. In her whirl to face the charging bear, feet planted, her body a small, battered shield. Maybe that was why her mother left her the lock of hair: to show her that when there was nothing left to be done, that abandonment could be an act of love. Maybe it felt like standing in the woods with blood running down your legs, knowing there was no other way to keep your child safe. These are the things they must do to survive.

Levi is nodding to himself. "We'll try again." He pats the seat back in front of him. "We've got this bus. Now that you're here, we can head back tonight. You've seen the signs, the world is falling apart. You can tell us what's coming. We'll be ready, and we'll be together." He thinks everything will be all right now, that she can walk back into that room full of singing and tell them they'll be a family again.

He takes her hand. "Come on. Everyone's waiting for you."

She shakes her head. "Levi—" All those years ago, when he told her she wanted to be normal, he was only half-right. She desperately needed to be special, too. That was an impossible thing to give up, the feeling that a light from heaven shone on her shoulders.

Nora gets to her feet, and follows Levi off the bus. She nearly slips on the wet steps leading to the basement entrance. The church, with its peeling plaster, its boarded-up windows, stinks of ruin.

She takes a breath and pushes on the door; it gives to her touch. There's a dark hallway cluttered with folding chairs on either side. The hum of music playing at the end, sliding out of a lit doorway. "Are You Washed in the Blood of the Lamb?" An old favorite. She steps slowly, feeling the pull of the sound. Her body belongs to that music.

There in the room at the end of the hall: a circle of chairs, a ring of waiting faces. There is the man from the parade, the stranger who pressed the verse pleadingly into her hand. Other familiar faces: Dinah and Kevin and Joan, Hannah and Sue, the loyal believers, her family.

Kevin stands and walks over to her, his hand extended, his gaze wide-eyed, full of reverence. "We've been waiting for you," he says. "We hoped you'd come."

Nora takes a step and stumbles, almost falls. She's never had to deliver her own sermon. It was always her father's work. What should she say?

The people here still think the world is going to end. They don't see that it already has, that the catastrophe has come. The world they're praying for is already gone, because it never existed. The disaster is here; the prophecy came true. The only question is what to do now: how to go on, how to live.

She'll begin with: prepare yourself.

And then she's going to tell them the truth. That the prayers were only ever hers. That the voice was only her voice.

Benediction

(3,100 days since the world didn't end)

She gets winded easily now, well into her second trimester; strange how a walk in the woods can rob her of breath these days, leave her woozy and faint. But she's come for good reason.

She stoops, huffing slightly, as she slips under the barbed wire—she still knows the secret spots. It's just past dawn, and the woods are cold and silent. She follows the old path to her childhood home and meets no one, not the few remaining members, not Levi. She arrives at the front door: the windows are dark, the porch sagging. Abandoned.

It was Alder who convinced her to return. After finally getting a letter back from his own mother, and with the baby coming, he's softened. He's all for closure now. He says a story isn't complete until it has an ending. He's trying to get Nora to seek out her mother, too. There are always breadcrumbs, he says, things people leave behind when they want to be found. It will take time, but she can see herself bending, especially when she has a baby in her arms, and feels the breathless fear of knowing her life is not fully her own anymore. She imagines she'll have questions. How do you hold a baby? How do you feed her, how do you love her? And she'll have things to say, too. She'll start with how angry she is. That will come first. Followed by mourning.

Alder told her, you need to bear witness to his life.

She doesn't want to linger; she has this one thing to do, and then she'll flee from the uneasy memories. In Henry's dusty bedroom, a faded Pentecostal flag still hanging on the wall, she pushes herself carefully under the bed, feeling around the notebooks he left there, searching. There it is, as she thought. He'd kept it all this time.

She has to hurry. Levi is probably waking up, wherever he sleeps now on the property; soon he'll be puttering around, beginning the diligent work of digging new shelters, stocking charcoal and cans of gasoline and long chains of dried garlic in his secret root cellars. She imagines by this time that there must be bomb shelters and buried rooms dotted all over the place, hidden with elaborate codes only he knows.

Sometimes, in the middle of the night, she wakes, heart thudding, Alder's warm arm heavy on her hip. She's been dreaming of Levi again. He is digging himself deeper and deeper into the iron-rich earth, burying himself the same way he buried Henry, and he's pulling her down with him. She wants to save him. But some things are beyond her powers. At her new job at Chicago Memorial, where Kiki got her in, the palliative care team leader said that you have to let go of the idea that you can save anybody.

At the ventilation shaft, she spends a long moment listening to the wind move over the opening. It's a lonely sound, a murmur that comes and goes. If she didn't leave that day, she could have ended up at the bottom of the pit with him. But she wishes—she wishes—

She pulls out the crumpled scroll of paper, brittle now with age. There were the notebooks, of course, Henry's private, vengeful writings. But those are such sad, brutal things to send down into the dark with him.

So she dug deeper under his bed, and found the Noah's Ark mural.

She unfurls it a little way: there are the giraffes and elephants and lions, all in a line. A child's hand, but with a personality, the animals all big-eyed, clumsy, beautiful. It looks like he added even more animals over the years, the animals of the north woods: deer and otter and moose and porcupine, all of them walking to their salvation. Beside them, a few expertly drawn animals: a horse that truly looks like a horse, a bear that looks like a bear. Her father's hand is everywhere in their lives.

"Rest," she whispers. She will not say a prayer. That language isn't hers anymore, she is learning new tongues. She hopes he understands, in the old, silent way they used to speak.

She tosses the mural in the hole. Listens to the soft *tic-tic-tic* of its descent, bumping on the walls of the shaft, no heavier than a falling leaf.

It feels like bearing witness.

Acknowledgements

Thank you to my agent, Chris Clemans, for his tireless championing of this book, and to my editor, Robert Lasner, for seeing what this book could be.

Thank you to Gary Paulsen, whose books taught me to love the literature of survival; to the fantastic early readers and wonderful writers who offered their endlessly helpful insights: Sash Bischoff, Daria Lavelle, Laura Hankin, Olivia Tandon, and Olivia Cerrone.

Thank you to my teachers and mentors, who taught me how to find the story I needed to tell.

Thank you to my family for their love, enthusiasm, and support: Dad, Margot, Suze, and Paul. And thank you to my mother, whose voice I long to hear every day.

Thank you to the Literary Retreat at Hawthornden Castle, which gave me the time and space to write an early draft of this work.

This work was generously supported by a grant from the Ontario Arts Council, and a grant from the Canada Council for the Arts.

Works cited in the novel

Biblical quotations in this book are from the King James Version. I was inspired by the fearsome poetry, the thought-provoking questions and the unsettling stories of this work of literature, which we must continue to question and interrogate in our own way.

This book references a mathematical problem now known as the "Angel Problem," formulated by the mathematician John Horton Conway, and first published in the 1982 book *Winning Ways* by Berlekamp, Conway, and Guy (Academic Press, pp. 607–634). The solution to this problem was found by András Máthé and Oddvar Kloster in 2007.

The quotation "There will be angels, and we will see the whole sky in diamonds" is from *Uncle Vanya* by Anton Chekhov, translated by Ronald Hingley (in: *Five Plays*, Oxford University Press, 1998).

The quotation "Oh, when she's angry, she's keen and shrewd! And though she be but little, she is fierce." is from Shakespeare's *As You Like It* (Bloomsbury, *Arden Shakespeare*, 2022).

The story about the girl who reads a cursed book is from John Bellairs' *The Ghost in the Mirror* (Piccadilly Press, 2019).

The quotation "Prophets have a way of dying by violence" is from Frank Herbert's *Dune* (New English Library, 1972).